Forcing herself not to sigh for the luxuries back home was as useless as trying to keep her thoughts from returning to Tom McCullough.

In his own way, Tom was as forceful as Jamal, but Shara hadn't resented his attitude, aware that Tom spoke out of concern for her, not out of a desire to control her.

He would have more subtle means of getting his way. A shudder of possibility shook her as her imagination worked overtime. In her country, women had a saying about men— Stillness Cloaks The Tiger Within.

Where Jamal's inner tiger was a rampaging beast, seldom cloaked, Tom's, she sensed, was immensely more powerful than that.

What would his tiger be like, once unleashed?

Dear Reader,

No doubt your summer's already hot, but it's about to get hotter, because *New York Times* bestselling author Heather Graham is back in Silhouette Intimate Moments! *In the Dark* is a riveting, heart-pounding tale of romantic suspense set in the Florida Keys in the middle of a hurricane. It's emotional, sexy and an absolute edge-of-your-seat read. Don't miss it!

FAMILY SECRETS: THE NEXT GENERATION continues with *Triple Dare* by Candace Irvin, featuring a woman in jeopardy and the very special hero who saves her life. *Heir to Danger* is the first in Valerie Parv's CODE OF THE OUTBACK miniseries. Join Princess Shara Najran as she goes on the run to Australia— and straight into the arms of love. Terese Ramin returns with *Shotgun Honeymoon,* a wonderful—and wonderfully suspenseful—marriage-of-inconvenience story. Brenda Harlen has quickly become a must-read author, and *Bulletproof Hearts* will only further her reputation for writing complex, heartfelt page-turners. Finally, welcome back Susan Vaughan, whose *Guarding Laura* is full of both secrets and sensuality.

Enjoy them all, and come back next month for more of the most exciting romance reading around—only from Silhouette Intimate Moments.

Enjoy!

Leslie J. Wainger
Executive Editor

Please address questions and book requests to:
Silhouette Reader Service
U.S.: 3010 Walden Ave., P.O. Box 1325, Buffalo, NY 14269
Canadian: P.O. Box 609, Fort Erie, Ont. L2A 5X3

HEIR TO DANGER
VALERIE PARV

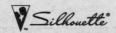

INTIMATE MOMENTS™

Published by Silhouette Books

America's Publisher of Contemporary Romance

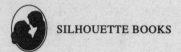 SILHOUETTE BOOKS

ISBN 0-373-27382-7

HEIR TO DANGER

Copyright © 2004 by Valerie Parv

All rights reserved. Except for use in any review, the reproduction
or utilization of this work in whole or in part in any form by any
electronic, mechanical or other means, now known or hereafter
invented, including xerography, photocopying and recording, or in
any information storage or retrieval system, is forbidden without
the written permission of the editorial office, Silhouette Books,
233 Broadway, New York, NY 10279 U.S.A.

All characters in this book have no existence outside the imagination of
the author and have no relation whatsoever to anyone bearing the same
name or names. They are not even distantly inspired by any individual
known or unknown to the author, and all incidents are pure invention.

This edition published by arrangement with Harlequin Books S.A.

® and TM are trademarks of Harlequin Books S.A., used under license.
Trademarks indicated with ® are registered in the United States Patent
and Trademark Office, the Canadian Trade Marks Office and in other
countries.

Visit Silhouette Books at www.eHarlequin.com

Printed in U.S.A.

VALERIE PARV

With twenty million copies of her books sold, including three Waldenbooks bestsellers, it's no wonder Valerie Parv is known as Australia's queen of romance and is the recognized media spokesperson for all things romantic. Valerie is married to her own romantic hero, Paul, a former crocodile hunter in Australia's tropical north.

These days he's a cartoonist and the two live in the country's capital city of Canberra, where both are volunteer zoo guides, sharing their love of animals with visitors from all over the world. Valerie continues to write her page-turning novels because they affirm her belief in love and happy endings. As she says, "Love gives you wings, romance helps you fly." Keep up with Valerie's latest releases at www.silromanceauthors.com.

For Lulu, Sunny and Merry
with love and appreciation

Chapter 1

The woman's scream reverberated around the steep canyon, dragging Tom McCullough's attention away from the deserted car he'd stopped to investigate. It was one of the old cars used for work around Diamond Downs, but why was it sitting in the middle of nowhere with plenty of gas and no obvious damage?

Tom's head snapped up. A scream wasn't a sound he expected to hear on a cattle property in the middle of nowhere, either.

Neither could he ignore it. As a ranger, he was sworn to protect both the unique environment of the untamed Kimberley region of northwestern Australia, and the people who came to marvel at it, from themselves if necessary.

Even as his mind raced through the list of possible threats, from deadly king brown snakes to wild dingoes and man-eating crocodiles, his long legs scaled the cinnamon-colored rock wall that rose like a submarine emerging from an ochre ocean. His feet skidded on the tangle of creepers and tree roots cascading over the jagged, layered rocks.

The difficult terrain made the shriek of terror even more disturbing. This wasn't a place where the unwary wandered. Usually the only people who made the climb were the Aboriginal custodians of a ceremonial site located among the rocks. He could see the entrance to the narrow gorge now, festooned in greenery.

Surely the scream hadn't come from the gorge? What would a woman be doing in a place reserved for initiated men only? The scream must have come from somewhere close to the rock enclave rather than inside it, he thought, knowing wishful thinking when he expressed it.

Tom braced himself to find some lost backpacker lying on the ground, staring in bewilderment at a snakebite on her leg or ankle. When his scan of the surroundings revealed nothing, he plunged into the greenery, coming up short at the sight of the most beautiful woman he'd ever seen, being held at spear point by a tribal elder with murder in his expression.

"What's going on, Andy?" he demanded. As well as being one of Tom's best friends, Andy Wandarra worked as a stockman on Diamond Downs. In the shadow of the rock wall decorated with ancient paintings, he had shed his veneer of civilization along with everything but a loincloth. Here, he was the upholder of eons of tradition stretching back in an unbroken thread to the dawn of creation, the Dreamtime.

The man brandished the spear at the woman who faced him down with a defiance Tom found admirable if foolhardy. "I found this one looking at the paintings. No woman can see them. The cave spirits say she must be speared in the leg as punishment," Andy said.

Tom's blood chilled. The cave spirits were embodied in the eerie figures adorning every surface of the rocks. Wandarra knew them as the creative beings of the Dreaming, makers of the world and everything it contained. According to his people, these spirit beings governed all aspects of human behavior, along with the rituals that were vital for living in harmony with the land.

It was Andy's responsibility to keep their images in good repair as his forebears had done for thousands of years. Without the benign influence of the spirits, his people believed, the land would dry up and the game would vanish.

"This little-bit woman didn't mean any harm. She's not from around here," Tom said, as if the woman was hardly worth his friend's notice.

Out of the corner of his eye he saw her draw herself up. She didn't like being described so dismissively, he gathered. If the situation hadn't been potentially lethal, he would have been amused. In contrast to his six-two, she *was* a little bit of a thing.

She stood about five-seven and wouldn't have weighed more than a hundred and twenty pounds wringing wet. Hair as dark as midnight hung halfway down her back. Her skin was the color of milky coffee and her violet gaze locked with his in silent challenge. She definitely wasn't from around here. Her cream shirt and tailored jeans, even caked in red dust, screamed European designer. The jeans were tucked into calf-hugging leather boots that Tom would bet were worth several months of his salary.

He sighed inwardly. Now he had an explanation for the deserted car, if not for its lovely occupant.

"I didn't mean to trespass by coming in here," she said in a cultured voice tinged with an exotic accent.

Tom struggled to place it. Where had he heard that voice before? "I'm Shire Ranger Tom McCullough. Who are you?" he asked quietly.

He detected the slightest hesitation before she said, "My name is Shara."

Had she been about to say Mrs. Somebody? He knew he'd have been disappointed if she had. No, she'd hesitated as if she wasn't accustomed to having to explain her identity. Who was she and what the devil was going on?

"This place is off-limits to all women, Shara," he said. "You're breaking indigenous law by entering."

"It wasn't intentional," she assured him. "I was merely—driving around. A kangaroo hopped in front of my car and I bumped it very slightly. I didn't think it was injured but I followed it up here to make sure. When I saw the opening in the rock and the paintings, I decided to take a closer look."

As a ranger, Tom knew a lie when he heard one. Not about the kangaroo, but what she was doing in the area in the first place. "Driving where?" he asked.

"Just—around."

There it was, that hesitation again. The growing impatience in Andy's body language put an end to Tom's probing. Not even their long friendship would stop the other man from doing his sacred duty, Tom knew.

He looked at the spear held unwaveringly on her. "She didn't know any better, Andy. Let me take care of this. I'll see she never makes a mistake like this again."

The other man's frown deepened. "You know our laws, Barrak."

Hearing his clan name used, Tom's heart sank and with it his hope of salvaging the situation.

To Wandarra's people, the cave spirits weren't gods, watching the people from on high. They walked among their people, controlling the natural world. If they were offended, they could turn nature against the people, causing untold misery and hardship. If Andy allowed her to walk away, the clan elders could hunt her down and possibly kill her for defiling the sacred place. Andy would also suffer for his part in the transgression.

Tom was uncomfortably aware of Wandarra waiting. "We've known each other long enough that you know some things can't be handled the traditional way anymore," he said carefully. He sensed the other man's resolve, but he had to try. "When someone does wrong, I talk to the wrongdoer, make sure they understand their mistake so they don't do it again."

Wandarra shot him a look of anger. "Talk won't help. This is sacred clan business." He tapped Tom's chest hard. "Your business, Barrak."

"What does he mean, your business? And why does he call you Barrak?" Shara asked. Her voice was thin with fear but held steady, earning his grudging admiration. Whoever she was, she didn't spook easily.

He grasped the lapels of his khaki uniform shirt and pulled them apart, hearing her breath catch as he revealed a pattern of whorls and cicatrices, the result of long-healed scars cut into his chest.

"The name means white dingo. I'm an honorary member of Wandarra's clan," he said.

"But you're not Aboriginal."

"Not entirely." Like many people in the Kimberley, he had a thin trickle of Aboriginal blood in his veins and sometimes wished he had more. It would have been an improvement on the heritage he did have.

As boys, he and Wandarra had been initiated into manhood together. For Andy, it had been a necessary rite of passage. No one had expected Tom to participate, but as teenagers he and Wandarra had been so close, he'd wanted to do everything his friend did. When the elders sent Andy into the desert for three days to survive on his own, existing on what food and water he could find, Tom insisted on undertaking his own survival trek, returning tired, hungry and dehydrated, but triumphant.

His feat had so impressed the elders that they'd agreed to include him in the final initiation rites. His foster father had tried to talk him out of it but Tom had refused to believe Des's description of the ceremony, thinking the older man meant to scare him out of doing what he wanted to do. When Des realized Tom was determined to undergo the ritual, he had locked the boy in his room.

Tom had slid a sheet of paper under the door, jiggled a penknife in the lock until he dislodged the key. When the key dropped onto the paper, he'd pulled them both through to his side and escaped.

By the time he found out that Des hadn't exaggerated the ordeal ahead, it was too late. Along with Andy and the other boys on the brink of manhood, Tom had forced himself to endure the grueling physical challenges, nightmarish confrontations to test his courage and the agony of having tribal markings carved into his chest. The alternative was to remain forever a boy in his friend's eyes, and that would have been far worse.

The elders had gone easy on him, he knew now. Andy's markings were far more extensive than Tom's own. Nevertheless, he had been a mess, feverish and delusional by the time Des found him and carried him back to the homestead. Without recrimination, Des had tended the cuts on Tom's chest until they healed into the pattern that now identified him as a man of Wandarra's clan.

A man with frightening responsibilities.

Shara recognized it in his face, and he saw the color leave her features. "What is this man going to do?" she asked.

"What he must," Tom said tautly. He saw Andy lift the spear as if testing the weapon's weight.

Her eyes saucered as she caught the gesture. "You're as mad as he is. You can't let him put a spear through me. This is the twenty-first century. There are laws even in the wilderness."

"Outback Australia has its own laws."

"And I'm to be punished for my ignorance by being speared?"

To her credit, although her voice faltered, she held herself proudly, her chin lifted.

"It is the traditional penalty," Tom said, remorse tingeing his tone.

She eyed the insignia on his shirt. "You're an officer of the law. Can't you stop this?"

"The outback has more than one kind of law. I try to uphold both kinds, white and traditional."

Disbelief shadowed her violet eyes. "You really mean to let him do this, don't you?"

His gut twisted. He had never seen eyes quite that shade before. They were ringed with some dark makeup that made them look huge in her heart-shaped face. He felt as if he was about to kick a puppy. "I have no choice."

He grasped her shoulder, noting how fragile her body felt beneath the thin shirt. Feeling the delicate outline of her bones, he amended his assessment of her weight downward by a few pounds. She felt as slender as a child. And she was shaking.

She was putting on a good act, but he felt her trembling like a leaf.

His throat felt dry as he pressed her back against the sandstone wall. "Brace your palms against the rock, and whatever happens, don't move an inch. Understood?"

The lambent gaze she turned on him was almost his undoing. "Please don't do this."

He roughened his tone, not wanting to drag this out. "Understood?"

A ragged breath escaped her full lips, making him feel even more brutal. "Yes."

"It might help to close your eyes," he said.

Wandarra made an angry sound of impatience and Tom knew he couldn't stall any longer. If he didn't take care of this, the other man would, and it would be far worse for Shara.

Her heart beat so hard Shara thought it would fly out of her chest. Some of her own country's older customs seemed barbaric to her, but this was a nightmare. First a man in a loincloth had threatened to spear her after finding her looking at the ancient cave paintings. When the ranger had arrived she'd expected him to intervene. Instead he seemed to condone the cruel ritual. What kind of men did this country breed?

Awesome ones, she concluded reluctantly. Primitive they might be, but both men were incredible examples of masculine perfection. Wandarra's loincloth hid almost nothing of his physical beauty. Tom's uniform was more concealing, thank goodness, but when he'd ripped open his shirt to reveal the tribal markings, she'd glimpsed solid muscle under the uniform.

Not that it was any help to her now.

Desperately she cast about for a way out, but Wandarra stood between her and the narrow entrance. The other end of the gorge was blocked by collapsed rock and only a shaft of sunlight penetrated the gloom. The walls were too steep to climb.

Could she try to fight her way out using the basic self-defense skills she'd learned as a teenager? The answer was obvious. She might have been able to tackle one man successfully, but not both. She was trapped.

As a student of primitive art, she understood that she'd broken Wandarra's law and she was prepared to make amends. But dear heaven, not like this.

Panic swirled through her but she resisted by focusing on how much she despised Tom for allowing his friend to act as judge and jury over her.

Her inner tension reached boiling point as Tom said something to Wandarra in an Aboriginal language. Probably deciding the finer points of her fate, she thought as a strange sense of disconnection settled over her, as if her mind was floating away from her body. Why didn't they just get on with it, she wondered from this new vantage point? Wandarra argued furiously, but Tom held his ground. She saw Wandarra give a grudging nod and back away, hefting the spear.

Then a shadow fell across her, jerking her back to full awareness as Tom stepped between her and the other man.

Finally, she understood.

Tom intended to take the spear meant for her.

"I won't let you do this," she said.

"You're not exactly in a position to stop me."

A moment ago she'd thought him despicable. Now she could hardly believe he was prepared to endure the penalty that would have been hers. In her own country she had bodyguards whose job was to put themselves in harm's way for her. But Tom didn't know who she was. He wasn't from her country. Yet she couldn't mistake his intention. His demeanor showed that nothing would dissuade him from following his chosen course.

"Why?" she asked, needing to know this at least.

"The cave spirits must be placated," he said.

She wondered if he'd deliberately misunderstood her question. "Is there no other way?"

"None," he stated. "Trust me. This is for the best."

For her, not for him. She couldn't let him suffer for her mistake. But moving past him was like trying to shift solid rock. He'd planted himself so she had no space to maneuver. All she could do was hold her breath and wait.

Over her shoulder she saw Wandarra balance the spear lightly in his hand, sunlight glinting off the tip. Tom had told her to brace herself against the rock wall. She was pressing so hard the grit drove itself into her palms but she hardly noticed. Her rubbery legs felt as if they wouldn't hold her up much longer but she refused to give her nemesis the satisfaction of fainting at his feet.

Everything in her screamed that this couldn't be happening, but it was.

She closed her eyes and prayed.

Tom fixed his gaze on Wandarra as the other man backed away as far as the limited space allowed. Under traditional law a transgressor was speared in the fleshy part of the thigh, causing maximum pain with minimum physical damage. The punishment was rare now, replaced by modern remedies, but Tom still encountered the occasional incident. He had never dreamed he would face the wrong end of a spear himself, and his insides churned. He was well aware of the damage the weapon could inflict.

Better to him than to the woman behind him.

Wandarra began to chant in his language, telling the spirits of the cave what he was about to do and why, so they knew that a wrong was being righted and they wouldn't take their wrath out on Wandarra's people.

The chant ended and Tom braced himself.

He hadn't counted on the woman's stubbornness. Instead

of staying safely sheltered by his body, she planted her palms in the small of his back and pushed with all her might, knocking him off balance for a crucial instant.

In the same instant, Wandarra let the spear fly.

Recovering his balance, Tom heard her let out the faintest whimper. Swearing profusely, he turned to see the spear jutting from her boot, the point having penetrated her calf. Her knees sagged but she stayed upright, staring in disbelief at the still quivering weapon. The blood had washed out of her face and he suspected her grip on the rock wall was all that held her up.

He whirled on Wandarra. "Enough. This is settled now." He didn't drop his gaze until the other man nodded and turned away.

Dropping to one knee beside her, Tom braced his hand on her thigh. Her sharp intake of breath told him she knew what he was about to do. He saw her close her eyes again and pull in a deep breath.

There was no easy way so he made it fast. In a fluid movement he pulled the spear out, hearing her choke back a cry of pain. Tossing the spear aside, he gathered her into his arms. "You stupid woman. Let's get you out of here."

Any moment now she would wake up in her curtained bed in Dashara with her personal servants fussing over her, Shara thought. She must have stayed up too late last night working. When she opened her eyes, the handsome stranger who had been willing to take a spear meant for her would be no more than a bizarre dream.

Experimentally she opened her eyes and almost closed them again at the sight of the man cradling her against his chest. Her imagination could never have conjured up such a breathtaking experience.

He was as tall and self-assured as the men of her country, carrying her down the boulder-strewn hillside as if he owned it. He held her effortlessly, her weight no more than an inconvenience. When he'd swung her into his arms, she'd automatically linked her hands around his neck and hung on. Under her fingers, the corded muscles of his neck felt as solid as a tree trunk.

Shadowed by his bushman's hat, Tom's eyes and hair were a matching shade of sable. Beneath thick sooty lashes, fine lines framed a hooded gaze, from years spent scanning these far horizons, she assumed. The grim line of his mouth hinted at a disturbing sensuousness.

Close up, the tribal markings on his chest looked even more awesome. What must he have endured to acquire them?

Heat radiated through her, not all of it traceable to her throbbing calf. She knew she was focusing on details to avoid facing the truth. This man she didn't know had tried to put himself on the line to protect her. By interfering, she'd offended his code of honor, she assumed. But she had her own code, and it precluded letting someone else pay for her mistake.

His hold on her stopped barely short of crushing. She dragged in a deep breath, regretting it almost at once as she was assailed by his musky man scent. This had gone far enough. "You can put me down. I can walk," she insisted.

His hold didn't loosen. "No need. We're almost there."

She strained to see anything around his daunting bulk, then stopped as the movement brought her into closer contact with his hard body. "Where is *there?*"

"My vehicle."

Shifting her weight to one arm, he opened the door of a four-wheel-drive Jeep with the other and eased her onto the front seat, leaving the door open. She closed her eyes for a moment as the stored heat inside the car stole what remained of her breath.

"Are you all right?"

She forced her eyes open. "For someone who was speared, I'm fine. What do you think?"

He retrieved a compact first-aid kit from the back of the vehicle and opened it on the floor at her feet. "If you'd stayed put, you wouldn't be injured."

"I couldn't let you suffer on my account."

He shrugged this off. "You don't take orders easily, do you?"

Did he sense that she was more accustomed to giving them? "Your friend Wandarra has his system of justice. I have mine."

"Well, next time, try not to let it lead you into trouble." He reached for her damaged boot.

She steeled herself, surprised to see him wince in sympathy when she was unable to suppress a cry. "You wouldn't have been any better off," she snapped, angry at herself for feeling so weak. Or was it because of the unwelcome feelings Tom's touch stirred up? "I suppose you're so tough that you would have walked away from the experience?"

"The spearing is meant to teach a lesson, not cause undue harm. By moving, you could have been killed."

His anger suddenly made sense. Something tightened in her stomach, beyond the pain of the injury which she saw was mercifully slight when he pushed back the leg of her jeans.

Slowly her own fury ebbed. "I haven't thanked you yet for what you tried to do."

Tom kept his head down. "No thanks needed. You didn't know what you were getting into."

She still didn't, she thought, trying not to flinch when he used a razor blade to slice the leg of her jeans open to just above her knee. She wouldn't be wearing them again. It came to her that this could be a problem. For the first time in her life, she didn't have a dozen more pairs where they came from.

As Tom cleaned her injury and wrapped a piece of gauze bandage around it, the touch of his fingers against her heated skin was deft, almost a caress. "Are you a doctor?" she asked.

"In the outback you have to be a bit of everything." He lifted his head. "That's the best I can do for now. I'll take you to Diamond Downs homestead where they'll do a more thorough job. I have some painkillers on me if you need them."

"The antiseptic stings a bit, that's all. I prefer not to cloud my thinking with painkillers."

He repacked the first-aid kit efficiently. "Pity you didn't think of that before you blundered into the gorge."

"You think I don't know that now? I may be many things, but stupid isn't usually one of them."

He rested an arm against the open door of the vehicle, trapping her within the angle of his body. His speculative gaze raked her, sending fresh waves of heat coursing through her. "You don't strike me as stupid. Naive, but not stupid." ·

"You're too kind." She laced her tone with regal sarcasm more reminiscent of her life in Q'aresh than her present situation.

Instead of quailing, as her subjects would have done when she took that tone, Tom gave a sharp laugh. "Why do I get the feeling you expect me to fall at your feet and beg your forgiveness?"

Because part of her did expect it. As the only daughter of the King of Q'aresh, she was accustomed to having her slightest wish obeyed. Here, she had to get used to being treated like everyone else. "You're imagining things," she said.

"I don't think so. You don't exactly fit in here, do you?"

"Not like Barrak, the white dingo." She couldn't help sounding bitter, knowing she was jealous because he so obviously belonged here, while she was the interloper.

"The name was given to me when I was initiated into Wandarra's clan. To everyone else, I'm Tom, the shire ranger," he informed her.

He waited for her to volunteer information about herself. When she remained silent, he shrugged. "Suit yourself. I'll find out who you are one way or another. You're obviously foreign, but you must have someone I should notify that you're all right."

Panic welled inside her. "No, you mustn't. I mean, there's no need. I can look after myself."

His gaze swept her slitted jeans and bandaged calf. "So I see." He gestured toward the car slewed at an angle a few yards behind his. "I assume you got here in that. Care to tell me what you're doing with Des Logan's car? Or is that classified information, too?"

"I'm a guest of Mr. Logan's."

Tom's dark eyebrows swept upward. "Des is my foster father."

Suddenly she remembered where they'd crossed paths before. Tom's familiarity had nagged at her. She had met him in the nearby township of Halls Creek when her father brought her with him on a cattle-buying expedition several years before.

Chagrin gripped her. Tom obviously didn't remember her. Not that she wanted him to. The fewer people who knew her identity, or where she was hiding out, the better. "I simply wanted a safe—that is, a place I could have some time to myself," she improvised. "Mr. Logan was kind enough to let me stay in the old cottage."

Tom didn't miss the hasty correction. Safe from what? "Des told me he had a guest staying out here, but that's all."

"Surely he doesn't have to tell you everything? I understand you don't live at Diamond Downs now."

He nodded. "I have my own place outside Halls Creek."

"What were you doing here?"

His mouth thinned. Then to her dismay, he said, "I'm not answering any more questions until you answer a few of mine, princess."

Chapter 2

Feeling the color drain from her face, she let her head drop against the leather headrest. What had he called her?

"That does it, I'm getting you back to the homestead."

She forced her head up. "I don't feel faint, just…" What? Alone in a strange land? Terrified that she would be caught by her fiancé, Jamal, before she could get evidence of his true nature to her father? If she hadn't been so distracted with these worries, she would have braked more quickly when the kangaroo leaped across her path. Then she wouldn't have needed to follow the animal to ensure it wasn't hurt, and come across the forbidden site.

A lot of ifs, she thought. She bit down hard on her lower lip to control the threatening tears, recognizing them as a product of mild shock. Tom didn't know who she was. He'd called her princess as a nickname.

"Have you had your tetanus shots?" he asked.

"I've had every immunization possible."

His eyes narrowed. "How long since you've eaten something?"

"I—I'm not sure. Breakfast, I think." She had eaten some crackers and an apple, too unsettled to face anything more.

"That was hours ago. Des should have warned you against setting off alone without water, at the very least."

"I have food and a water bottle in the car."

He unscrewed the top of a canteen and handed it to her. As soon as the water spilled down her throat she realized how thirsty she'd been. How hungry she was.

He watched her grimly. "You really are a babe in the woods, aren't you, princess?"

She lowered the canteen warily. "Why do you call me that?"

"Because of your haughty manner, as if everyone else is a rung or two beneath you on the social ladder."

It was truer than he knew, at least in Q'aresh. "I'll try to appear more sociable," she said as much to herself as to him.

"I recommend it if you want to last long in the outback. And speaking of lasting long, if you run into any more trouble, the first rule of survival is to stay with your vehicle."

His warning sent a stab of alarm through her. She'd never intended to last long in the outback, as Tom put it, only to eavesdrop on a meeting between Jamal Sayed and some of his cronies aboard the private plane Jamal would take to Australia on an assignment for her father.

She'd planned to leave the plane when it dropped the other men off at a coastal airstrip, but Jamal had caught her taping his conversation, and forced her to accompany him to Australia, telling her father she couldn't bear being separated from her fiancé for so long.

Before he'd searched her bag, she'd managed to push her taped record of his treasonous meeting into a secret compartment under a seat. With luck, the tape was still on the plane. Her only hope of convincing her father that the man he expected her to marry was a traitor.

When the king had brought Shara with him to the Kimberley eight years before, she had never imagined she would return under such circumstances. Or that she'd find her life depending on the Logan family whom she'd met on that visit.

She was sure that the Logans, and by extension Tom, weren't involved with Jamal. Shara had remained in touch with Judy Logan after meeting her at Diamond Downs on that first visit. Drawn together as the only teenage girls in the party, they'd discovered a mutual passion for rock art. Shara had been fascinated by the ancient sites in Q'aresh, deciding to set up an exchange program between the traditional artists in Australia and her country as soon as she came of age. Judy had become the scheme's contact in Australia. Judy had been the logical person for Shara to turn to, although getting away from Jamal at the airport hadn't been easy.

Claiming a need to visit the ladies' room, Shara had squeezed out through a tiny window into the open air. By the time Jamal became impatient waiting for her, she'd persuaded a taxi driver to take her to a bank where she'd used her credit card to obtain some Australian currency, then paid the driver to take her to Diamond Downs.

Had it only been two days ago? It felt like an eternity. The seat gave as Tom got into the Jeep. She opened her eyes. He was a lot like his foster father, she thought. Not in looks, since they weren't related by blood. But in his cool decisiveness. Not domineering, but no pushover, either. Qualities she admired in a man. In Tom.

His foster father had reacted as if having a runaway princess land on his doorstep was an everyday event. A room at the homestead was hers for as long as she wanted. Too risky for them if Jamal traced her to the Logans, she'd argued. In the end she'd agreed to stay at the original cottage some distance from the homestead, and accept Des's offer of the use of an old work car.

In it she'd been checking out escape routes from the cottage, when she and the kangaroo had their fateful disagreement.

She rubbed her aching calf. "Where are we going?"

Tom gunned the engine. "I'd prefer to take you to a doctor, but since you've vetoed that idea, and you evidently don't want to have me arrested, I'm taking you home where there's a better medical kit on hand. We can send someone to fetch the car later."

This time the fluttering in her chest was easier to subdue. "What you've done feels fine. You don't have to worry about me."

"Looking after stray princesses is part of my job."

She was getting used to hearing her title used as a nickname, feeling as if it eroded some barrier between them. Australians gave nicknames to people they liked, she recalled her grandmother telling her. And she found the idea of Tom liking her oddly appealing. "Do you come across many of us out here?" she asked.

"Not normally at spear point."

The concerned tone of his voice pulled at her. He really hadn't wanted her to get hurt, and tried to save her from greater harm. "I was a fool to go into the gorge without knowing the correct protocol," she said.

"You couldn't have known what would happen."

"I should have. I've studied rock art for long enough to understand that traditional people have their own ways of doing things and their own reasons. The taboo on women entering the area has probably existed for hundreds of thousands of years."

The look he gave her was thoughtful. "Are you always this forgiving?"

She guessed he was referring to her reluctance to press charges against him. "Only when I know I'm in the wrong."

"Are you really female under those classy clothes?"

She felt the blush all the way to her toes. "Excuse me?"

He looked equally disconcerted, she saw, when she forced herself to meet his heated gaze, as if he'd blundered into territory where he had no business going.

"I mean, I can see that you're female." He pushed his bush

hat far back on his head, tousling his dark hair. "A man would have to be blind not to. You're bloody beautiful. I only meant…hell…how many women do you know who're willing to admit when they're wrong?"

The awkward compliment warmed her. So he thought she was beautiful, did he? The clumsy words meant more to her than all of Jamal's eloquent flattery, and were probably far more sincere. "You obviously haven't heard the women's rules," she murmured, letting him off the hook. "Rule one, the woman is always right. Rule two, if the woman is wrong, refer to rule one."

He gave a theatrical groan. "Don't let Judy hear you say that. I'll never hear the end of it."

"Judy's my friend. Perhaps I owe it to her." Shara was amazed to feel jealousy scraping along her nerves. Was there any romantic interest between him and Des's daughter? Again she asked herself why she cared.

"She's okay," he admitted grudgingly. "When we were kids, she considered it her mission in life to give me as hard a time as possible. Do you have sisters?"

She shook her head. The lack was a source of sorrow to her. "I have one older brother, Sadiq. Our mother died when I was born. We were raised by our grandmother who was born in Australia." She didn't add that Noni had crossed swords with their father about almost everything to do with their upbringing. Where his son and heir was concerned, King Awad had won every battle. Not for the first time, Shara wondered if he had done his daughter a favor, letting Noni have her way when it came to raising Shara herself. Would she have found it easier to accept her father's plans for her if her upbringing had been more conventional?

"Tough break. My mother's gone, too. I still miss her," Tom said, interrupting her thoughts.

"Were you very young when she died?"

"Twelve. It should never have happened." His voice held a rasping quality she had already begun to recognize as emotion, quickly suppressed in the manner of Australian men. She also sensed there was something he wasn't telling her. It sounded as if his mother had died in an accident. Did he blame himself? This was certainly something she could understand.

"I never knew my mother, but I felt responsible for her death," she said.

"You didn't ask to be born. If anyone deserves blame it's fate, or your father."

Again she had the uncanny feeling Tom was speaking of his own experience. She didn't know him well enough to ask, but it didn't stop her wanting to. "What about brothers?"

"I have three foster brothers. Blake runs the local crocodile farm. Ryan is a jackeroo on a property farther north. We don't see much of him or Cade, who's a wildlife photographer for magazines. Judy is the only girl. After she was born, Des and his late wife, Fran, found out they couldn't have any more children so they became foster parents."

Shara nodded. "And your real family?"

"They *are* my real family."

Taking a hint from his gruff tone, she turned to the scenery jolting past the car window as he steered the heavy vehicle over the corrugated track. Since she wasn't prepared to open up to him about herself, respecting his privacy was the least she could do.

"Am I keeping you from your work?" she asked.

"I started a couple of weeks' vacation today. Most days I start work at dawn, before the heat builds up, take a break and catch up on paperwork about now, then finish anything that needs doing when the day cools down."

"What were you doing out here?"

"Heading to the homestead for dinner with Des and Judy."

At least she wasn't dragging him out of his way.

"How long have you been here?" Tom asked.

"Two days. Des said I can stay as long as I like."

Tom nodded. "He would."

His gruff tone didn't disguise his obvious affection for his foster father. "Judy told me he makes a habit of taking in strays," Shara said.

"Like me and my foster brothers," he agreed.

Like her, too, she thought with a pang. "Are they all as big as you?" she asked.

Tom slanted a grin at her. "We're all taller than Des."

"And you're all from different families?"

"Yeah." He didn't seem to want to elaborate, then surprised her by adding, "My real mother was Irish and my dad's one-eighth Aboriginal, if you hadn't already guessed."

His smooth skin had a tanned look she found disturbingly attractive. "Is it a problem?"

"Not around here. Maybe in the big smoke, the city," he elaborated for her benefit. "Out here, you're judged by your actions."

What did his actions tell her about him? First condoning a barbaric punishment, then being prepared to endure it in her place? More hero than villain, she decided.

Carrying her, his arms had felt strong and supportive. Tending to her leg, his touch had been almost unbearably gentle. And she hadn't missed the gleam of male response to the shapely calf her torn jeans had revealed. He had made her feel feminine and, yes, beautiful, restoring some of the pride in herself Jamal had threatened to crush.

She found herself warming to Tom, wanting to tell him the truth about herself, but still felt unsure. She knew nothing about him beyond what her instincts told her. Could she trust them?

"You've had a pretty poor welcome to the Kimberley," he said.

He was making amends without knowing it. She put a hand on his arm, feeling the muscles tighten and her pulse skip in response. The temptation to trust became a certainty. "It's over now."

Tom wished he could dismiss his part in her injury so readily. Seeing the danger she'd been in, he'd tried his best to protect her, but doubt wracked him. Could he have talked

Wandarra into letting her off? Or would Andy's people have come looking for her later and inflicted worse harm?

According to the outback credo, what was done was done and you moved on. Tom knew he should also be moving on. But something about Shara made him wish the drive to the homestead was twice as long. Her touch on his arm felt like a fresh brand. Amazing that there wasn't a mark on his skin.

Her skin was the color of milk coffee, satiny and soft in contrast to his own. Scratches marred her skin where she had tracked the kangaroo through the bushes into the gorge, more concerned for the animal's safety than her own. He felt an uncharacteristic urge to kiss them better.

Not sure what impulse drove him, he asked, "What are you afraid of, Shara?"

"What makes you think I'm afraid?"

"Before you thought better of it, you started to say you came here to be safe. Are you running away from something?"

"Not something, someone," she confessed, sounding relieved by the admission.

"A man?" She nodded. Feeling a surge of jealousy, he asked, "A lover?"

She shrank closer to the car door. "Never. I'd die before I'd let Jamal touch me."

Not liking the way she shied away from him, Tom said quietly, "You'd better tell me what this is all about."

"Why? I'm nothing to you."

He'd been asking himself the same question without coming up with an answer he wanted to hear. "I'm the nearest thing to the law out here for the moment. Maybe I can help."

She shook her head, black hair tumbling like silk around her face. "You can't. Jamal is too powerful. He has friends everywhere."

"Not among my family."

He had the satisfaction of seeing her uncoil a little, although the screen of hair still hid her expression. The sight whirled him back eight years. As if a door had opened in his mind, he remembered who and what she was. When he'd last seen her, her face had also been screened, but by a scarf crossing under her chin, the fringed ends tossed over her shoulders. The glimpse of beauty he'd gained had fired his imagination for weeks afterward.

Amid the heat and dust, she'd stood out like the rare desert flowers that sprang up only after rain. He'd felt sorry for her, forced to attend her father when she must have been bored witless. Judy had noticed and struck up a conversation, he remembered. If he was right about her, she and Judy had kept in touch ever since.

Only one way to find out. "I've seen you before, haven't I?" he asked.

She nodded resignedly. "Eight years ago. A lifetime."

"Princess," he said slowly, his changed intonation bringing her head up, her eyes glittering with fear. "No wonder you looked so startled when I called you that. You *are* a princess. Shara—" he searched his memory "—Najran. Your father, King Awad, buys bloodstock for his breeding program from our neighbors, the Horvaths."

She buried her face in her hands as memory flooded back. Her father had asked about some new breeding techniques being used in the Kimberley, and Clive Horvath had arranged for them to visit Diamond Downs.

While their entourage was being shown around the cattle yards, a handsome young man had ridden in, commanding Shara's attention. The dust and heat had been choking but Tom had looked comfortable, happy, even, in the stifling atmosphere. She'd seen his gaze linger on her as he was being presented to her father. Tom wouldn't have seen much of her face beneath her silk scarf, but she had certainly noticed him.

Des had invited Tom to join them, but he'd murmured his regrets and ridden away. She remembered admiring the easy way he'd melted into the landscape, wishing she could have gone with him, although her father would have been scandalized beyond words. As it was, he'd only allowed her to accompany him to Australia after she'd argued that she would need a broader experience of the world to share with her children one day.

Although the discussions about cattle had been tedious, her imagination had been captured by the beautiful, limitless vistas of the Kimberley. Finding a kindred spirit in Judy had been a high point. Almost making up for the slight she'd felt over Tom's refusal to stay, Shara thought.

Almost.

From Judy, she'd learned that Diamond Downs covered over a thousand square miles. Now Shara wished it were larger, putting more distance between herself and Jamal.

"Tell me about Jamal," Tom prompted, as if reading her thoughts.

"I'm promised to him in marriage, but he's the most corrupt man in my father's ministry. After he caught me trying to gain proof of his treachery, he forced me to accompany him to Australia. Under our law a wife can't speak against her husband, so he intends to marry me before we return to Q'aresh."

"Nice touch," Tom murmured. "Can't your father protect you?"

"He has no idea what Jamal is really like. Years ago he saved the life of my brother, the crown prince, putting my father in his debt."

Tom nodded. "And you're the payment. I see."

She wound her fingers together. "I don't think you do. As soon as Jamal gains access to my titles and dowry, he means to take the throne from my father."

Tom released a whistling breath. "Have you told the king what you suspect?"

"I tried, but at that point I had no evidence beyond what I'd overheard. He thought I was making it up to get out of the marriage." She gave a derisive snort. "In my country, a woman's word—even that of a princess—counts for little against a man's."

"What happens if you don't marry this man?"

She couldn't suppress a shudder. "My father will keep me locked in the palace until I change my mind."

"Talk about a rock and a hard place. What are you going to do?"

"Before I was caught, I recorded Jamal talking about his plans. The tape is hidden aboard the private plane that brought us here. I have to stay out of his clutches long enough to get the tape back and send it to my father."

"Today's adventure isn't going to help."

She straightened her leg, wincing at the pain of reminder. "Probably not, but I'm not going to let it stop me."

"Do Judy and Des know what you're embroiled in?"

She inclined her head. "They wanted me to stay with them, but I won't expose them to more danger than I must."

"So you exiled yourself to a rustic cottage, intending to take on Jamal all by yourself."

"If I have to."

"With respect, Princess, you're crazy. If this man is as dangerous as you say, he'll do whatever it takes to stop you getting that evidence to your father."

Breathing deeply to bring her temper under control, she lifted her chin. "Do you have a better idea?"

"Quite a few, starting with going to the police."

"They'd want to return me to Q'aresh for my own safety."

"They could be right."

"Without the tape, I may as well marry Jamal here and now."

Tom didn't approve, she saw, as his frown deepened and he tightened his grip on the wheel. His sense of justice must be offended, she decided. At least he was on her side. Realistically she couldn't expect any more from him. If she found herself wanting more, it was her problem.

He drummed on the steering wheel. "Can't the police get a warrant to search the plane?"

"As a member of our government, Jamal has diplomatic immunity."

"So we find another way to get it."

Her eyebrow arched. "We?"

He directed a steely gaze her way. "I told Wandarra I'd take responsibility for you, and I meant it. Whatever happens now, Princess, we're in this together."

Chapter 3

What had made him decide to get involved with her? he asked himself. The answer was in her fight with Jamal. Tom knew only too well how it felt to be threatened by someone with all the power on their side. At the very least, he wanted to help her even the odds.

Her beauty and courage had nothing to do with his decision.

Although Des's homestead was over sixty years old, the Australian sense of irony meant it would be forever referred to as new, he told her as they neared it. The house sprawled across a ridge of grassland between river and rain forest, raised on a raft of concrete beyond the reach of the spreading floodwaters that would come with the monsoon rains of the wet season.

From the moment Des and Fran had taken Tom in, their house had felt welcoming. The only solid walls belonged to the bedrooms and bathrooms. The living areas were soaring, open spaces with vaulted ceilings and insect screens for walls. Translucent shutters could be pulled down over the screens to shield the house during the monsoon rains. A deep veranda shaded the house on all sides.

The room he'd first occupied was on this side, with a view of the McKellar Ranges. The gum tree he'd occasionally climbed down after lights-out leaned more toward the house these days, but was good for another hundred years.

Much as he liked his own home at Halls Creek, this house still gave him a sense of homecoming. Scared as he'd been arriving as a foster child, unmanageable as he'd acted toward Des and Fran Logan, he'd felt safe here. Fran had died from appendicitis six years after Tom arrived, but Des had made it clear the family would stay together no matter what. Tom wanted Shara to feel the same sense of security.

Shara watched Tom's expression soften as they neared his former home. The palace where Shara had grown up was a low, sprawling complex of rooms opening into one another, with the main building at the heart of a cluster of other buildings. While far from palatial, the Logan homestead was also low and rambling, with the same sense of being the focal point of a small community, although her father's thoroughbreds lived in more luxury than the Australian family. The Logans' stock horses were corralled in a fenced yard with only basic amenities, but the sound of them whickering to one another as she passed made her feel homesick.

Accustomed to lavishly maintained homes, she was troubled by the signs of neglect visible everywhere on Diamond Downs. However rich Des Logan was in generosity and compassion, money was evidently in short supply. Shara's heart ached. She hated adding to the strain on his resources. Her private fortune wouldn't be hers to control until after she married, but one day she would return Des's generosity, she promised herself.

At the sound of Tom's car pulling up, Des appeared on the veranda. In his mid-sixties he was still a handsome man, the gray peppering his hair lending him an air of wisdom.

He was a couple of inches shorter than Tom, she saw when

they greeted each other, but the older man had a commanding presence. His face was darkly tanned and creased, but she saw welcome and concern in the blue eyes behind his dark-framed glasses.

If Des was surprised to see her with Tom, he didn't show it. He looked more alarmed when he saw Shara limping and Tom dragging out a substantial medical kit. From her interactions with Judy, Shara knew you had to be equipped to treat almost any medical emergency yourself in the outback.

"Should I put in a call to the flying doctor?" Des asked as he took them inside.

Tom intercepted Shara's panicked look. "Not yet. Shara wants me to take care of it."

Judy appeared in the kitchen doorway, drying her hands on a towel. She took in the situation at a glance. "Let me. I'm the one with paramedic training."

As a pilot she would be, Shara thought. Des's daughter had inherited his perceptive blue eyes, but her coloring was lighter, perhaps from her mother's side. She was about Shara's height, with short blond hair, a trim figure and muscular legs shown off by denim cutoffs.

Shara didn't miss the reluctance with which Tom handed her into Judy's care, but refused to read anything into it.

Judy took her into the huge, airy bathroom and sat her down on a chair before opening the kit at her feet. "What happened to your leg?"

"I hurt myself while scrambling around a gorge looking at some cave paintings. Tom took care of me," she said, wondering if he would tell them the rest.

Judy frowned. "Men! Did it occur to Sir Galahad that he might have rolled up your jeans instead of ruining them."

"He did what he thought was right," Shara said, referring to more than the clothes.

"He usually does," Judy agreed, her hands busy. She frowned. "This doesn't have anything to do with your friend Jamal, does it?"

"I haven't seen or heard from him since I moved into the cottage."

"But you expect to."

She flinched as much at the prospect as at Judy's ministrations. "He's not a man who gives up easily." Like Tom, came the unbidden thought, although Jamal's motives were purely selfish. "I can't stay much longer. I'm putting you all in danger from him."

Judy finished fastening a bandage around Shara's calf. "You're not going anywhere just yet. Tom did a good job. The wound is clean and doesn't need stitches, but it will take a few days to heal."

She closed the kit and stood up to wash her hands. "You'll stay to dinner tonight, at least?"

Royal reserve gripped Shara. "I can't in this condition."

Understanding lit Judy's gaze. "Come with me. I'm sure something of mine will fit you."

Shara felt color seep into her cheeks. "As soon as I'm able, I'll repay you for all your kindness."

"Put Jamal out of commission, and your happiness will be payment enough."

Des waited until the two women disappeared into the bathroom, then turned to Tom. "What really happened out there?"

Tom kept his face blank. "That's between Shara and me."

Des glowered. "Look, son, my heart might be defective but my brain isn't. I won't be wrapped in cotton wool just because of what some fool doctor told you."

"He told you the same thing he told me. Too much stress can kill you."

The older man's eyes narrowed. "And a transplant won't?"

"The success rate—"

"Requires some other poor soul to die to give me a chance at life," Des interrupted, "so I can hardly feel happy about it. Not that there's any hurry to decide. The doctor reckons my age puts me well down the priority list."

Judy, Tom and their foster brothers had all tried to convince Des that if he was given a chance at life, he should grab it with both hands. He was still far from convinced. At the thought of being without him, Tom felt a reaction as if someone had kicked him in the gut.

"You sure Shara wasn't trying to outrun her intended?" Des persisted.

Another kick, this time a little lower down. "What makes you ask?"

"One of Judy's colleagues told her he flew Jamal's retinue and a ton of baggage out to the Horvath place yesterday."

"Jamal came to Australia by private plane. He can't have been happy leaving his flash plane at Halls Creek airport because Horvath's runway can't handle a decent-size aircraft," Tom said, betraying how much he already knew of Shara's situation.

Des's eyebrow lifted, but he let it go. "I told Clive he should do something about that apology for an airstrip. He never listened. Now it's too late."

The sadness in Des's voice betrayed how much he still missed his friend and neighbor. They'd known each other for most of their lives, until Clive was bucked off a horse and killed five months before.

"I don't suppose Max Horvath will upgrade the airstrip," Tom commented.

Des's face twisted. "Max isn't half the man Clive was. No wonder his father disowned him."

"I didn't know he had."

"He meant to, but changing his will was another thing he never got around to doing."

Something in his foster father's voice alerted Tom. "So?"

Des hesitated then said quietly, "You may as well know. Max now holds a mortgage over Diamond Downs."

"You never mentioned a mortgage before."

"It was a private arrangement between Clive and me when the medical bills started piling up and the income fell off, to be forgiven in his will."

"But if he never changed it…"

"Max isn't likely to. He reckons I convinced his old man to stay on instead of moving into a retirement home. Can you imagine Clive Horvath in a retirement home?"

Tom's gesture swept the question aside. "How much are we talking about?"

Des named a sum that pulled an oath out of Tom. It was more than he and his foster brothers could put together in a hurry. "You should have told us things were that bad," he chided.

"You boys have had enough struggle in your lives. I'm supposed to ease your way not complicate it."

"You haven't. If Max starts pressuring you for the money…"

"He's already started."

"Refer him to Blake or me. It may take time but we'll find a way to repay him."

Des shook his head. "He doesn't want repayment. He wants this land so he can look for my grandpa's diamond mine."

Tom and the others had grown up with the legend of Jack Logan's rich find. The trouble was, Jack had disappeared before revealing the location to anyone. Andy Wandarra's people were said to know the secret but believed Jack's spirit haunted the site and refused to speak of it. "Assuming the mine really exists, how does Max expect to find it?" Tom asked.

Des popped the top on a can of beer, ignoring Tom's automatic frown of disapproval. "Eddy Gilgai works for him now."

Eddy was a cousin of Andy Wandarra's and had been on Diamond Downs's payroll until he was caught stealing. He'd been cautioned several times, including by Tom. When the thieving didn't stop, Des had no choice but to terminate his employment. Even then, he could have remained on the land, but the clan elders had banished him. Later Tom learned that Eddy had been seeing girls from his clan who were taboo to him under the complex laws governing relationships. "If anyone knows the location and would violate the site, it would be Eddy," Tom agreed, mentally adding another worry to his growing list. "One problem at a time. Let's hope Max and Jamal keep each other occupied until Shara's leg heals."

Des took a swallow of his beer. "Clive had a contract to supply cattle to King Awad of Q'aresh. As the new owner, Max won't have any choice but to deliver on it."

Tom massaged his chin between thumb and finger. "You have to wonder why the king sent someone his daughter warned him wasn't trustworthy."

"Maybe that's why he did it."

"To get Jamal out of the way, you mean?"

Des nodded. "He couldn't have known Jamal would drag Shara along with him."

Thinking of the tape hidden aboard the plane, Tom said, "We have to keep him from finding out she's here."

"It won't be easy. You know how fast news travels in the outback?"

"Only too well." As a boy, Tom had been the subject of enough gossip to last him a lifetime. Even today, stares occasionally followed his progress down the main street of Halls Creek and murmured voices told each other, "That's the man who's father..." His arctic look silenced them at least until he was out of earshot, when no doubt the rest of the story would be poured into eager ears. Gossiping was human nature, but he thought they should have found something else to talk about by now. Evidently they hadn't.

Tom was right. On Diamond Downs, Shara stuck out like a sore thumb. An idea began to form in his mind of how he could help her, and make amends for hurting her at the same time. He reached for a can of beer and took a thoughtful drink.

"You're very kind, but I can't take your things," Shara insisted as Judy dragged an assortment of clothes out of her closet and dumped them on the bed.

The other woman planted her hands on her hips. "Your

clothes are out of reach aboard the plane. You're going to need a few things to see you through this."

Her friend was right, but Shara didn't like admitting it, even to herself.

Judy frowned. "I understand pride. When Tom first came to us, he was a walking mass of it. So stiff-necked, you couldn't say a word to him without offending him. If he could learn to bend, surely you can, too?"

"I don't think he bent very far."

Judy grimaced. "It didn't take you long to work that out. What happened between you two in that cave?"

Half in and half out of her jeans, Shara tensed. "He took care of me, nothing more."

Judy made a face. "He must be losing his touch."

Shara didn't ask her to elaborate. If by "his touch" Judy meant he was charming to women, Shara had already worked that out for herself. Their first meeting might have been far from romantic, but she couldn't deny his power-house effect on her. Her grandmother would say he turned her on.

No amount of telling herself she was adrift and vulnerable made any difference. Whatever his true background, he ex-uded an air of assurance that marked him as a leader, tripping every female hormone she possessed without even trying. She didn't intend to do anything about it, but she was woman enough to feel the impact.

Careful of her injury, she pulled the ruined jeans off and dropped them on the floor. The black pair Judy proffered were tighter than those Shara normally wore and sat low on her narrow hips. When she zipped them up they fit as if molded to her.

Shara lifted a filmy white top over her head. It settled like a cloud over her shoulders, the soft material drifting down to outline her breasts. The cowl neckline revealed the deep cleft between them. In her country, she would never have worn such revealing clothes. Could she overcome years of conditioning and dress as Judy did so naturally? Yes, she decided with a defiant glance in the mirror. For better or worse she was in Australia. She would do as the Australian women did.

Wanting to earn Tom's admiration had nothing to do with her decision.

"Take that outfit with you, it looks great," Judy urged. "You can have the other stuff, too."

"Won't you need them yourself?"

Judy glanced at her well-filled closet. "What for?"

Thinking of Tom, Shara said, "To please the man in your life."

"I'd rather dress to please myself. Besides, there's no one on the horizon at the moment. At least, there was. But he doesn't seem all that interested."

"And you're—what do you call it?—holding a candle for him?"

"A torch," Judy amended. She shook herself like a puppy shedding water. "He'll either come back or he won't. Dad's my priority at the moment."

Shara shot her a look of concern. "Your father is ill?"

"He has a serious heart problem. The only cure is a transplant."

Thinking of the run-down state of the buildings, Shara asked, "Forgive me for asking, but is money the problem?"

"Partly, but throwing yourself on your father's mercy won't help, so don't even think about it. In this country everyone has access to medical care through the public hospital system. And Tom and the boys can come up with whatever Dad needs if he's treated privately. But they can't guarantee that Diamond Downs will be here when he recovers."

Shara stilled in front of the mirror. "How can land not be here?"

"Max Horvath owns the property bordering ours. He wants control of our land and he won't rest until he gets it."

"I know the name. Horvath has supplied bloodstock to my father for many years. I understood he is a good man."

"Clive Horvath *was* a good man, one of Dad's oldest

friends. But he died five months ago in a riding accident. His son, Max, is a different kettle of fish."

Ignoring the confusing metaphor, Shara said, "He doesn't have enough land of his own?"

Judy perched on a corner of the bed and folded her arms. "Oh, he does, but he isn't interested in raising cattle. Too much like hard work. According to legend, my great grandfather, Jack Logan, found a fortune in diamonds on our property. Max wants the diamonds."

Hearing the scorn in Judy's voice, Shara said, "You don't think the legend is true?"

Judy shook her head. "When I was a kid, I did. But the only evidence we have is the journal entry Jack left about a fabulous new diamond mine he was going back to explore. He disappeared before telling anyone where the mine was. The local Aboriginal elders are said to know the location but they won't go near it."

"Why not?"

"They say the place is haunted by Jack who supposedly died at the site of his discovery. All I know is his body was never found, and the aboriginal people working here clam up if the diamonds are mentioned. Now Max wants them, and it's my fault."

Judy held out a pearl silk top. "Try this on, it's more your color than mine."

Reluctant to spoil Judy's obvious enjoyment, Shara shimmied out of the white top and into the second one. She stood patiently while Judy gathered the loose folds and knotted them at Shara's waist, exposing a good inch of midriff. "How can Max's actions be your fault?" she asked.

"Max wanted to marry me and I turned him down. He thinks I was poisoned against him by his father. Max can't see that his attitude is what turns me off."

"Not to mention the torch you're carrying for this other man," Shara said.

"Right." Judy stood up. "You should wear that. It looks better on you than on me. I have too much up front to do it justice."

Shara thought Judy was being unnecessarily modest about her appearance, as she said, "I wish I could help you and your family. You're being too kind."

Ignoring Shara's protests, Judy scooped the white top into a plastic carrier bag, adding a pair of camel moleskins and a sweater. "Don't worry about us. The boys won't let Max stand over Dad. We were going to ask Tom to go over and talk with Max this afternoon."

Shara shifted uneasily. "Instead, he got held up on my account."

Judy grinned. "Max isn't going anywhere. And when Tom sees how you're dressed, I don't think he'll have too many regrets."

Shara's hands fisted uneasily in the silky fabric. "Perhaps it's better if I don't distract him."

"Relax, I'm joking. In any case, Tom's bombproof when it comes to women."

A sharp sensation gripped Shara. She wasn't interested in romance. Her life was already complicated enough without it. Yet the thought that Tom might be involved with another woman had a staggering impact on her.

She had spent only a few hours in his company. How could she feel anything toward him, far less this stomach-twisting dislike of an unknown woman?

She masked her reaction with a polite smile. "Is he engaged to be married?"

"Good grief, no. By bombproof, I meant he doesn't want a lasting relationship."

The relief that washed through Shara was tempered by curiosity. "Why not?"

"It's Tom's story. I'll let him tell you himself when he's ready."

If he was ready, Shara interpreted. She took a last look at herself in the mirror. She looked almost Australian. Only her dusky complexion and kohl-rimmed eyes hinted at eastern mystique. The combination was startling she saw, and unwillingly pictured Tom's reaction. Not that she wanted to have an effect on him.

Even so, his reaction was hardly the one she'd expected. When she and Judy rejoined the men, Tom's voice trailed off and his eyes went cold as he stood to acknowledge her. "That isn't going to help," he stated.

At least Shara wasn't alone in feeling puzzled. Des and Judy looked equally baffled. "I think she looks fabulous, don't you, Dad?" the young woman asked.

"Like a magazine cover girl," Des agreed.

"You may as well serve her up to Prince Jamal on toast," Tom snapped.

A chill frosted Shara's spine. "He can't have found me already?"

"Not yet, but he's staying with a neighbor, Max Horvath," Tom stated. "Looking like that, you'll be the talk of the area. Word will get back to him so fast your head will spin."

Shara shivered. Her head was already spinning, partly with the awareness of her own foolishness. She had let herself feel safe at Diamond Downs, when nowhere was safe from a man like Jamal. Trying on Judy's clothes, she had been so carried away anticipating Tom's reaction, that she had forgotten who and what she was.

She was a princess on the run, and it was only a matter of time before Jamal found her and forced her to return to Q'aresh as his bride. Her brief taste of freedom would be over before she had brushed the traditional bridal rice and rose petals out of her hair.

And if Jamal used her to usurp her father's throne, the consequences for her homeland would be disastrous.

Chapter 4

"Remind me again why I let you talk me into helping you on my vacation?" Tom said as he followed Blake into an enclosure containing a twelve-foot female crocodile his foster brother wanted to introduce to a male.

It wasn't Tom's first experience of handling big crocs. He had helped Blake to set up Sawtooth Park as a tourist and research venture. Tom still had shares in the park. They'd worked together until Tom decided that he preferred a career as a shire ranger. Not out of fear of the man-eaters, as Blake joshed Tom, but because spending his life hip deep in mud had turned out to have limited appeal.

Blake reveled in the life. At just over six feet, Blake was as tall as Tom, with hazel eyes, longish brassy-gold hair and a cowboy's rangy build that belied his muscular strength.

Today, Tom welcomed the dirty, dangerous work and he wouldn't be surprised if Blake had guessed as much before asking for his help. Finding out about the mortgage Max Horvath held over Diamond Downs had given him nothing but a colossal headache.

Shara's refusal to stay with Des and Judy at the homestead wasn't helping either.

The woman had as much of a death wish as Blake, Tom decided. Learning that Prince Jamal was so close by should have spooked her, but no, she had to prove she wasn't afraid of her would-be fiancé, insisting on being driven back to the old cottage. Thinking of her alone there had kept Tom awake for a good part of the last two nights since the dinner with Des.

How long would it be before Jamal found out she was on Diamond Downs land? Staying with Des and Judy, she had some protection. On her own in the middle of nowhere, she had none.

Not that it was any concern of his, Tom assured himself. She might be a sloe-eyed beauty with more fire than most women he knew, but it didn't mean he wanted to get any more involved with her problems. Driving by the old cottage and keeping an eye on her from a discreet distance yesterday was part of his job as a ranger, nothing personal.

Now all he had to do was convince his raging hormones.

Because worrying about her wasn't all he'd done while lying awake long into the night. Part of the time was spent imagining her small, firm body pressed against him. In her own clothes, she'd looked every inch a princess, regal and untouchable. In Judy's clothes, showing off that tantalizing flash of café au lait midriff, she'd made his mouth water.

Fear shot through him, and not because he stood within feet of an unseen crocodile. That kind of fear he could handle. The prospect of a serious relationship alarmed him much more. And in spite of his personal history, he wanted to be close to Shara.

Her pride, boldness and insistence on living her life her way no matter what the cost sent his blood pressure soaring higher than her beauty did, and that was fast enough.

In a matter of hours she'd slipped well and truly under his skin where she had no business being. No woman had. Leaving her alone at the old cottage had taken almost more grit than he possessed. Everything in him had urged him to follow her inside.

Maybe he should hope that Jamal *would* whisk her back to their magic kingdom, then she'd stop filling Tom's thoughts.

He felt a sensation like a punch in his midsection, momentarily grabbing his breath. He didn't like the idea of her returning to Q'aresh as Jamal's bride. As anybody's bride. Except maybe—

No, he halted the thought in its tracks. With his background, he wasn't in the marriage market now or ever. The more attracted he was to Shara, the more reason he had to keep his distance, emotionally *and* physically.

Nobody said he had to enjoy it.

Blake turned from studying the muddy water. "You're here because you'd rather wrestle an amorous crocodile than try to convince Max Horvath that the diamonds he's so anxious to possess exist only in legend."

Tom shot his foster brother a look that said "smart-ass." But Blake was right. "Andy Wandarra has always said the mine is real and the elders of his clan knows how to locate it. Only the spirit of our great-grandfather keeps them from revealing the secret. If it's true, Eddy Gilgai might be able to lead Horvath to the place."

Blake used a long pole to probe among the reeds at the water's edge. "Max must have promised him a lot to get him to betray his clan. Shows how strongly Max believes in the legend."

Tom kept a wary eye on the deceptively still waters. "If he didn't, he would have sold out right after his father died. This way he gets to stay in the area and keep looking." He made a sound of annoyance. "He has a law degree. Why can't he use it to fleece rich clients instead of harassing a sick man?"

Blake ventured ankle deep into the mud. Without turning, he said, "Max likes the idea of being a wealthy landowner. The trouble is, he has too much land and not enough wealth."

"When did you get your psychology degree?" Tom's tone was grudging but his foster brother's assessment of their neighbor sounded valid. Max Horvath had never liked the demanding life of a cattleman. He and his father had fallen out because the younger man hadn't wanted to follow in his father's footsteps. He'd been more interested in making money, but even law hadn't made it as fast as Max liked to spend it. "If there really is a mine, why wasn't it located long before this?"

"You know the taboos as well as I do," Blake said.

"Yeah, yeah. Great-grandfather's spirit haunts the place. That might have worked on the tribal people, but not on some of the current generation, like Eddy. Unless there's nothing to be found."

"Is that why you stopped looking?"

Blake's casual question didn't fool Tom. As boys, he and his foster brothers and Judy had talked about finding the mine and becoming rich beyond their wildest dreams. As Tom grew older, the dream had never completely died, although it had been pushed aside in favor of more grown-up pursuits.

"I stopped because I had more pressing things to do. What about you?" he asked Blake.

Before Blake could respond, the pool exploded into a mass of leathery scales and snapping jaws. Although he'd expected this, Tom's heart slammed against his ribs and he stepped back instinctively.

Blake was ready. On the end of the pole was a catching rope that he looped expertly over the crocodile's top jaw, settling it behind the strong back teeth before pulling it tight. His muscles bulged with the effort of keeping the rope taut as he hauled the creature out onto the bank.

Tom dodged the thrashing tail that could snap a man's legs off, and waited for the right moment before throwing himself on the crocodile's back, using brute strength to restrain the animal until it had expended its initial burst of energy. His job was to control the massive head while Blake draped a wet sack over its eyes, the darkness meant to have a calming effect.

Under him he felt the powerful saurian try to launch itself into the death roll crocodiles used to drown their prey. He kept his elbows locked and jammed against his sides, his splayed fingers gripping the torpedo-shaped body as he fought the movement. If he was tossed off before Blake got the croc's massive jaws tied, they were both in trouble.

A croc could snap its jaws shut like a steel trap, but had little muscle strength to force them open, Tom knew. With Blake's rope wound around its snout, the crocodile couldn't do much damage.

He stayed put while Blake tied the animal's back legs, before jumping clear and expelling a huge breath of relief. "I hope lover boy in the next pen is up to handling this lady. She's got plenty of fight in her."

"Delilah," Blake supplied, looking at the crocodile with what Tom thought was almost fatherly pride. "I caught her near Three Rivers Crossing after she developed a taste for cattle. Don't worry, Hambone can handle her. He's sixteen feet of pure crocodile testosterone."

Tom slanted his eyebrows upward. "Hambone? Let me guess, he likes wild pigs."

"His favorite food." Blake bent over the trussed crocodile, checking to ensure all was well. "Come on, Delilah. Time for your blind date."

Tom rolled the crocodile toward himself to let Blake slide a carrying board under the animal, then they hefted it between them to the next pen. By the time they'd followed the catching routine in reverse and Delilah was splashing her way into Hambone's pond, Tom was soaked in mud and perspiration.

"I need to get more exercise," he said, rotating his arm at the shoulder and grimacing with pain as he saw the sixteen-foot Hambone surface and make his first courtship moves.

"You need to get more of something," Blake countered wryly. His head jerked toward the fence between them and the new couple. "Even a crocodile with a brain the size of a pea knows it's not meant to be a solo act."

"You think I should set something up with Delilah?"

Blake looked at the male crocodile arching his tail and head out of the water, and setting the water dancing with shivers from his powerful body, a ritual designed to arouse the female's mating instincts. "She's already spoken for. I was thinking of someone from your own species."

Tom rotated the other arm the female croc had almost jerked out of its socket. "You wouldn't have anyone specific in mind?"

Blake looked studiedly casual. "I don't know. You seemed taken enough with a certain Middle Eastern princess."

"She's a stunning looker. I may not be involved with anyone right now, but I'm not dead."

"Then the interest Judy detected at Des's place the other night was purely academic?"

Tom kept his gaze averted but felt himself redden. Of his three foster brothers, Blake knew him the best. Soon after Tom joined the Logan family, Blake had managed to get through to him when nobody else could. Tom didn't exactly endorse taking your new brother out to the woodshed and fighting him until he agreed to communicate, but it had worked. Tom had learned that he wasn't the center of the universe. Nor was he such a bad apple that nobody would want to bother with him.

He owed Blake a lot, but some things weren't meant to be shared. "Purely academic," he insisted.

Blake nodded. "Like Tonia Winters."

"Tonia was a mistake. A man's entitled to one."

"One? What about Susan and Jemma? You're starting to look like a rolling stone, brother."

"And you're starting to sound like Judy. 'When are you going to settle down? When are you going to get married?'"

His falsetto imitation of their foster sister didn't deter Blake. "Tonia and Susan I can understand. They were only marking time until they could get away from the Kimberley to the bright lights. But what was with you and Jemma? She shared your interests and your lifestyle. You could have had a good thing going with her."

"She was the one who ended it," Tom stated flatly, his tone suggesting an end to this line of discussion.

Blake propped a booted foot on a crossbeam of the enclosure fence. "Her decision wouldn't have had something to do with your real dad?"

Tom whirled on Blake, fists raised before he realized what he was doing. An icy sensation shafted through him as he studied his clenched hands before lowering them slowly. Over the years they'd had this conversation several times in different forms. It always pushed his buttons, and for the same reason. "If you must know, I was in love with her. When I told her, she said I scared her. She was afraid that if we got too involved, I could blow up and hurt her the way my father did my mother."

"Did you give her a reason to think you might?"

"She said it was in my manner. What the blazes is that supposed to mean?"

"It means you probably came across to her the way you're doing now, as if you'd like to take somebody apart with your bare hands," Blake suggested.

"Then she was right to leave."

Blake shook his head. "If she hadn't known your background, she wouldn't have read so much into it. You're not the violent type, Tom. You could have slugged me just now but you didn't."

"Doesn't mean I won't if I'm provoked far enough. My dad never meant to hit my mother and he always felt like a louse afterward. But sorry didn't mend her bruises or broken bones. Any more than it could bring her back to life the day he used a knife instead of his fists."

Blake watched the crocodile courtship ritual for a few minutes before saying quietly, "By now I know it doesn't help to remind you that you're not your father. But I'll say it again anyway. You're different. I've seen you risk your neck to rescue idiots who should know better than to cross a river in flood in an ordinary car. I've been around when you nursed sick animals for half the night, and suffered when they didn't make it despite your best efforts. None of that suggests you'll wind up in a prison cell for killing someone."

Tom felt his features harden. "Jemma left me because she was afraid of what I might do. Can you guarantee she wasn't right? Unless you can, there's no point having this discussion. I won't put any woman at risk of my mother's fate."

"Not even a woman you really care about?"

"Especially a woman I care about."

Blake slapped him on the shoulder. "If you don't get cleaned up, the problem will solve itself. No woman wants a man who smells as rank as you do right now."

Tom wrinkled his nose, well aware of the fishy odor of crocodile clinging to him. "News for you, brother, that's not a smell, it's an echo. Race you to the shower."

A short time later he was clean, wearing the change of clothes he'd brought with him and already tasting the beer Blake was opening, when his cell phone rang. He dug the muddied and battered object out of its holster. "McCullough."

He ended the call as Blake placed two cans of Foster's on the table. "Trouble?"

Tom gave his beer a regretful glance. "That was Judy. She was flying over Cotton Tree Gorge on the way back to the homestead airstrip when she spotted a truck heading for the old cottage. It belongs to Max Horvath."

A slight sound outside made Shara almost drop the battered copper kettle she was filling to make coffee. From the window she saw a kangaroo leap away into the scrub. She told herself she had to stop jumping at every sound, but it was hard not to when Jamal was so close by. He wouldn't leave her alone until she was his wife and couldn't get in the way of his ambitions.

He needed to own things to prove his worth to himself. Palaces or people made no difference. First he would own her in marriage, then he would go after her country. Then a neighboring country. Every new conquest would sate his insecurity but only for a limited time.

She frowned, remembering a personal assistant Jamal had hired two years before. The young woman, Amira, had been fresh from the country, extraordinarily beautiful and naive. Shara had assumed the woman hadn't been hired for her office skills.

Shara had no way of knowing what went on within the walls of Jamal's apartments, but gradually Amira's vivacious beauty had waned. She became painfully thin and edgy, shadows darkening her lovely hazel eyes. The fearful glances she gave Jamal were enough to tell Shara the reason. He had taken the young woman as his mistress and had mistreated her when the novelty wore off. The doctor Shara had ordered to check on Amira had diagnosed overwork, and sent her home to her province. Jamal had a new assistant the next day.

Shara felt her jaw firm. There was no way she would let any man bend her to his will until her inner fire was quenched and her spirit broken. Under Q'aresh's ancient laws, a man could physically discipline the women in his household if they betrayed him in some way. Women had the same right, but their strengths were rarely equal, so it was inevitably the woman who suffered at the hands of the man. No matter that the law was rarely used these days. It had never been repealed and Jamal took every advantage of the fact. When she had petitioned her father to change the law he had readily agreed, but always there were more pressing concerns. Nothing had changed.

No matter, she was in Australia now, she told herself. For the moment she was free.

Ironic laughter bubbled up inside her. If she was so free, how come she was hiding out in a rustic old cottage in the middle of nowhere, spooning the tasteless powder the Logans called coffee into a thick ceramic mug? In her apartments at her father's palace, servants would be doing this, and the heavenly aroma of real coffee would envelope her before she took her first sip out of a china cup so fine it was practically translucent.

Stop it, she ordered herself. When she had dealt with Jamal, she could return home to her good coffee and her own fine china. They were trifles. Her thoughts were a disservice to the kindness Des Logan and his family had extended to her.

Stirring two spoonfuls of sugar into the steaming coffee to disguise the taste, she carried the mug to the couch where a ceiling fan churned the air, making little impact on the stifling afternoon heat.

Forcing herself not to sigh for the air-conditioning back home was as useless as trying to convince herself the coffee was delicious. Or keeping her thoughts from returning to Tom McCullough.

"You can't stay there by yourself," he'd insisted when she'd asked him to drive her to the cottage after dinner with his foster father.

In his own way Tom was as forceful as Jamal, but she hadn't resented his attitude, aware that Tom spoke out of concern for her, not out of a desire to control her.

He would have more subtle means of getting his own way. A shudder of possibility shook her as her imagination worked overtime. In her country, women had a saying about men— stillness cloaks the tiger within. Where Jamal's inner tiger was a rampaging beast, seldom cloaked, Tom's was leashed but, she sensed, immensely more powerful for that.

What would his tiger be like, once unleashed?

She rubbed her calf absently, having had a glimpse when his friend threw the spear at her. Only a slight ache reminded her of where the point had penetrated her flesh. A lesser man would have allowed Wandarra to punish her, and she would have suffered more as a result. Tom's bold action had saved her. A desert warrior indeed.

Irritated with herself for letting him dominate her thoughts, she reached for her notebook. In case she was unable to re-trieve the tape of Jamal's meeting, she had decided to reconstruct what she could remember. The task would take her mind off everything, including Tom.

On impulse she got up again and fetched the loaded rifle he had left with her when he couldn't persuade her to remain at the homestead. She had assured him she knew how to use a firearm, having been taught to shoot in Q'aresh, although she had never targeted a living creature. Wasn't sure she'd be able to. But she felt better having the weapon near at hand.

How long would she have to endure this hunted existence? If Judy's prediction proved true and their neighbor gained control of this land, Diamond Downs might not provide a sanctuary for much longer. What would she do then? What would all of the Logans do?

Their connection with this place evidently ran as deep as hers to her native country. She wished there was something she could do to help them.

Some time later she closed the notebook with a feeling of dissatisfaction. She had a reasonably clear account of the plans Jamal and his cronies had talked about, but it still wasn't enough to convince her father. To do that she had to get hold of the tape hidden aboard the plane. Easier said than done, she was sure.

Taking a sip of now-tepid coffee, she lifted her chin. Where there was a will, there was a way, as her Australian-born grandmother had told her often enough.

A fierce longing for her grandmother gripped Shara. In spite of her love of Australia, Noni was fiercely loyal to her adopted country. But having her close by even for a short time would have made the cottage feel more like home to Shara.

The sound of a car pulling up outside made her pulse spike. Jamal? If it *was* him, he was in for a shock. She hadn't come this far to let him win now. Dragging the rifle across her knees, she aimed it at the door and waited.

When the door creaked open and a bulky male shape filled the opening, she lifted the rifle. "Take one step closer and I'll shoot."

Chapter 5

"**I**'d rather you didn't," said a husky voice.

"Tom?"

He lowered the hands he'd raised to shoulder height and came to take the gun from her. He had to pry it from her tense fingers. "You would have used it, wouldn't you?"

She nodded, blinking hard, letting anger chase away tears. "You'd better believe it. Why didn't you call out to let me know it was you?"

"Everything was so quiet that I thought you must be resting." Or gone, he'd thought but didn't add. His heart had started to race at this possibility.

She massaged her eyes as if they were tired. When she lowered her hands, he saw the fear in her liquid gaze. He eased on the safety catch and propped the rifle against the couch before grasping her hands and bringing her to her feet. "I'm sorry I scared you."

A tremor shook her. "I thought you were Jamal."

"If you're this worried about what he might do, why insist on staying here alone?"

She looked away. "Haven't you ever wanted to prove something to yourself?"

He pressed one finger under her chin, making her look at him. "You got yourself out of a bad situation that could only have gotten worse. What else do you need to prove?"

"That I'm not a total coward."

Her husky voice purred through him, warm as molasses. With her hands trapped in his and less than a heatbeat of space between them, his breathing caught. Under different circumstances, he'd have accepted the invitation of her parted lips without hesitation.

Feeling another tremor ripple through her strengthened his resistance, for now anyway. A man could resist temptation only so long. He looked pointedly at the rifle. "You're not a coward. In another second you'd have put a bullet in me."

She tossed her head, spilling a river of raven strands over his fingers. "Anyone can be brave with a gun in their hands. Forcing my father to listen to my concerns about Jamal would have shown greater courage."

"Without proof, you'd only have gotten yourself locked up in the palace for the rest of your life." His tone rejected the waste.

"It might not have been forever."

"The other night you said the king meant to lock you away until you agreed to his marriage plans for you. Parole hardly sounds likely."

Her sigh whispered between them. "No, it doesn't. But this isn't freedom, either."

Her bleak tone made Tom remember a time, many years ago, when he'd felt as if his life was over, too. With his mother dead and his father in prison for her murder, he hadn't been able to imagine drawing a whole breath again. The muscles used for smiling and laughing had frozen forever, or so he'd believed.

He suspected Shara was staring into a similar abyss now. Without thinking, he bent his head and brushed his lips over hers. The kiss was meant as reassurance, to tell her she wasn't alone and that somebody cared. The somebody being him.

She steadied herself by placing her hands on his waist, accepting the touch of his mouth without returning the pressure.

As a result, the kiss was chaste, brotherly and completely one-sided. But the contact sent liquid fire searing along his veins. He made an effort to even his breathing, and took a step back. Her hands dropped away but she didn't move. "We have to get you out of here," he said, annoyed with himself for delaying. The arousal he felt told him the time hadn't been wasted, but that was beside the point.

She ran her tongue over her lips as if tasting him, oblivious to the effect the small gesture had on him. "I can't keep running away."

"From the air, Judy spotted one of Horvath's cars heading this way. It's likely to arrive any minute."

Her face paled. "Was Jamal in the vehicle?"

"No way to tell, so let's assume the answer is yes."

She crossed her arms. "I'm not running from him."

"Oh, yes you are. I'm not risking him bundling you into a private plane and taking you back to Q'aresh against your will." The prospect shook her, he saw, as well it should. From her description of Jamal, the man was capable of abduction—or worse.

Still, her head came up. "You can't force me to do as you say."

He got a glimpse of the royal princess in her determined stance and outthrust chin. She was magnificent. He could imagine her in a palace, giving orders to a bevy of servants. He slanted her a smile that his foster sister would have read as a warning and been off before he could blink. Not having Judy's understanding of him, Shara foolishly stood her ground.

Not for long.

"Put me down, you peasant," she yelled, drumming her fists against his back as he tossed her over his shoulder. "You're hurting my injured leg."

Hit right in the conscience, he almost complied until he remembered that she hadn't so much as limped since he arrived. "Nice try," he said.

"I'll have you thrown in jail, publicly flogged, maybe both."

Having her small, nicely rounded rear pressing against his cheek was punishment enough, since he couldn't do anything about it. Except enjoy it, a not unreasonable benefit, considering he was trying to save her life. If his palm lingered on her firm flesh longer than strictly necessary, he could hardly be blamed.

With his free hand he restrained her flailing legs before her drumming feet bruised his ribs beyond repair. "Not in Australia you won't. In my country we're equals, Princess."

"Never." Like the female crocodile, her struggles weakened as her initial energy was spent, but Tom maintained his hold. Where was a wet sack when he needed one?

As he picked up the rifle, he diverted himself by imagining her trussed up on a carrying board and being delivered to him for what Blake had called a blind date. Bad idea, Tom decided when his internal temperature immediately soared.

Dismissing the fantasy, he also snagged a leather satchel from a table near the door. "Is everything you're likely to need in here? Squirm once for yes, twice for no."

Her violent lunge almost took out his eye. "Yes, damn you. What about the rest of my things?"

"They'll have to wait until the coast is clear. It's nearly an hour since Judy called. Jamal—if it is him—must be practically on the doorstep."

"Then put me down and I'll walk to the car."

"No time." Certainly not to argue with her over the proper time for heroism. He carried her outside, kicking the door shut behind them. Dumping her and the bag on the back seat of the Jeep, he closed the door and jumped into the driving seat, placing the rifle near his feet. Before she could react, he activated the central locking system and the tires spat gravel as he floored the accelerator.

Pinned down by the sudden acceleration, Shara struggled to right herself. Her eyes glared fire at him as she clung to the back of the seat.

"Fasten your seat belt," he said over his shoulder. "This is going to be a rough ride."

"Any more orders?" she snapped, but he heard a metallic click as she complied.

He ignored her murderous tone. "Not right now, but if Jamal shows up, be ready to duck out of sight when I tell you to."

"Of course, Master," she said, the words dripping sarcasm. "Anything you say, Master."

He grinned. "Keep it up, I could get to like the sound of it."

As he'd anticipated, her mouth snapped shut, but not for long. "You're the most heartless, insensitive, uncivilized…"

"Peasant?" he reminded her helpfully.

"Barbarian. In my country, no one manhandles me without my permission and lives."

He deliberately chose to misunderstand. "What does it take to get permission to manhandle you?"

The rabbit punch she delivered to the back of his neck almost ran them off the road. "Do that again and I'll tie your hands," he cautioned, fighting to keep the Jeep on the rutted surface. It wasn't much smoother than the ditches on either side, but at least they wouldn't get bogged in the talcum powder-like dust known locally as bulldust.

"What am I supposed to do, let you treat me however you will?" she demanded.

If he did that, she wouldn't be alone in the back seat, he thought, feeling an instant, powerful surge of response. "You're supposed to let me do my job," he said through clenched teeth.

"Which includes getting women stabbed with spears, assaulting them and then carrying them off?"

The Jeep bounced off a tree root the thickness of his arm and he winced as her head lashed around. He didn't dare slow down. "In some traditional cultures, a start like that would have us practically married."

She'd stopped complaining about the rough treatment, fixated on their conversation, as he'd intended. "I don't consider any of this amusing."

"And you think I do? I'm not the one with a murderous fiancé on my tail."

"You have only my word that he means to harm me," she said. "For all you know, I could be shirking my royal obligations by avoiding this marriage."

Seeing her pale face reflected in the mirror, he doubted it. "No one goes to this much trouble to avoid doing their duty."

"Thank you," she said simply.

"For what?"

"Trusting me. Believing me when my own father wouldn't."

"Maybe he would have been convinced if you'd had more evidence against Jamal."

He saw her shake her head. "You and your family required no evidence before you were prepared to help me."

"Code of the outback," he said, wrenching the wheel to avoid another tree root snaking across the road.

She grabbed the back of the seat. "What?"

"Something my foster brothers and sister made up when we were kids. Under the code of the outback, you don't back down, you don't give up and you stand by your mates." Blake had also insisted on a clause that said "no mushy stuff," to keep Judy in line, but Tom didn't think Shara would appreciate that. Besides, his attitude toward women had changed since then. He might not want a permanent relationship, but mushy stuff was definitely on the agenda.

He caught the first glimmer of a smile. "Do you consider me one of your—mates?"

The word sounded foreign on her tongue, but deliciously so. "Anyone who turns to us for help is a mate, so long as they're innocent of any crime."

"Is it a crime to want to live your life your own way?"

"Not in this country."

"Then I'm innocent."

She meant of any wrongdoing, but Tom had a feeling the description fitted her in every way. No amount of royal pig-headedness could completely disguise her fear of the fate Jamal had in store for her and her country. The ache in Tom's bruised ribs was easier to tolerate suddenly. It was nothing compared to what she must be going through.

"Are we going to the homestead?" she asked.

"Too obvious."

"Then where? Oh, no, not to your place."

He cocked an eyebrow at her in the mirror. "What's the problem? Not good enough for a princess?"

"Stop throwing my rank at me. I can't help being born royal."

"A minute ago you were threatening to have me flogged for laying hands on you."

He saw her reflected frown. "Yes, well, I'm not accustomed to having men touch me so intimately."

"Trust me, Prin...Shara, that kind of touching is not what I call intimate. One day I'll show you the difference."

Her reply was drowned by the crash of the Jeep as they became briefly airborne before returning to the dusty road surface on the far side of a jump-up. The gullies pitted the surface at irregular intervals where the floodwaters of the wet season had swirled across the road. Over the engine's roar, he thought he caught something about, "Over my dead body."

He was going to show her the meaning of intimacy, was he? Shara muttered a response, not sure if Tom heard her over the laboring engine. She was furious with him for treating her so cavalierly.

She felt heat surge into her face. Being thrown over his shoulder like a sack of rice was bad enough. He deserved to be boiled in oil for such disrespectful treatment. Far more mortifying was the hot, weak way his touch had made her feel.

Much as she had hated being carried, for one mad moment she had fantasized about sliding down his body and pressing herself against him until he kissed her again. Not in brotherly reassurance this time, but fiercely, passionately.

The stress of avoiding Jamal must be the reason for her weakness. Remaining unresponsive to Tom's kiss at the cottage had been surprisingly difficult, but she refused to accept that she'd welcomed his touch. Not because she was as innocent as he believed, but because she had her own code of behavior.

In her country, affairs before marriage were less common than in Tom's, but they did happen. She wasn't proud that she had been tempted herself three years before. Forbidden by her father to travel overseas to study, she had been matched with a female professor who came to her at the palace. The professor had been assisted by a handsome young undergraduate only five years Shara's senior.

She'd thought him the most attractive and fascinating man. He had returned her feelings, kissing her with a passion that was hardly the norm between teacher and student. But when he'd wanted to go further she'd refused, not because of any noble ideals of chastity, but because she hadn't loved him enough.

Now here she was, imagining herself in Tom's arms. Hardly noble, she thought on a hollow laugh.

He'd been affected, too. She hadn't been so traumatized by the threat from Jamal not to notice Tom's arousal. Lying across his shoulder she'd felt the caress of his hand over her bottom and his shuddering response. Yet unlike her tutor, Tom had been strong enough to resist temptation. Why?

Wasn't she beautiful enough? Worldly enough? Or did his code of the outback preclude relationships with "mates."

Trying to push Tom out of her head, she concentrated on her surroundings. She had never experienced anything like this drive. In her country, roads were arrow-straight, blacktopped highways financed by the bounty of oil. Being bounced around in a motorized tin can with a hell driver at the wheel was entirely new to her. How could Tom tell what was road and what was trackless desert?

He was like the nomads of Q'aresh, she decided, able to read the country the way others read newspapers. Ranger's training or an affinity with his land? Probably a bit of both. He was a curious mixture in other ways, too, part warrior bearing the scars of pagan initiation on his chest; part healer, tending her injured leg with an amazingly gentle touch.

Now he was a rally driver, fighting the Jeep over a road barely worthy of the name. She looked back but all she could see was the cloud of dust generated by their passing.

"Relax, he isn't following us," Tom said, catching her glance through the driving mirror. "Not enough bulldust."

"How can you tell through the clouds of the stuff." Although the car windows were closed, the dust seeped into every crevice. Her mouth and nose were choked with the powdery particles. She couldn't imagine how a second car could churn up much more.

"Trust me, we aren't being followed." Over his shoulder he handed her a canteen of water and she drank thirstily, wetting a handkerchief with a few drops to clean the grit from her mouth. She may as well not have bothered. Within seconds the dampness dried and the dust was back.

His confidence and skill helped her to relax although she would probably be covered in bruises by the time this drive was over. She hoped his home, cabin, whatever he lived in had a decent bathroom.

For a moment, nostalgia for her apartments at Dashara Palace swept over her again. There, the bath was as deep and wide as a child's pool, the water perfumed with attar of roses. She had servants to assist her and to help her dry and dress afterward. Her hair was coiffed by the most skilled of her attendants, and her clothes prepared by her personal maid. In her wildest dreams she'd never imagined a simple shower seeming like a luxury.

"You live underground?" she asked when he stopped the car at last. They were on the outskirts of Halls Creek Township. Tom's home was cut into the side of a steep hill with a garden of succulents and sedges extending over the roof.

He got out and opened her door. "It's called earth-integrated. I built it this way so the house is protected from the heat without the need for air-conditioning."

"You built it." Was there no end to his talents?

Inside there were more surprises, such as a panoramic view of the surrounding country, and a surprising amount of natural light from the windows and a series of cleverly placed light shafts.

All the woodwork was fifty-year-old recycled Oregon, he told her, showing her the kitchen, bedrooms opening onto a shared patio, a shower and composting toilet. Best of all there was a luxurious spa bath located on a platform overlooking the living room.

"So I can enjoy the view while I soak the dust away," he explained when she queried the location.

She didn't ask how she was supposed to take advantage of the spa without providing him with a view of a different kind. One way or another she intended to try that bath.

First she needed to get something straight. "I appreciate your help getting me away from Jamal, but if you ever manhandle me like that again, your ability to procreate will be in serious jeopardy."

"Ouch."

He sounded more amused than threatened, she thought as her annoyance rose. "It's no idle threat. At the palace I was taught self-defense by experts." In a blur of movement she flicked her foot up and sideways, stopping the kick only inches from his groin.

This time his flinch was genuine. "Bloody hell, Princess. You could do a man an injury."

She lowered her foot. "Do we understand each other?"

He didn't cup himself protectively but looked as if he wanted to. "I understand if I want to touch you, I'd better make sure you're bound hand and foot first."

"You're impossible."

"Then we're well matched." His mouth sloped into a teasing smile. "There *is* another way to disarm you."

He had already found too many ways for her liking. "What?"

"Close in, so you don't have room for any of those fancy moves."

She wasn't the only one capable of fast action, she discovered. Before she could react, he had taken her in his arms, holding her so tightly that she was molded against him. Not only was she captive, but the desire to escape had deserted her suddenly. She waited, trembling, for Tom to make his next move.

Chapter 6

Whatever had possessed him to bring her to his home? Tom asked himself. He should have taken her to the homestead. She could have hidden there and Tom could have protected Des if Jamal decided to play rough. Or to a hotel in town. Anywhere away from temptation. Now there was nothing Tom could do—nothing he wanted to do—except give in to it.

Not that he hadn't wanted to for a long time. Shara didn't know it, but the reason he'd turned away so abruptly after meeting her and her father on their cattle-buying spree years before was because he'd been fairly sure the king wouldn't approve of having his daughter thrown over Tom's saddle and carried off.

The scene, like something out of an old Hollywood movie, had played in Tom's head long after their first brief encounter. Having her beauty largely masked by a silk scarf had only added to her mysterious allure. He'd been unable to tear his eyes away from a figure as perfect as a goddess's and movements as gracious as any dancer's.

She'd been stroking a horse's head, her long, aristocratic fingers playing over the muzzle. The horse had whinnied its pleasure and Tom had been instantly, insanely jealous. Of a horse. So like a true hero, he'd ridden away as fast as he could.

It hadn't stopped him from asking Judy about her afterward. Or taking an interest when Judy and the princess had launched an indigenous art-exchange program, telling himself his fascination with rock art was the only reason. In a pig's eye, he'd told himself.

Now Shara was in his arms and her long fingers were tugging at his shirt. He looked down into eyes that were cloudy, not with anger, but with desire. She wasn't trying to break free. In fact, she was as close to him as she could get without them both being naked.

So he wasn't the only one wanting this. The thought made him feel light-headed.

When she wriggled her hands up inside his shirt, her nails lightly scraped his back, and heat pulsed through him. Fighting the urge to devour her mouth, he forced himself to shape her lips gently under his.

"You don't have to be so careful. I won't break into little pieces," she murmured against his mouth.

Maybe not, but he might if he didn't drink his fill soon. In spite of her invitation, he didn't want to risk hurting her. He tangled his fingers in her hair, sliding them down her soft nape to bring her mouth closer, deepening the kiss without giving in to the urge to plunder. The slight taste he allowed himself was pure honey.

When she locked her hands behind his head and opened her mouth to him, his resistance ebbed faster than a northern Australian tide. He was left high and dry with one thought in his head. He would be a fool not to take what she was so blatantly offering.

Okay, so he was a fool.

Her tongue touched his for a brief, giddy moment, and he bucked as the rest of him went on full alert. As a gentleman of sorts, he usually tried to allow a little more time to elapse between first course and mains, but Shara's kiss gave him no chance. "I want you so much," he growled, stirring against her.

She purred softly. "How can I not know?"

He felt a desperate need to be closer still, to bury himself in her until they were both gloriously sated. "We can't," he said, hearing more than regret in his tone. "Because you're not free."

Her wide-eyed look at least got that delectable mouth doing something else besides taunt him. "My father might consider me engaged to Jamal, but I don't."

He was definitely a fool, he thought as he unhooked her hands from his neck and held her at arm's length. Her lips were moist from their kiss and her cheeks glowed with hectic color. There were stars in her lovely dark eyes and it didn't help to know he'd put them there. "You're alone in a strange land, unsure of your future. And Jamal is still out there."

He hated himself for replacing the stars in her eyes with a sudden jolt of fear, but his words had the desired effect, he saw, as she wrapped her arms around herself. "And if he was not?" she asked in a hollow voice.

He owed it to both of them to be honest. "If he was not, and you weren't doing this for all the wrong reasons, nothing would keep me from making love to you."

"You have no idea what my reasons are," she said.

He ticked them off on one hand. "Fear, loneliness, the need to feel safe for a while. They'll do for a start."

Her gaze darkened. "Do you have to be right all the time?"

He cupped her hands in his. They felt chilled. "It doesn't give me any joy. Believe me, right now I'd far rather show you how I feel than stand here discussing it."

She turned away. "I have to be content with that, I suppose."

"Until we can change the future."

"Do you think we can change it?" Her tone was dubious.

He nodded grimly. "If the desire is strong enough."

* * *

Her desire was more than strong enough, Shara thought. Now its magical power was tempered by frustration at being unable to do anything about it.

All because of Jamal.

She felt Tom's hand under her chin. "Look at me, Shara. I know how you feel at this moment. Right now you want to kill him, don't you?"

Unable to speak for the hatred gorging her throat, she nodded.

Tom's gaze bored into her as if he could see into her very soul. "Don't let him do this to you. There was someone in my life, someone very close to me, who almost warped my life. I wanted to kill him, too. I wasted several years on that hatred, and you know what? It didn't even touch him."

"How did you deal with the feeling?"

"I went to see him. I'd believed my life would be fine if I never set eyes on him again, but it wasn't true. Seeing him, and how little my hatred affected him, helped me to move on."

Her mind worked overtime. Had this man abused Tom as a boy? He'd said they were close. She knew her eyes were full of questions, but he shook his head before she could voice them. "You have enough problems of your own. You don't need to hear about mine, not yet. Maybe someday. Just remember what I've said and don't let hatred drive you, or Jamal will have won more than your hand in marriage."

She forced the words out. "I know." Tom was right. Had she been compelled to marry Jamal, he may have owned her body but she would never have surrendered her spirit. Not to him or any man.

"Hungry?" Tom asked.

The question caught her unawares. Then he gestured toward the kitchen. He meant for food. If they did something as mundane as preparing a meal, perhaps it would give her time to subdue the yearnings gripping her. She could live in hope. "A little," she said then added, "I'm afraid I won't be much help with the cooking. Making coffee is about all I know how to do."

At the kitchen door, he turned. "Living in a palace, surrounded by servants, wouldn't give you much practice. Doesn't matter. I can throw together a pretty mean Spanish omelette."

She'd never eaten one but it sounded interesting. "As long as it isn't made of witchetty grubs."

He responded to her attempt at humor with a teasing smile. "Don't you know? In the Kimberley, they're a key ingredient of every omelette."

He began to move about the kitchen and she settled herself on a wooden stool, content to watch him. Her experience of domesticity might be limited, but she doubted if many Australian men were as at home in a kitchen as Tom looked.

He cracked eggs one-handed into a bowl then began to chop green peppers, onions and tomatoes. "Where did you learn to cook?" she asked.

He handed her a block of cheese the size of her fist and a three-sided metal grater, demonstrating how she was supposed to use it. "Des expected all of us to take turns cooking, making beds, doing laundry and cleaning house. At first I accused him of being a slave driver who fostered kids so he'd have someone to do his dirty work. Now I'm grateful. He made sure we could all take care of ourselves."

Feeling clumsy, she steered the cheese up and down the grater, her fingertips in danger of joining the growing pile of shredded cheese. "Des doesn't seem like the slave-driver type."

Tom poured cooking oil into a skillet and added the chopped vegetables. Almost immediately the delicious aromas made her mouth water. "Hardly. He said his mother had done everything for him, and he'd had to struggle to find his way around the kitchen. He didn't want any of us to be at a similar disadvantage."

"Wise man." Wiser than her own father, who'd never considered such a thing. "I was taught to run a palace but never to actually get my hands dirty. My father assumed we'd always have servants to take care of us."

Tom stirred the vegetables around in the pan. "Regrets, Shara?"

"A few. But not because I've been pampered. Mostly for what I haven't had the chance to learn and experience. I feel so inadequate when it comes to the most basic tasks. Such as how I'm supposed to grate this last sliver of cheese without my fingers going with it."

Removing the skillet from the heat, he took cheese and grater from her. The brush of his hand sent powerful sensations arrowing along her arm. She had to stop herself from clutching her chest near her heart, as if the arrows had actually lodged there.

He winked at her. "You've just identified one of civilization's most elusive secrets, how to grate the last of the cheese."

"You're making fun of me."

"It's true. We can send a man to the moon but we can't make a cheese grater that doesn't take fingers with it."

"Maybe I'll become an inventor and solve this great mystery," she mused aloud, her heart beating faster at the closeness the cooking task engendered. Preparing the meal was supposed to put some distance between them. It was having the opposite effect on her.

His gaze lingered on her face as if he was committing her features to memory. "Something tells me you're destined for bigger things, Shara."

She could hardly speak. "As a princess?"

"As whatever you choose to be."

She hadn't thought of herself in such a way. Suddenly she felt less inadequate. Her gaze blurred. "Thank you."

He gave her a look of being found out. "For showing you how to grate cheese?"

"For making me feel as if I'm not totally useless. I already feel like a fish out of water in the Kimberley."

He slid a hand along her arm. "Practically everyone in

Australia was a fish out of water here at one time, or their fore-bears were. The country was founded by immigrants. Even the Aboriginal people can only trace their history back forty thousand years or so."

"Only?"

"Recent research suggests maybe sixty thousand," he conceded. "So you see, you're not the only one."

For a moment she thought he was going to lean over the counter separating them and kiss her again, and her heart thudded in anticipation. Instead, he tipped the cheese into the frothy eggs and mixed them together with a spatula.

She should be glad he was stronger than she was, but she felt cheated. Why couldn't he sweep her into his arms and teach her all he knew of lovemaking? Showing her how to cook was a poor substitute.

But he was pouring the egg mixture into the skillet while he gave a running commentary about how to slide the spatula under the cooked parts to allow the uncooked egg to run underneath. She looked and listened dutifully, but inside she wanted to scream with frustration.

Tom was well aware of her dissatisfaction. Hard not to be when he shared her feelings. He wasn't especially noble and was glad she didn't know it wasn't the first time he'd cooked an omelette for a woman, as a substitute for lovemaking.

Des had wanted his boys to learn to cook for their own good, never suspecting what a turn-on it would be for the women they met. At least Tom didn't think he suspected.

More than one female had licked her lips in anticipation of more than a meal as they watched him potter around this room. Something about a man who was at home in a kitchen made them weak at the knees. Feeding them bites of the one dish he could cook really well finished the job. By the time he suggested they move on to the bedroom, they were practically melting.

So why was he so intent on keeping Shara *out* of his bedroom? Could it be because she touched parts of him no other woman had come close to touching? And he wasn't thinking of the more sensitive parts of his anatomy. If he wanted to be dramatic, he'd say she touched his soul. And that scared the hell out of him.

She wasn't the type a man could love and leave, and there lay the problem.

"I think the omelette is done," she observed quietly.

Startled, he dragged his mind back to his task. His hand had stilled long enough for the underside of the omelette to start to crisp. He moved the pan off the heat. "See, you have the right instincts."

She laughed. "Having a nose for when something is cooked hardly makes me a gourmet chef."

He regarded the omelette ruefully. "Makes two of us. There goes my chance to impress you."

"I'm sure it's perfectly fine. By now I'm hungry enough not to care."

"A lady after my own heart," he said, thankful that she didn't know how truly he spoke. He sliced and buttered crusty rolls from the local bakery and brought them to the dining table on the bread board he'd carved and polished from a round of fallen log.

At his request she carried cutlery and paper napkins to the table. While he tossed some salad greens in a bowl with bottled dressing, she pleated the napkins with deft fingers. By the time he had everything on the table, the napkins had become elegant swans, their long necks dipping over the plates.

He stared at them in fascination. "How'd you do that?"

"I may not have learned any useful domestic arts, but I was taught how to be decorative."

His mouth dried. "Sweetheart, I doubt you needed any lessons."

She dipped her head, the casual endearment more touching than he probably meant it to be. "You keep saying those things, yet you don't seem to find me decorative."

She sounded angry. He reached across the table and took

her hand, marveling at how soft it felt in his. "Does it help if I say I find you more decorative than is good for me?"

Her head lifted and her shining eyes dazzled him. "You mean it?"

"It's taking me all my strength to sit here and eat a meal with you, instead of what I'd really like to do."

She must have read his desire in his expression, because she didn't ask what he'd prefer. "I should be grateful for your strength," she said.

"But you're not."

"Yes—no—I don't know. When you're accustomed to having every decision made for you, and you finally taste freedom, you resent any suggestion that someone else knows what's best for you."

His eyebrows lifted. "Do you think that's why I'm not taking you to bed?"

"Isn't it?"

His breath gusted out. "This isn't what's best for you, as much as what's best for me."

She toyed with a piece of bread. "I don't understand."

"I don't expect you to, since I barely understand it myself." He served her then himself, leaving the singed bits of omelette in the pan. "Tell me about Jamal. What is his master plan for overthrowing the crown?"

She forked the food into her mouth and was gracious enough to look appreciative. Swallowing, she said, "The countries around Q'aresh are always warring about something or other. My father has kept us neutral and at peace with everyone including the West."

"The Switzerland of the Middle East."

She nodded. "A valid comparison. Jamal argues that we should ally ourselves with more belligerent regimes in order to gain power in the region."

"And your father objects."

"He feels we are peaceful and prosperous with no need to covet the land and resources of others."

Tom offered her the salad. She took a small amount then watched as he piled his plate high. "Unless you're power hungry," he observed.

"A good way to describe Jamal."

"Why hasn't he staged a coup?"

"He lacks the necessary following. As King Awad's son-in-law, he would gain access to the treasury and would be able to buy the support he needs to depose my father and then attack our neighbors."

Tom ate thoughtfully. "Charming man. No wonder you don't want to marry him."

She pushed her plate away with a savage gesture. "His lust for power is not the only reason I hate him. He uses people, especially women. Our law still permits a man to chastise the women in his household. No self-respecting man takes advantage of this law, but Jamal openly glories in it."

Tom's appetite had also deserted him suddenly. "He beats women?"

"I knew a woman he'd abused. She told me he becomes violent and sadistic with very little provocation. One day I fear he will kill a woman for some fancied misdemeanor. How could I have any feelings for such a man?"

He felt his jaw tighten. "You couldn't, of course."

She gave him a gentle smile. "I'm glad you understand."

He understood all right, more than she imagined. Tom's family history made him more like Jamal than was good for either of them. Blake's assurance that Tom was different from his father didn't help. How could Blake know, when Tom didn't, that under pressure he wouldn't turn into a violent monster, even though at this moment the thought of laying a hand on Shara made him sick with horror.

His father, too, had reacted with repugnance when he realized what he'd done, Tom recalled. But always too late, after Tom's mother lay on the floor sobbing and nursing a newly inflicted injury.

"I'll clean up here then I have some work to do in my office. You can use the spa bath if you like," he said brusquely, still haunted by the vision.

A frown made a small valley in her forehead. "You're angry. Do you think I should do my duty and marry Jamal?"

The denial exploded from him. "Good grief, no. You'd never know peace with a man like him."

She touched his hand, her frown deepening when he couldn't stop himself from recoiling. "What is it, Tom? I feel as if there's something you aren't telling me."

"Some things you're better off not knowing." He pushed his chair away from the table and began to gather up the dinner things.

She watched for a moment in wounded silence, then stood up slowly. "All my life I've been protected, told what's good for me and steered in the way others thought I should go. But I won't allow it anymore. Especially not from you."

She had his full attention now. "Why especially not from me?"

"Because I'm starting to care about you, and for some reason, that troubles you. You can do me the courtesy of telling me your reason and letting me decide for myself if it's justified. But you may not command me in what I should or shouldn't feel."

Tom's blood chilled. His worst nightmare was standing right in front of him. A woman who wouldn't take no for an answer. He debated whether to tell her exactly what she risked if she let herself care for him, but the words stuck in his throat. He couldn't bear to see her turn away from him in revulsion, any more than he could stand the thought of hurting her if his father's genes gained the upper hand.

Yet he couldn't have it both ways.

With that parting thought, he turned and left the room.

Chapter 7

After Tom disappeared into his office, Shara wandered around the house feeling unsettled. He'd definitely been as aroused as she was. She wasn't such an innocent that she couldn't recognize when she affected a man.

Following him and demanding he share his secret wasn't likely to wring a confession out of him. In his way he was as stubborn as Shara herself.

Was he afraid of Jamal? Unlikely. Make that impossible. As they drove into the town he'd told her about helping Blake to move the crocodile. Such a man would never let a bully dictate his actions.

She picked up a beer can sheathed in an insulated covering boasting Halls Creek, the Most Lawless Town in the State. Trust her to seek sanctuary in such a place. So far, the place was anything but comforting.

From behind Tom's closed door she heard the tapping of a keyboard. He might not want to make love to her, but he was nearby if she needed him. Small consolation, but it would have to do.

Her gaze went to the spa bath overlooking the living room. Tom had said he'd be busy for some time, and had told her to make herself at home. She'd intended to freshen up in the shower, but every muscle ached from the rough ride to get away from Jamal. A spa would be far more relaxing.

While the bath filled, she went to Tom's bedroom and retrieved a khaki ranger's shirt. He had several identical shirts, so she assumed he wouldn't mind her borrowing one, especially since she had no other clothes until they could return to the cottage for the rest of her things. She resisted the temptation to explore his bedroom. She was unlikely to find the answers to her questions here. They were more likely to be inside Tom himself.

In the living room she shed the dust-streaked shirt and jeans she'd borrowed from Judy and wriggled out of her underwear. Silk was definitely not suited to outback living, she decided as she dropped the bra and panties into the hot spa so they could soak while she did. No doubt in the outback heat they would be dry in no time.

She draped a towel from the shower over a chair, then stepped into the steaming water. At the touch of a button the water churned to foaming bliss and she sank up to her shoulders, a moan of pure pleasure escaping her parted lips.

The bath was large enough for three people, so she stretched luxuriously, letting her head drop back and her hair stream out around her, floating away the dust and aches of the day. She kept her injured leg propped on the edge, the spa's wide rim making this surprisingly comfortable.

Tom had been right about the view from the spa. From his sandstone ridge, the surrounding ranges possessed a lunar sparseness. When she lifted her head she could see a high collar of bare white rock surrounding a checkerboard of red- and black-soil plains. Tufts of spinifex decorated the hilltops while grasses and eucalyptus trees dotted the plains. The color and texture was as different from Q'aresh as Tom was from Jamal, but she found a comforting similarity in the landscape teeming with life on the edge of a baking desert.

Halls Creek was a small town but provided all the essential services in a Wild West atmosphere and she promised herself she would explore thoroughly after Jamal ceased to be a threat. From what she'd seen of the Kimberley, she wanted to spend more time here before returning to Q'aresh. Once she'd convinced her father to have Jamal's activities investigated, there would be nothing to stop her.

Remembering Tom's fear that Jamal might try to drag her back to her country and marry her by force made her shiver in spite of the heated bath. Jamal would have to kill her first.

He must have been furious when he reached the cottage and found she'd gone. She'd hate to be responsible for him taking his anger out on Des and Judy, and she resolved to ask Tom to call them to make sure everything was all right. Judy hadn't said a lot about Des's illness, but Shara gathered that they were worried about him. Shara would never forgive herself if such a generous man suffered because of her.

This bath wasn't proving as relaxing as she'd hoped, as the worries continued to churn through her mind. In desperation she began to sing a desert lullaby a nanny had taught her. Shara couldn't have been more than four when she'd first heard it, but the song was strong in her mind.

> Sea of stars, silver moon,
> Light your dreams
> And bring them soon.
> Shifting sands warmed the day,
> Now peaceful night
> Keeps fears at bay.
> The tent is still, still as night,
> As here you drowse
> Till morning light.

The song conjured up such a vivid image of the desert sands of her homeland lapping at the fringes of the modern cities, that a wave of homesickness made her voice catch. How long would it be before she could safely see it again?

Shara's song reached Tom in his office and his hands stilled on the keyboard. When he'd taken her in his arms he'd noticed the bloom of bruises on her skin from the rough ride and felt like a heel because it was his fault. In spite of the danger from Jamal, he should have treated her with more care.

He'd hoped Shara would avail herself of the hot spa. And he really did have work he wanted to do. But when he'd heard the spa start up, he'd been surprised by the strength of his desire to abandon his task and join her. He wasn't making much progress here.

He was halfway out of his chair before he forced himself back into it. Bad enough to have her kiss lingering on his mouth and his arms aching for the pliant feel of her. So he'd retreated to his office to avoid the temptation to take more.

Her voice lifted, the notes pure and bell-like, and he caught something about a tent in the desert. As a boy anxious to be accepted into Andy Wandarra's clan, Tom had gone into the Great Sandy Desert, spending a week alone sleeping under the stars and living off the land.

In her position, Shara probably hadn't spent much time alone. He would like to show her his desert sometime. Of all the women he'd met, she was the one most likely to appreciate the great silences and a velvet canopy crowded with more stars than he'd known existed.

What was he thinking? Just the idea of being alone in the house with her was making him rock hard. Taking her into the wilderness was not likely to help him keep his distance. Propping his elbow on the desk he cupped his chin with one hand, letting his mind join her in the spa.

He was probably crazy but he couldn't resist. And a fantasy couldn't hurt either of them, right?

In the fantasy she'd see him watching her and ask him to turn away so she could get out of the water. He'd never known a woman so unaware of her own beauty. Rising like Venus, the bubbles streaming off her, she'd take his breath away.

He'd say softly, "I have a better idea."

Before she could ask him what he had in mind, his clothes would be scattered on the floor and he would step into the water beside her. She wouldn't say anything but he imagined how her pulse would spike as she sat down again.

The water level would surge as he sank beneath the bubbles on the opposite side of the bath. As he stretched out his long legs they would tangle with hers. He could practically hear her gasp of surprise but she wouldn't pull away. It might be the first time in her life that she'd shared a bath with a man, but she would soon get the hang of it. In his dreams, anyway.

When they were kids, Judy and his foster brothers had used a rainwater tank on the property as a swimming pool, tumbling naked together in the tepid water. Like most people in the Kimberley, the Logans lived so close to nature that modesty was a waste of energy. Was it similar in Q'aresh? He would dearly love to find out.

Except that he wasn't moving from this chair until he heard her turn off the spa and retire to bed.

Don't even go there, he ordered himself. He'd shown her around. She knew where she was to sleep. She didn't need him to tuck her in.

Damn, but he wanted to.

The phone rang, shattering his fantasy and not a moment too soon. "McCullough," he said sharply.

"Interrupting something?" a voice asked.

"No, Blake, you aren't interrupting anything," he told his foster brother.

"But you wish I was."

"How in the devil...? You bastard. I'm at my desk catching up on paperwork. What did you think I was doing? On second thought, don't answer that."

Blake did anyway. "Keeping a certain lady company."

The last of Tom's arousal ebbed away. "How do you know she's here?"

"Jamal came to the homestead demanding to know where we were hiding her. I put two and two together."

Relief swept through Tom. "Then he doesn't know she's with me?"

"He didn't learn it from us. He's such an arrogant swine that I wouldn't give him the time of day if he asked me for it."

"Is Des okay?"

"He's all right, although not surprisingly, he was troubled by Jamal's visit. For that alone, I may have to kill Mr. Do-You-Know-Who-I-Am Sayed."

Tom couldn't help chuckling. "Is that how he introduced himself?"

"Not in so many words, but it's how he acted. He drove up to the homestead in a huge black Range Rover, the effect a bit spoiled by the red dust messing the showroom shine. Brought a couple of beefy blokes with him for backup when they blazed up to the house."

"Employees of Max's?"

"I only recognized one of them as Max's man. The other was probably Jamal's bodyguard."

"Was Max with them?"

"Not this time, but I'll bet he wasn't far away. Those two are made for each other."

Tom's hand tightened around the phone. "They can be in bed together for all I care, provided they leave Des out of this."

"I don't think they will as long as you have what Jamal wants."

"You're not suggesting I hand Shara over to him?"

"You know me better than that, Tom. I'm only saying this guy means business. You have something he wants and he isn't the type to give up easily. You need to watch your back."

"Always do, big brother. And thanks for not letting on where Shara went."

"It's the least I can do. There's one more thing you should know. Jamal made Des an offer. My guess is he's already offered Max financial backing in exchange for help getting his fiancée back. Last night he insinuated that the mortgage over Diamond Downs would vanish if Des cooperated, and he'd be generously compensated for the trouble he's been put to."

Tom whistled softly. "No more worrying about the future of Diamond Downs, money in the bank for his transplant. Des must have been sorely tempted."

"For all of about five seconds."

Tom dragged his fingers through his hair. "Just as well Shara doesn't know. She's noble enough to throw herself to the wolves to help Des."

"Don't let her. We can't trust any cartel that has Max Horvath in it. He's likely to accept the deal then go after the diamond mine as soon as Jamal drags Shara back to Q'aresh."

"Then we're agreed, we don't tell her," Tom said.

"I'm sure you'll find plenty of other things to talk about," Blake said. "You go back to whatever it was that I didn't interrupt, and have a good night."

"Remind me to slug you one next time we meet."

"You and which army?" Blake asked in a pleasant tone.

After he said good-night to Blake, Tom's warm glow was overwhelmed by hot-blooded anger. How dare Jamal try to bribe Des into betraying Shara? He knew his foster father well enough to be certain he wouldn't be tempted for a minute. The code of the outback had been bred in the older man's genes long before Tom and her foster brothers and sister concocted their own version.

The callousness of the offer chilled Tom's soul. Jamal was rich enough to get Des out of financial trouble with change left over. Yet the price he had put on his help was Shara's freedom. No wonder Shara was appalled at the idea of marrying such a man.

Tom looked down at his hands. They were so tightly clenched they shook. What he wouldn't give to get his hands around Jamal's throat right now. He'd take positive pleasure in throttling the life out of him.

"No." The agonizing protest was wrenched from him. Was this how his father had felt before he abused Tom's mother? Had he rationalized his urge to do violence just as Tom was doing now? Tom could argue that Jamal deserved whatever he got, but the arguments rang hollow in his mind. He couldn't deny that he wanted to hurt Jamal for his own reasons.

Just as well he hadn't given in to the urge to go to Shara. She deserved a better man.

Bathed, her hair dried using a masculine gun-shaped drier she found in the bathroom, and wearing the ranger's shirt, Shara felt a little better. She would have felt a lot better if Tom hadn't spent the evening locked in his office, but she was in bed by the time she heard him emerge.

Wide awake, she listened to him humming as he went around the house, snapping off lights and locking doors. As he passed her door on the way to his own room she recognized the Q'aresh lullaby. He must have heard her singing in the spa.

Her impatient sigh ruffled the darkness. What exactly did she want? Not a relationship when she was still under threat of an arranged marriage. And definitely not the constant attention she'd occasionally found trying at her father's palace. Something in between, she decided, although the thought of Tom as a friend wasn't satisfying either.

He went to his room without stopping and she heard nothing more after he closed his door. She took deep breaths, trying to slow her breathing and slip into sleep.

An hour later she was still wide awake.

Back home she would have summoned an attendant to bring her a glass of herbal tea. Here, she had no one to fuss over her. She slipped out of bed and pulled on the ranger's shirt, then padded out to the kitchen, careful not to make a noise and disturb Tom.

His kitchen didn't run to herbal tea, but there was cold milk in the refrigerator. Glass in hand, she wavered. Returning to bed made sense, but she was still too alert to sleep. It was daytime in Q'aresh. She would telephone her grandmother and assure her she was all right. Shara had already decided to stand by Jamal's story that she was in Australia of her own volition, at least for the moment. No need to burden the older woman with the truth when there was nothing she could do to help. But Noni knew her granddaughter well enough to be suspicious of the message, and Shara hated the thought of her being worried.

She also wanted to hear the beloved voice for her own sake.

Tom's study door was ajar. She could use one of the phones in the kitchen or living room, but her voice might carry and wake him. No sense in both of them having a troubled night. She went into his study and closed the door behind her.

The desk was at right angles to the door. As she sat down she tried not to notice the way the chair carried the imprint of his body. Photos and notes littered the desk. She recognized some of the rock art she'd seen during her fateful visit to the gorge, and she rubbed her calf absently. These pictures were not for female eyes, so out of respect for local custom, she covered them with a sheet of paper and pulled the telephone toward her, keying in the direct number, which bypassed the palace switchboard and connected her with Noni's apartment.

At the sound of her grandmother's personal assistant, Shara almost wept. The land of her birth had never seemed so remote. She hoped it wasn't lost to her altogether. She had to put on a good show for Noni, she reminded herself, banishing the tears. When her grandmother came on the line, Shara made sure she sounded bright and cheerful.

Twenty minutes later she was glad she had called. Noni was far from convinced that Shara had chosen to accompany Jamal, but trusted her granddaughter's judgment. She always took her side, Shara mused, wishing she possessed as much wisdom as her grandmother.

Shara's grandfather had valued his wife's counsel, in spite of his conservative ideas about the roles of men and women. Noni had been working as a governess in his palace when they fell in love and married. He'd professed to be exasperated by his foreign wife's desire for equality for women, but had gradually acceded to her gentle pressure to allow his female subjects greater freedom.

Thanks to Noni, the women of Q'aresh now enjoyed a high standard of education, drove vehicles, pursued careers and no longer had to conceal themselves under voluminous garments. Their lives were still largely controlled by men, but as her grandmother said, drops of water could wear away stone.

Her grandparents' love had bloomed for half a century until her grandfather died of a sudden brain hemorrhage. Sixteen years later, Shara still missed him although she knew he'd never valued her as highly as he did her brother.

Would Shara's life have been different if her father had also married a foreigner? Family history described Vivani Najran as stunningly beautiful but delicate and submissive, probably why her father had chosen her as his bride. He'd never been happy about his mother's liberal views and probably wanted a wife as different from Noni as possible.

No one would ever label Noni delicate or submissive, or her granddaughter for that matter, Shara mused as she drank the milk. She didn't care. She would rather follow Noni's example and live her life her way. Being submissive hadn't done her mother much good.

A choking sensation gripped her. Was she determined to avoid emulating her mother because she believed in equality for women, or because she was afraid of dying young like her mother, Vivani, who had died giving birth to Shara?

She snatched up the phone then made herself put it down, unwilling to disturb Noni again with stupid fears spawned by sleeplessness. At this very moment thousands of women were having babies safely and joyfully all over the world. So would Shara when the time came. *If* it ever came.

Suddenly her gaze was caught by one of the photographs still visible amid the clutter on Tom's desk. Torn between knowing she wasn't supposed to see it, but unable to tear her eyes away, she set the glass aside and lifted the photo for closer study. The rock art on the cave wall had faded with the centuries but was still clearly discernible. Several other photos showed the same style of art.

Her heart picked up speed. She was sure she'd seen figures like these in the caves in Q'aresh. If only she was at home, she could be certain. But all she had at present was her memory.

"What are you doing?"

Startled, she looked up to see Tom looming in the door-way, his raking gaze taking in her long legs and bare feet, the uniform shirt ending at her thighs. His short black silk robe hung open over matching sleep shorts and his feet were also bare. Her heart began to beat double time. "I couldn't sleep so I called my grandmother in Q'aresh."

"You what?"

She recoiled from the fury in his tone. "I'll pay for the call."

He gestured in savage dismissal. "That could be truer than you think. The charge isn't the problem. If anyone knows you were the caller, they could trace the number."

"I only spoke to my grandmother and her personal assistant. She's completely loyal to Noni," she said, annoyed at hearing a tremor in her voice.

He came in and stood over her. "You'd better hope so."

She resisted the urge to jump to her feet and meet him eye to eye. Without something to stand on, it was a lost cause anyway. Instead, she summoned years of royal training to say primly, "It's done now. Any consequences are on my head."

Instead of defusing his anger, her comment seemed to fuel it. He grasped the arms of the chair and leaned over her, sparks flaring in his dark gaze. "I'm sure you're used to doing as you please back home, but this isn't Q'aresh."

She blinked furiously, unwilling to give him the satisfaction of reducing her to tears. "What have I done that's so terrible this time?"

"Because you're not in this alone, Princess. My whole family could pay for your indiscretion. Earlier today, your intended went looking for you at Des's place."

Her heartbeat stuttered. "Jamal didn't do anything to harm Des?"

"Fortunately not or he would have had me to answer to. But the stress isn't helping Des's condition. Nor is Jamal's offer to buy off Max Horvath and take care of my foster father's medical bills if he hands you over."

She dragged in a strangled breath. How could she let Des turn down such an offer? She had to give herself up and hope she could make her father believe the truth about Jamal. Youth and time were on her side. Des had neither. "He should accept."

In Tom's gaze she saw a glimmer of respect. "Yes, probably, but he won't. Any more than I would in his shoes. Or any of us."

The code of the outback again? Or was it plain stubbornness? Guilty of the failing herself, she couldn't condemn it in Tom or his family. The closeness of Tom's mouth to hers made her thoughts spin. Heat exploded through her. He was magnificent in his anger, the sense of power and danger only heightening her desire for him.

"You can't stop me from surrendering to Jamal in return for honoring his promise," she whispered.

Tom's eyes glittered. "Want to bet?"

Chapter 8

His mouth descended on hers, strong as his anger, hot as her desire, negating any argument she might have made. She wanted nothing more than to lose herself in the kiss and whatever might follow.

If she did, she would truly be pleasing herself, but oh, she was tempted.

Unable to resist, she allowed herself a long, sensuous taste, feeling his lips soften against hers when he met compliance instead of objection. Desire shivered through her, swelling unbearably when he brought her to her feet and pulled her against him.

His chest was every bit as hard and muscular as it looked. Beneath the sculpted flesh the powerful beat of his heart kept time with hers and she burrowed deeper, feeling his robe settle around her like enfolding wings.

His masculine aura invaded her senses, blended with shower scents and the tang of peppermint toothpaste. On the brink of overload, her reason shut down. She forgot that she wanted to give herself up to Jamal, and gave herself up instead to everything Tom made her feel. She was all emotion, all sensation, all desire, surrendering to his embrace and wanting more.

His mouth answered her unspoken plea, his tongue dancing with hers in an unbelievably erotic braille. Flame tore through her until she expected her hair to crackle with the effect. Instead, she sizzled inwardly, his accusations and her dire situation swamped by the need to give from the deepest well of her being and take all she could from his.

Tom put into the kiss all the concern for her that he'd fought against acknowledging. Hearing that she'd contacted the palace in Q'aresh, his blood had chilled at the risk she was taking. If palace security traced the call to this number they could notify Jamal who'd be here with his henchmen before daylight.

Maybe it wasn't up to Tom to stop her giving herself up to her fiancé, but he was going to anyway. Much as he admired her willingness to sacrifice herself for the Logans, he couldn't let her. In the first place, invalid or not, Des was likely to kill him. And in the second, she would end up bound to Jamal for nothing. Because Tom knew what she didn't: that a man like Max Horvath wouldn't be content with Jamal's payment when an even bigger one in diamonds might be his for the taking.

More alarmingly, if Shara was right and Jamal coveted her father's throne, the stakes climbed even higher. She might be handing him the means to take over her country with who knew what consequences for peace in the region.

They were all noble reasons for restraining her, Tom rationalized, knowing that not one of them explained why she was in his arms. He wanted her there, pure and simple.

The sight of her curled in his chair, wearing nothing but his shirt, and with a faint milk mustache beading her upper lip, had aroused all his protective instincts and most of his other instincts as well. Telling himself he was no good for her didn't help. Never having been a candidate for sainthood, he simply had to touch and taste.

He should have known this would happen sometime. Until now he'd been able to separate women into those he bedded with their enthusiastic approval, and those he could care about and therefore avoided if he could.

Where did Shara fit in? His gut clenched. He'd desired her since his first, arousing glimpses all those years before. Her grace and beauty had haunted him since forever. Hearing of the work she'd done with Judy had earned his respect. Meeting her again had only banked the fires higher. But she wasn't the type a man loved and left. By touching her he was breaking all his own rules.

So why didn't he stop?

If she objected in the least he would, he vowed to himself. He might not be a saint, but Des had raised his boys to be gentlemen, up to a point.

On her side she had admitted to some skill in self-defense. All she had to say or demonstrate was "no." A tiny struggle, a well-aimed kick, and it would be over. A bit of pain might just bring him to his senses because it sure as blazes wasn't happening any other way.

He lifted her to her feet, pulling her into the shelter of his robe. Her breasts flattened against him, the feel of her hardening nipples against the marks of his initiation sending his pulse into overdrive. He licked at the milk traces on her mouth.

Come on, come on, he urged silently. *Show me what you want before it's too late for either of us.*

She showed him by sliding her hands around his neck and pulling his head down to deepen the kiss. A growl like a tiger's rumbled deep in her throat.

He watched his scruples sink without trace.

Unable to contain himself any longer, he plunged and she opened to him, her tongue twining with his as he flexed his fingers in her glorious hair. The blood thundered in his veins, making him forget his self-imposed rules, banishing all thought except how good she felt in his arms.

* * *

She was losing her mind and in danger of losing a lot more, Shara realized in the part of her brain still capable of rational thought. She hadn't known she could feel like this, as if some other wanton creature had taken over her body. Whatever Tom gave her didn't seem nearly enough. She ached to be part of him in the way she had learned that men and women came together, but only in careful euphemism, for fear of too much detail corrupting her innocence.

There was nothing innocent about the way she writhed against him now, feeling the power of his desire through her thin shirt. Visions of pressing him back against the couch in his office and tearing away his clothes crowded her mind. She wanted to experience for herself what her tutor had only hinted at. She wanted Tom. And the sheer physicality of his response left her in no doubt what he wanted.

Sweet reason, what was wrong with her? Had she lost her mind when Jamal brought her to Australia? She didn't even have the excuse of greenness, as she'd had when she fell in love with her tutor. With Tom she knew perfectly well what she was inviting.

Shocked at herself, she flattened her palms against his chest. As if a current had been cut off, he released her and took a step backward. His chest heaved and his eyes were wild, and there was no concealing the state of his arousal. But then he stepped back. Without a word he walked out, the door rocking on its hinges as he jerked it shut behind him.

No, she wanted to cry. Don't go. She felt as if she had been toiling up an enormously steep hill, then just as she was about to reach the crest, the force pulling her upward had pushed her back down before she could glimpse the glory awaiting on the other side.

Why had he stopped at her slightest touch? She hadn't been sure herself whether she'd been resisting or exploring, but he'd reacted as if she'd screamed a rejection at him.

What was it about her that aroused him then made him

break off before taking things any further? Was she not beautiful enough? Sexy enough? Experienced enough?

That had to be the explanation.

A man like Tom must want a woman of the world who could match him in the bedroom arts. Not a pampered, protected princess he'd have to coax every step of the way. Where was the pleasure in that for him? Shara already knew he was a man of great passions. Going slowly and gently while she caught up probably wasn't on his agenda.

She tried to feel grateful that he'd been strong for both of them, but instead she seethed with frustration. How was she supposed to become experienced if he wasn't prepared to teach her how to satisfy him? Well, damn him. This time she'd been vulnerable, her emotions in turmoil after the call to her grandmother. She wouldn't give him the chance to reject her again.

With head high she emerged from the office to find him slumped on the sofa, watching what looked like a sales pitch on TV for some complicated exercise equipment. Not something he would ever need, she thought, then remembered her promise to herself. No matter how attractive he looked—and with his shirt open and his chest and feet exposed, he looked good enough to eat—she wasn't going to let him get to her.

She took a seat opposite him, crossing her legs at the ankles and tugging the shirt over as much of herself as she could, although it wasn't much. "Good program?"

Without looking at her he aimed the remote at the set and muted the sound. "Not as good as the one that was on before it."

Her heart picked up speed. "The one you turned off?"

"The one we should never have turned on in the first place."

"Wrong channel?" she asked, wondering how long he would keep this up before he told her outright that he preferred a woman with experience. Then she could assure him that she wouldn't sleep with him now if he was the last man in the Kimberley. Whether she meant it or not was beside the point. Pride demanded the pretense.

"Wrong everything," he said tersely. "Time, place, couple."

"Then why didn't it feel wrong?" she demanded. So much for pride.

He did face her then, his measuring look shriveling her defenses to nothing. In spite of her promise to herself, if he kissed her now she would be his for the taking. When had she become so pathetically needy?

"Because it's late, we're alone and you're vulnerable," he said.

"You make it sound as if I'd throw myself at any man in the same circumstances," she snapped. "Well, you're wrong. I have my standards. Why do you think I pushed you away?"

As lies went it was a beauty. She hadn't pushed him away as much as tried to give herself breathing space before plunging in again. Thankfully he wasn't to know.

"Good, I'm glad we're in agreement," he said heavily, re-activating the television's sound.

On the screen a woman in a skimpy sports top and leggings was pushing and pulling cords, and talking about how the machine strengthened her already luscious body without building unsightly muscles. Shara might be naive but she knew that wasn't possible. Any more than she could move the immovable object that Tom had become.

The woman on the screen was welcome to him. A blond Amazon, she was probably more his type anyway. "I'm going back to bed," she said, her tone dripping ice.

He didn't look up. "I wouldn't get undressed if I were you."

Was he warning her that he might be overcome by desire after all? Instant betraying heat washed through her and she struggled to keep the effect off her face. "I'll lock my bedroom door," she said with a calmness she was far from feeling.

"That flimsy lock won't do you much good if Jamal and his goons show up."

Fool, she told herself. How could she have forgotten that her call to Q'aresh might have been traced? Tom had made her forget, driving everything from her mind except how much she wanted him to make love to her.

Her Royal Highness Princess Shara Amelia Vivani Najran

al Dashara, Hope of Q'aresh, Daughter of Light, had allowed a man not her husband, not even her fiancé, to kiss and caress her until she was mindless with lust.

Thank goodness he'd stopped. It still hurt knowing she hadn't been able to drive him mad with desire for her. Or that he could walk away and watch television, for pity's sake. Her ego would take some time to recover from that. But the sane part of her knew he'd done the right thing. When this was over, she would probably never see him again. What if she'd gotten pregnant? Her life was difficult enough right now without involving an innocent child.

"The risk of the call being traced isn't great," she said, fighting a vision of herself cradling a baby.

"How can you be so sure?"

"My grandmother's private line bypasses the palace switchboard. It's encrypted against bugging."

"So the only weak link is the personal assistant."

"She's been with my grandmother for twenty years. I'd stake my life on her loyalty."

"Let's hope that isn't what you've done," he said. "Either way, we'll know by morning."

With his dire words ringing in her ears, Shara hadn't expected to sleep a wink during the night. She followed his advice and dressed before stretching out on top of the covers. But she must have been more exhausted than she realized, because the next thing she knew, Tom was placing a cup of coffee on her bedside table. She had forgotten to lock the door after all.

"Relax, I'm not Jamal," he said, noting her startled reaction. "Although if I had been, you'd be on your way back to Q'aresh by now. You were dead to the world."

She sat up. Not used to being awakened by a man, she was glad she'd slept in his shirt tucked into Judy's jeans, so there was nothing untoward for him to see. Soon she would have to shop for clothes of her own, she thought. She was starting to look like a fugitive as well as feel like one.

Tom hadn't changed clothes either, although the rumpled look suited him. With stubble shadowing his face, and his eyelids heavy from their late night, he looked disturbingly sexy. She hadn't heard him return to his room, she realized. "Did you sleep at all?"

His expression became shuttered. "Some."

She was used to being guarded but not by someone with nothing to gain. "You sat up all night in case Jamal showed up."

"I slept on the couch. No big deal."

It was to her. Later she'd have to think about what Tom's actions might mean. Logic told her he wouldn't have wasted time bringing her coffee if there was any immediate danger. "He didn't find out about the call," she surmised.

"Looks like you got away with it this time. But we have to find you a safer bolt-hole. It's only a matter of time before he learns about this one."

Tom sounded as if he wanted rid of her, yet he'd kept watch over her all night. What was going on here? "You don't have to worry about me. I got away from Jamal once, I can do it again," she insisted. "As long as I have to, in order to convince my father of Jamal's true nature. I'll never belong to such an evil man. I'd kill myself first."

"He isn't worth it."

As a ranger Tom was duty-bound to protect the vulnerable, probably why he'd watched over her last night, she rationalized. Still, his explosive assertion warmed her. "I know he isn't. I wouldn't give him the satisfaction."

"Good. Drink your coffee while I clean up, then we'll have breakfast and decide your next step."

"I've told you, it's not your problem. I'll find a way to get the tape of evidence back from Jamal and to my father."

"Are you always this difficult first thing in the morning?"

Only when she'd been aroused to dizzying heights then abruptly rejected the night before, she thought furiously. "It's early for me," she said.

He frowned. "It's after eight-thirty. Perhaps you'd prefer

breakfast on a tray and your bath scattered with rose petals?"

His offer was so close to the way she'd started her day in Q'aresh that her face heated. "Sarcasm doesn't become you," she snapped.

"It's the best I can do right now, Princess. Drink your coffee."

He turned on his heel. A few minutes later she heard a door slam and a shower running. She lay back. A few hours' sleep had done little to alleviate her exhaustion. Tom's contradictory behavior was also wearing. Telling herself he was only doing his job didn't explain the kissing, or the strength of his effect on her.

With a sigh she got up. A change of clothes was out of the question, and she didn't feel greatly refreshed by the time she'd showered and dressed again and found her way to the kitchen. While showering, she'd made up her mind to ask him to take her to town, supposedly to buy clothes, but in reality so she could slip away rather than put him and his family at any more risk. She already knew he wouldn't agree. So she wouldn't tell him.

He must have finished showering. His office door was closed and she heard the murmur of his voice on the phone. She looked around. His comment about serving her breakfast in bed rankled. Time to show him she wasn't completely useless.

His refrigerator yielded eggs and milk, bread and butter. She located an electric toaster and popped the slices in to toast while she whipped all the eggs she could find into a fury with some of the milk and pepper from a grinder.

She began to hum to herself. Why did people make such a fuss about cooking? It wasn't all that hard. She had never scrambled eggs before but she'd seen servants do it. Nothing to it.

Saucepans hung from a stainless-steel rack above an electric stove. Choosing a small pan, she set it on a burner and turned the heat to high, then continued beating the eggs. When they looked sufficiently frothy, she poured the mixture into the saucepan, the sizzling sound encouraging. A few drops spilled onto the burner and she wrinkled her nose at the unappetizing smell, but decided it would soon burn off.

The burning smell wasn't only coming from the spilled eggs, she discovered as smoke drifted across her vision. The toast was burning. She grabbed the toaster and turned it over, trying to shake the bread loose, but her reward was a loud bang. Flames licked at the charcoal slices. With a screech of alarm she dropped the appliance.

"What in the devil…"

Tom stormed into the room just as the eggs surged over the rim of the saucepan and onto the floor like lava from an erupting volcano. She reached for the handle but his command stopped her. "Don't touch that, you'll scald yourself."

He snapped off the burner and the volcano subsided. Stepping over the mess on the floor, he turned off the toaster at the power point and hauled it back onto the counter by the cable, his expression grim. "First rule of accidents in kitchens, turn off the power."

"I knew that." She tried to sound as if it would have been her next move.

"Yeah, right." A slice of toast continued to smolder on the charred linoleum and he stomped on it. "I wasn't far off the mark with the rose-petal bath, was I?"

Refusing to answer, she wrapped her arms around herself, appalled at the devastation a few minutes could cause. "Maybe I should have started with something easier."

"Like McDonald's," he said, the laugher in his voice taking any sting out of the suggestion. He dumped the ruined saucepan into the sink and filled it with water. A cloud of steam hissed from it. Then he took her arm. "Come on."

"Don't you want me to clean this up first?"

"If your cleaning skills are on a par with your cooking, I might not have a house left. I'll do it later. Let's go."

"Go where?"

"Somewhere they can cook breakfast without needing the fire department on standby."

She had wanted him to take her to town, but not because she was spoiled and useless. "If I could change my background, I would," she threw at him.

He gave her a long, assessing look. "Sweetheart, that makes two of us."

A short time later she emerged from her room with her hair coiled into a chignon, and the ranger's hat he'd loaned her jammed over her eyes. "How do I look?"

He considered. "Like a princess disguised as a ranger."

"Be serious."

He was being serious. No man in his right mind could mistake her slight figure for a man's. An undernourished boy, perhaps. He handed her a pair of dark glasses and she perched them on her nose. "A bit better. From now on you're Nudge, a high-school kid doing work experience with me because you want to be a ranger when you grow up."

She didn't like that part, he saw as her mouth thinned. When had he started to read her moods so easily? She walked toward the hall mirror to check her appearance, her narrow hips swaying in the snug jeans. No boy could pull off that walk, he thought, feeling himself heat up all over again.

Last night she'd shown him how grown-up she was, tempting him to break every rule in his book. He still wasn't sure how he'd found the strength to resist, but he'd need every bit of it to prevent a repeat. Shara was everything he'd dreamed of in a woman. Too bad he was more like her nightmare.

He followed her. "Put some of this on."

Turning from the mirror, she inspected the bottle he handed her. "Aftershave?"

"To disguise your perfume."

She looked at him, puzzled. "I'm not wearing any."

He was close enough to smell it in her hair. Soft, feminine, faintly flowery. Could it be Shara herself? He had to stop himself from inhaling deeply, and said brusquely, "Use the aftershave."

They were almost ready to leave the house, when she balked. "Last night when I was using the phone in your study, I couldn't help seeing the photos lying on your desk. The style of the rock art in them looks familiar. I meant to tell you in case it's useful."

"But we got sidetracked, I know." If he went into the office with her now, it was likely to happen again. "Wait here, I'll get the photos and we'll discuss them over breakfast. It will add to the fiction that you're working with me."

Having something to focus on besides how much he wanted her in his arms was a good idea, he decided. He slid the photographs into a folder and jammed it into his day pack. Shara already had her satchel slung over one shoulder.

"Cut that out," he grouched.

"Cut what out?"

"You're standing like a model. Scuff your feet. Slouch a bit. Trail your bag as if it's too heavy to carry."

"Is this better?"

She did as he instructed but still looked like a beautiful sheep in wolf's clothing. He dragged in air. If he was to be any use to her, he needed to start thinking with his head instead of his hormones. She was Nudge, the work-experience kid. He didn't really think she had learned anything useful from the materials on his desk, but discussing them would help keep his mind where it belonged.

On his job instead of on her.

He jerked his head toward the front door. "Let's go, kid."

Chapter 9

Kid? Learning to answer to her name instead of a title was challenging enough, but *kid?* In Q'aresh, she could have had Tom arrested for taking such a liberty. Of course, in Q'aresh she would never have dressed like this.

Seeing her wearing men's clothing would have scandalized her father. His response to her wearing Judy's figure-hugging jeans didn't bear thinking about. And the red dust coating her top-of-the-range sports shoes would have cost some poor palace servant her job. But since the king wasn't going to see her, she didn't have to take his feelings into account. Why couldn't she dismiss Tom's opinion so readily?

He'd become important to her, she realized with a jolt. Despite her vow not to let him get to her, somehow he had, and it had to stop.

The thought depressed her so much, it was easy to slouch and scuff her shoes in the dust like a teenager. She was aware of Tom watching her, with mild amusement, as if he hadn't believed she could carry off the act.

The café he took her to was little more than a room at the front of an old weatherboard cottage. The front was sheltered by an iron-roofed veranda and inside were a few tables and chairs upholstered in plastic. Shelves of secondhand books lined one wall, and a table of hand-knitted items for sale was displayed in a corner.

"It's dreadfully hot in here," she said, wishing she could remove the hat as sweat trickled down her cheek.

"There aren't many people around this early. We can sit out on the veranda," he said.

Outside wasn't much cooler but at least more air was circulating. She waited for Tom to pull a chair out for her, then remembered she was supposed to be a teenage boy. Annoyed with herself for forgetting, she dragged a chair out and sat down opposite him. He was already looking at a menu, so she retrieved one from another table and began to study it, keeping her head down.

From beneath the hat brim she saw a motherly-looking gray-haired woman in her fifties approach the table. "My usual bacon and eggs, thanks, Betty," Tom said.

The woman smiled. "And two slices of thick toast with extra butter."

"You know me too well. My young friend here will have the same."

"He looks like he needs feeding up. You going to be a ranger too, son?"

Shara nodded without looking up. Answering would be too much of a giveaway.

Betty didn't seem fazed by the lack of response. "His first day out with you, Tom?"

He nodded. "I've promised not to feed him to the crocodiles. His name's...Nudge."

The woman took no notice of Tom's hesitation, and patted Shara on the back. "You're in good hands, son. Tom's shown lots of kids the ropes, and they all survive the experience." Barely pausing for breath, she went on, "I heard that Alan

Beckett, the last youngster who worked with you, ran away to Derby."

"Not on my account, I hope."

Tom's irony was lost on the woman. "Hardly. His mother says he has a sweetheart on the coast. The family used to live in Derby, you know, until the father inherited his parents' place in Halls Creek."

"Breakfast?" Tom suggested gently.

The woman seemed unperturbed. "I'm getting carried away as usual. I'll get your food."

Hearing the screen door slam, Shara looked at Tom over the menu. "I gather you make a habit of taking young people out with you on your rounds."

He shrugged. "It's called work experience. Gives them a chance to find out what a job's really like. Soon knocks any illusions out of them."

"Or shows them if they've made the right career choice."

"Whatever."

"Do you get paid for the extra work?" she asked.

He shook his head. "Part of my job."

Somehow she doubted it. "Your foster father must be pleased that you're following his example."

"I could do unpaid work for the rest of my life, and never be the man he is," Tom denied.

He was already as good a man as his foster father, she thought, but could see that Tom didn't know it. Why not? What was in his past to make him so self-doubting? And why on earth did she care?

The silence lengthened, although Tom didn't seem to mind. He was probably used to being alone with his thoughts. Accustomed to having people chattering at her all the time, Shara knew silence would take some getting used to. She refused to allow that some of her uneasiness stemmed from wanting more attention from Tom.

When it arrived, the breakfast was enormous. "Enjoy," Betty said as she set the plates down. Tom overpaid her, overriding the waitress's objections. She seemed inclined to say more, but a phone rang in the café, and she went inside to answer it.

Shara let out the breath she'd been holding. She felt horribly conspicuous. The café owner seemed pleasant enough but was just as obviously the town gossip. Wasn't Tom worried that she'd stumble on Shara's real identity?

"You're thinking too much," he said, watching her. "We'll work this out, trust me."

Oddly enough she did. She picked up a fork and prodded the heap of bacon, eggs, mushrooms and tomatoes on her plate. "I can't possibly eat all this."

Tom was already eating with gusto. "Nudge wouldn't think twice."

She sighed. "You're right."

"Have you any idea what it does to a man when you do that?" he asked, and forked most of the remaining bacon from her plate onto his.

"Do what?"

"Make that little sighing sound, as if life is too much for you."

"I don't do any such thing."

"You do, and it tears me up inside."

So she was having an effect on him after all, even looking like this. Her spirits rose unaccountably and she began to eat. The food tasted delicious. Between bites, Tom explained that most of it was locally grown or produced.

"All the same, the serving is far too generous," she insisted.

Her fork clattered against the plate and she looked down, astonished. A few bits of bacon, a mushroom and traces of the egg were all that remained.

Tom grinned. "The outback air gives everyone an appetite."

He made no comment when she helped herself to a slab of his toast and spread it with creamed honey. The heat was building up and the honey was almost liquid. She bit into the toast, leaving teeth marks in the butter. The taste was heavenly.

"The honey comes from Betty's own bees," Tom said,

seeing her blissful expression. "She'll be glad you appreciate her food."

Anxiety gripped her. "And everyone for miles will know you have a new protégé called Nudge."

The idea didn't seem to bother him as much as Shara thought it should. "Betty would give you her last dollar if you needed it, but she's an incorrigible gossip. What she knows, the whole town soon knows."

"What happens if word gets back to Jamal?"

"So what? He won't care that a scruffy teenager is hanging around learning my job. You'd be more at risk without a cover story. Halls Creek is a small place and strangers tend to attract attention."

His behavior started to make sense. "You brought me here to provide this cover story."

He leaned closer. "What we haven't told her, Betty will make up. By day's end, your entire life story, or her version of it, will be common knowledge."

Shara's spirits rose, although she told herself he was only being practical. He would have done as much for anyone who needed his help. "Perhaps your friend should be a writer."

"I told her the same thing. She said she's thinking of writing a gossipy saga set in the Kimberley."

The last of the toast and honey disappeared and Shara reached for a glass of orange juice to wash it down. "You really care about these people, don't you? And don't tell me it's your job. Your job doesn't include encouraging a middle-aged woman to start a new career." Or going out on a limb to protect a runaway princess, she thought. Instead of putting himself at risk, he could have handed her over to the local police for protection.

"When my mother was—died, Betty took me in and I got to know her better. After her husband left her for a younger woman, Betty bought this place with her divorce settlement. She taught me that you can either lie down and let life beat you, or you can take the lemons you're given and make lemonade."

Shara had the feeling he'd made a lot of lemonade in his life. Could she do the same? "Why didn't you stay with her?" she asked.

"She was too softhearted, and I was too young and stupid to know when I was well off. I made too much trouble and was hauled off to an institution. It took Des Logan's no-nonsense foster parenting to set me straight."

Hard to imagine Tom as a troublemaker. There was so much she didn't know about him, and wanted to. His shuttered expression told her she wasn't going to learn any more now. If ever. She pushed her plate away. "I haven't eaten this much at one time in years."

"Time you started. As Betty said, you need feeding up."

"You think I look scrawny?" She'd known this outfit was a problem.

He eased his chair back from the table. "You have a figure like a fashion model." Spoiling the compliment, he added, "Most of them look undernourished to me."

Ridiculous to feel slighted. She didn't need his approval. She looked at the empty plate in front of her. "I won't be if you keep feeding me like this."

His eyes narrowed. "You won't be in the Kimberley long enough for it to be a problem."

Butterflies jumped in her stomach. "Because?"

"As soon as this situation is sorted out, you'll go home to Q'aresh."

"Returning home isn't an option until I can prove Jamal's treachery to my father." Bitterness rang in her tone.

"By now your father might have missed you enough to see things your way."

A snowstorm in the Kimberley was more likely, she thought, feeling her heart grow heavy. "You obviously don't know my father. He's as stubborn and single-minded as…" About to say "as you are," she trailed off, not wanting to evidence too personal an interest in Tom. "…as your greedy neighbor," she substituted.

He frowned, distracted. "Then you have my sympathy."

It wasn't what she wanted, but it was all she was going to get. Reaching for a change of subject, she said, "Last night in your study, I couldn't help noticing your pictures of rock art from the gorge."

"Like you couldn't help going into the gorge itself?"

She felt heat flood her face. "All right, I have a scientist's curiosity. This subject fascinates me. Imagine if someone had placed a new plant or animal species in front of you. As a ranger, could you resist taking a look?"

His gaze grew warm, with approval she hoped. "Probably not," he said.

"I probably wasn't supposed to look at them."

"As it happens, you can. They're not from the gorge, but from another cave system that isn't off limits to women."

Her excitement grew. "They look the same as those I glimpsed before Wandarra caught me. I saw you bring the pictures, right?"

Pushing the plates to one side, he delved into his pack, coming up with a folder which he opened on the table. "These ones, you mean?"

She bent over the pictures showing a variety of ancient rock paintings. In broad daylight she was even more sure of her ground. "In Q'aresh, I've been researching the tradition of Uru, the Great West Land common to the mythology of many people, including the Australian Aborigines." She tapped the photos. "The people of Uru had a unique culture and social order."

His forehead creased. "The local clans have many culture heroes, as they call them. One of them is a being called Uru."

"According to my research, wherever the Uru legend persists—in places such as New Zealand, China, Tiahuanaco in the Andes—you also find people with different facial features and blood groups to the local people. Their language incorporates similar words, whether they're found in Q'aresh, Peru or Australia."

"You think some of the Uru migrated to what is now Diamond Downs, and left these paintings behind?"

She traced outlines with a finger. "This figure is also found in other parts of the world. See, the clothes appear almost Egyptian."

"You're not suggesting they were aliens who came to Australia in their flying chariots?"

She smiled. "It's one of the wilder theories. In my country we have paintings of supposed astronauts, but I don't think aliens explain them. The evidence suggests an ancient race migrated across several continents, taking their art and culture along."

"If Diamond Downs was home to these Uru people, it would be a significant cultural find," Tom said. "To prove it, we'd need more than a few ancient paintings. They're found all over the Kimberley and nobody knows who painted them. Wandarra's clan credits the people of the Dreamtime."

"If these Dreamtime figures were part of the Uru, wouldn't that prove they were the original inhabitants of your land?"

"It might. We'd need more information."

"But if the information supports my theory, Diamond Downs would become famous. People would come from all over the world to look at these sites."

Tom looked thoughtful. "Other than the gorge, most of them aren't taboo to outsiders. The present custodians can control where people go and what they see."

"Your foster father's place would prosper without Max Horvath's goodwill or the need to find a mythical diamond mine."

Tom nodded, his eyes gleaming. "Des would love it. And in his state of health, running tours would be a lot easier on him than cattle ranching." Then he sobered. "All very well, but how do we prove this art was done by your Uru?"

"When Jamal caught me aboard the plane, I'd been recording a meeting between him and his associates. They talked about staging a coup in Q'aresh."

Tom frowned as he gathered the pictures into the folder.

"You told me you stashed the tape aboard the plane as evidence. What does that have to do with the Uru?"

"Before that, I used the recorder to take notes about each of the rock-art sites I visited in my own country. One of the tapes was still in my bag when I decided to spy on Jamal. Once you hear it, the similarities will become obvious."

"So Jamal has the tape now?"

Her heart picked up speed. "No. He listened to enough of it to assure himself it didn't contain evidence against him, then he gave it back to me. He said it would keep me out of trouble during the flight here."

His friendly look warmed her. Only friendly, nothing more, she cautioned herself even as her pulse skittered.

"Where is the tape now?"

"I took it out of my bag at the cottage, and didn't have time to put it back before you—persuaded me—to accompany you." The memory of being tossed over his shoulder and carried to the car made her feel uncomfortably heated.

The corners of his mouth twitched, as if at the same memory. He didn't seem to find the thought nearly as discomfiting as she did. "Since it's my fault the tape was left behind, I'll go back and get it," he said.

"Jamal could have someone watching the cottage. He wouldn't care that he's trespassing on your family's land."

"I can deal with him if I have to. You'll be safer here."

She didn't like the idea of him going alone. "I'm not safe anywhere as long as Jamal remains free," she reminded him. "If I come with you disguised as Nudge, no one will think it strange that you're showing your current protégé around."

He toyed with the corner of the photos. "It *will* look strange if Nudge disappears soon after Betty broadcasts news of his arrival."

Triumph shrilled through her, tinged by anxiety. "There, you see? If you don't take me with you, you'll probably be accused of disposing of me in some evil way."

"Wouldn't be the first time someone disappeared without trace in the desert," he observed.

She suppressed a shiver. As a woman of the desert herself, it should hold no terrors for her. Normally it didn't. Only since she had been on the run from Jamal was she prey to irrational fears. Last night she'd dreamed of being chased over featureless dunes that eventually closed over her, burying her.

Tom's hand covered hers. "You okay?"

She nodded, unable to speak for a moment.

He looked at their joined hands and grinned as he withdrew. "Betty's gossip will have nothing on the rumors that'll start if we're spotted holding hands with you looking like that."

She saw his point, but hadn't minded the comforting touch. Comfort, friendship, she thought, taking stock. What next? Brotherly affection? "There's no one around to see us."

"You'd be surprised who's watching."

She knew Tom hadn't meant to fuel her unease, and heard him curse as her expression clouded. "Sorry, I meant in the gossip sense. Oh, hell."

Alerted by his tone, she asked, "What's wrong?"

"Don't look around, but Max Horvath just got out of a car across the road."

The butterflies in her stomach started fluttering again. "As you said, it's a small town. He probably has business here."

"He does, with me. He's coming this way."

She started to rise but he grabbed her wrist. When her nod indicated she'd stay put, he released her. "Running away will only tip him off. You're Nudge, remember? Just do as you did with Betty and keep your head down. Leave the talking to me."

She was only too willing. Jamal had befriended Max Horvath. She buried her face in the folder, although the pictures swam in front of her eyes.

A shadow dropped across the page. She made an effort not to tremble. But Max barely glanced at her before turning to Tom. "I've been looking for you, McCullough."

Her surreptitious glance revealed Tom balancing on the

back two legs of his chair, his fingertips resting lightly on the tabletop. How could he look so relaxed? "I'm not hard to find," he told the other man.

"It's not you I'm interested in, as much as a certain lady you're entertaining."

"I entertain a lot of ladies."

Her heart felt as if a giant hand had closed around it. A man as attractive as Tom was unlikely to lack female companionship, she knew, but hearing it from him so bluntly sliced through her like a knife.

Max Horvath roared with laughter. If she hadn't known he was an unpleasant man, that cold, humorless laugh would have told her. He was half turned away from her but the profile she glimpsed was fleshy and soft, and his coloring was pasty, as if he spent too much time in artificial lighting.

She told herself not to underestimate him. He might be soft but he was as tall and broad as Tom, and possessed far fewer scruples. Like Tom, Horvath had been bred in a country not known for turning out weak men.

"The particular lady I'm looking for is a princess," Horvath stated. "Not just your average spoiled heiress, but an honest-to-goodness royal. A certain friend of mine is willing to pay handsomely for help in finding her, for her own good, of course. She's a stranger to the outback, and he's afraid she'll come to harm."

"My brother tells me you're willing to tear up Des's mortgage if I help you find this princess, for her own good, of course." Tom sounded sickeningly agreeable.

Every muscle tensed as she waited for the inevitable betrayal. How could Tom go on protecting her when the price might be everything he and his family held dear? Could she let him do it?

Tom was no longer holding her in place. What was stopping her from giving herself up to Horvath in return for leaving the Logan family in peace? The certainty that neither Horvath nor Jamal were men of their word, she accepted. She would be giving herself up for nothing. Worse, she would be betraying the people who counted on the royal family to keep them safe. With Jamal running the country, no one would be safe.

But ultimately, it was knowing what Jamal might do to Tom if he thought his woman had been dishonored, that kept her from speaking out. Jamal would never believe nothing had happened between them. Jamal would see in her gaze how much she wanted Tom, and her foolish desires would become Tom's death warrant.

"I could be persuaded to do your father a favor, for the right consideration."

"You'd give up on the diamond mine as well?"

"We both know that's only a myth. But assuming it isn't, I might consider a partnership to find and exploit it." Horvath's sly tone belied his statement. She wondered what Jamal had offered the man to make him so conciliatory suddenly.

"If you believe the mine is a myth, why are you so anxious to get your hands on our land?" Tom asked.

"Some of my men have traditional ties to that land."

"Men like Eddy Gilgai?"

"I gave him a job and a place to live after he was banished from his traditional land. You can't blame him for wanting to return to his own country."

"He was fired for stealing. His own people banished him."

"He tells a different story. I'm simply ensuring he gets justice."

"The kind you'd deny to Des Logan?"

"It's no more than he deserves. He and his daughter think they're so much better than anyone else."

At the slur against his foster family, she saw Tom's body go tense. Then she saw his awareness that his response was what Horvath wanted, and Tom made himself relax. "Not bad, coming from someone who has barely worked a day on the land in his life."

His shot had hit home, she saw when it was Horvath's turn to tense. "I didn't choose to be dragged to the city when my folks split up. This land is my birthright, far more than it is yours. I may not have gotten along with my father, but at least he isn't serving a life sentence in prison for killing my mother."

She barely suppressed a gasp of shock. What did he mean? Was this the tragic past Judy had hinted at? No wonder Tom refused to talk about it. Her heart constricted in empathy with him.

If ever a man stood inches from death, Horvath was that man, she thought. Every muscle in Tom's body was corded with tension. She wouldn't have blamed him for smashing his clenched fist into Horvath's fleshy features. She wanted to do much the same thing herself, on Tom's account.

She saw Tom restrain himself by a superhuman effort of will. She doubted if many men could have withstood such provocation. "Get out of here, Horvath," he snarled. "You'll never get Diamond Downs while I'm still breathing. And you can tell your royal friend to get the hell out of Australia. There's nothing for him here."

"Too bad." Despite his nonchalant demeanor, Horvath sounded shaken. "It would have gone easier on you and your ragtag family if you'd handed the princess over." He thumped Shara on the shoulder. "I wouldn't stick around this loser too long, kid. Unless you want tips on street brawling and spouse abuse."

"Don't, Tom," she murmured as Horvath stalked away. "He isn't worth it."

Tom looked as if he'd like nothing better than to follow his adversary and pound him into the dust. Never had she seen a man more primed for violence. Oddly enough, his behavior didn't frighten her, although it probably should, given what she'd just learned about him.

She knew him, she realized. Without knowing how, she sensed that whatever was in his past wasn't in Tom himself, although she doubted if he had the same certainty.

Like a bomb being painstakingly defused, she saw him

claw himself back from some unknown edge. "You're right, he isn't worth it." He pushed his chair back so hard it almost toppled. "Let's get the hell out of here."

Chapter 10

The heavy breakfast felt leaden in her stomach as she followed Tom back to the Jeep. His past was a heavier burden than she had suspected. She longed to put her arms around him in silent support, but in her present disguise, she could imagine the attention they would attract. So she kept her head down and the ranger's hat pulled low as the town stirred to life around them. Everybody seemed to know Tom, but he returned their greetings with grunts.

He didn't open the door for her but this time she was prepared, and got into the passenger seat without hesitating. Pretending to be male had its advantages, she decided. No worrying about how you sat or sprawled, or waiting for someone to open a door when you were perfectly capable of doing it yourself.

Tom didn't start the engine right away, but clamped his hands on the steering wheel, staring unseeingly out at the street. She felt anger radiating off him in waves.

"Tom?" she probed gently. "Was it true, what Max Horvath said about your parents?"

"You mean, am I the son of a murdering wife beater? Yes, it's true."

Hearing the bitterness in his tone, she flinched.

He saw and misunderstood. "Now you understand why I wouldn't make love to you last night. You deserved to know the kind of man you were getting involved with."

"I already know," she said, her tone ringing with certainty.

He swung around to glare at her. "Do you? You were born in a palace and raised as a pampered princess. You've never had to dodge a father who wanted to beat out of you where your mother was hiding. Or lived through his trial for murdering your mother, knowing you betrayed her to him because you couldn't hold out against the pain."

The image shocked her to her core, but not because she thought any less of Tom. Somehow she had to make him understand. "You're not responsible for your birthright any more than I'm responsible for mine," she insisted. "Life is a lottery."

"Then you must have drawn the winning ticket."

She could hardly believe what she was hearing. "Listen to yourself, Tom. I'm on the run in a strange country. I'm being stalked by a man I'm supposed to marry against my will And you think I'm fortunate?"

"You're alive," he said, but she heard his tone thaw fractionally.

"For the moment," she agreed. "Because of that, I intend to live every minute as fully as I can, without regrets or self-recrimination."

"Being alive is better than the alternative," he said, sounding as if he didn't really believe it. Like a man coming slowly back to life, he gunned the engine.

At the sound, she let her breath rush out. No regrets, she repeated to herself. Whatever Tom could be to her was in the future, not the past, his or hers.

Tom didn't know what he had expected from Shara, but it wasn't understanding. He hadn't been surprised to see her flinch. Hell, after his father's trial, there were times when he'd turned away from his own reflection in a mirror. Then over the years, he'd made something of himself, gradually convincing himself that he had a right to breathe the same air as men like Des Logan.

His confrontation with Max Horvath had shaken that belief for the first time in many years. He hadn't felt driven to solve a problem with his fists for a long time, and he knew what had baited him this time. He had wanted to tell Shara about his past in his own way and time.

She'd tried to cover it up but he hadn't missed her shocked reaction when Horvath blurted out the ugly truth. Not that Tom blamed her. There was no easy way to explain that your father had killed your mother, but Tom had let himself fantasize about telling Shara in a way that made her look at him with tenderness instead of horror.

As a princess, she'd probably been taught to conceal her true feelings, but her calm reaction made him wonder if she'd heard him properly. His father might have wielded the knife, but Tom had aimed it by telling his father where his mother was hiding. The counseling he'd undergone after the murder may have convinced him he'd been too young to fight off his father, who had broken Tom's arm trying to get answers from him. But it hadn't stopped Tom agonizing over what else he could have done to help his mother. Lied to his father. Endured the punishment without breaking. Anything.

"No." Tom wouldn't give Horvath the satisfaction of twisting him around like this. There was nothing he could have done to change what happened. As a child, he'd lacked the physical strength to deal with his father's drunken rage. As it was, it had taken three burly police officers to arrest Dave McCullough.

Tom had heard later that his father had torn his cell apart, raging until he collapsed from exhaustion. Unfortunately, knowing he couldn't change history didn't stop Tom from wanting to.

He could, however, change the present.

"Where are we going?" Shara demanded. "This isn't the way to Diamond Downs."

"I'm taking you to the airport."

"Excellent. We can get our hands on the tape incriminating Jamal."

He shook his head. "Not we, me. After you tell me where you hid the tape, I'm putting you on a plane to Derby. I have friends there who'll take care of you. I'll contact you as soon as I have what you need."

"I'm not a parcel to be consigned wherever you wish."

At her imperious tone, he almost smiled. *Once a princess,* he thought. "You can't stay here. That getup won't fool anyone for long."

"It fooled Max Horvath."

"We can't be sure. He could be on his way to report to Jamal right now."

The thought shook her, Tom noticed. Good. He didn't want to add to her difficulties, but sometimes shock tactics were the only way to get results.

"Are you so anxious to be rid of me?" she asked in a lowered tone.

"Good grief, no." The answer was wrung from him before he could debate the wisdom of it. After what she'd learned she might not want to be around him, but it didn't mean he felt the same way.

Despite his strict rule against getting emotionally involved, he wanted to keep her with him. All the more reason to put her on the next plane out.

"Stop the car now," she insisted.

He slammed on the brake, almost slewing into a parked car. "What's the matter?"

She said the first thing that came into her head. "I need clothes."

"What?"

"If I'm leaving, I need a change of clothes. I can't go anywhere dressed like this."

His anger swelled. She could practically hear him thinking. He was trying to protect her, and she was worried about how she *looked?* But she couldn't let him send her away while he put himself in danger to get the evidence against Jamal, and she couldn't be much use from a safe haven, hundreds of miles from Halls Creek. Wanting to stay at Tom's side had nothing to do with her reluctance to leave.

"You look good enough to me," Tom said. He didn't think she'd appreciate hearing exactly how good. The too-large man's shirt only hinted at luscious curves, and the hat concealed her wonderful hair, leaving his imagination working overtime.

Her mouth remained taut. "But not for me. The things Judy lent me are still at the cottage."

"I'll send them to you."

She didn't miss a beat. "In the meantime, I'll need toiletries and undergarments."

"You're going to get some interesting looks, buying women's things dressed like that."

"The alternative is for you to buy them for me."

He lifted his hands. "Oh, no you don't."

Her chin came up. "Then I'm not going anywhere."

Before he could summon a fresh argument, a battered utility pulled up alongside them. Judy leaned out the window. "That open space up ahead is a car park," she said helpfully.

Tom shot his foster sister a wry look. He was well aware that they were still double parked. "Very funny," he said to Judy, then had another idea. "Hey, you can do me a favor."

Which was how both cars ended up pulling up outside a cottage on the edge of town ten minutes later. "This is Tracey Blair's place," Judy said when they got out. "The shop isn't open yet, but wait until you see her hand-painted T-shirts and swimwear."

Tom made an effort not to roll his eyes. "I can hardly wait."

He'd gone along with this craziness because it was safer

than taking Shara into one of the local shops. Or doing the deed himself. On the other hand, the princess didn't look too pleased by Judy's offer of help. "If I was a suspicious type, I'd think your sudden passion for new clothes is a stalling tactic," he told Shara as they got out of the car.

Her face remained impassive. "What would I have to gain?"

"You'd remain in town longer. Well, it isn't going to work. I'm putting you on a plane as soon as we're done here."

"We can't be done here. You're forgetting I have little available cash, and my credit cards can be too easily traced to use safely."

"So you *are* stalling. Too late now. We'll use my card, and don't argue," he said when she opened her mouth to do just that. "Your safety is what matters now."

According to Judy, she'd known Tracey Blair for some time although the woman had only recently moved into town. This explained why, in a town where everyone knew everyone, he hadn't met her yet. Judy performed the introductions and Tracey invited them into her residence, adjoining what would be her shop. They dodged the packing cases littering the hallway as they were shown into her living room. "Forgive the mess, I'm still getting organized," Tracey said.

The woman was in her early sixties, Tom judged. Small and round and simply dressed in a cream dress with a narrow red belt at the waist, she had brunette hair peppered with white, and her deeply tanned face was creased with laughter lines. Her eyes, the green of a shady river, invited trust.

She didn't so much as blink when Shara removed the ranger's hat, revealing her long, dark hair. "Judy tells me you make and sell clothes," the princess said.

Tracey inclined her head. "I do it to raise money for my mission."

"You're a missionary?" Tom hadn't meant to blurt out the question but he was taken by surprise. As Judy had intended, he saw from her impish smile. *Later for you,* his expression warned her.

"I used to be," Tracey said. "I was teaching at a mission in the desert until I was diagnosed with diabetes, and was advised to move into town to be closer to medical treatment."

"Tracey and I met when I flew one of her colleagues to Derby," Judy contributed. "Before we left, she showed me some of your handiwork. I told Shara, and she'd like to buy some of your work before she leaves."

The woman smiled. "No problem. I don't have much stock unpacked yet." She sized Shara up with a practiced eye. "But I'm sure I can find some choices for you. What are you mainly looking for?"

"A couple of bikinis and some T-shirts, maybe a dress," Judy volunteered when Shara hesitated. To Shara, she said in a low voice, "The bikinis can double as underwear for the time being."

At any other time Tom would have made an excuse to escape the female business of buying clothes. He'd never understood why they couldn't take the first garment that fit and did the job. But the chance to see Shara in the lovely things the older woman brought out was irresistible. He settled his long frame into an overstuffed armchair and waited.

When Shara came into the room wearing a dress like a long T-shirt, his breath was taken away. The knee-length dress was perfectly plain and virginal white, skimming her figure like a dream. Down the front Tracey had painted a spray of red and green kangaroo paw, the floral emblem of Western Australia.

The crimson flowers studded with black throats wound between Shara's breasts, starting at her waist and ending at the neckline. They looked ripe enough to pick. The flowers, he reminded himself hastily, the flowers.

He tugged at the open neck of his shirt. Was it getting hot in here suddenly? After the camouflage of the man's shirt, she seemed to be wearing nothing at all. It was no more or less than many women wore in the outback heat, but on Shara the effect was unsettling.

"You can wear that over the jeans," Judy suggested.

Sacrilege to hide those incredible legs, he thought. To him, Shara looked fantastic just as she was.

"Good idea," Shara agreed.

Judy turned back to Tracey. "If you have another in a different design, we'll take that as well. And two of your bikinis in Shara's size."

"Is that all right?" Shara asked, looking to Tom.

Judy was ahead of both of them. "Of course it's all right. You need these. Before you go, I'll lend you my credit card. That way Jamal won't be able to track your movements," she added, her expression daring Tom to disagree.

Shara's eyes filled. "You're all so kind. I won't forget this."

Kindness had little to do with it, Tom thought. He wanted her to have the dresses. Giving her the moon had a lot of appeal.

He was still dealing with the fact that she knew the worst secret he possessed, and still looked at him as if he had a right to walk the earth. The thought of her leaving made him feel hollow inside. He should be glad she was going, before she made him do something stupid, like forget his own rules of engagement. He couldn't make himself believe it.

While he was busy with his thoughts, Shara had changed out of the dress and back into the shirt and jeans. The ghost of the bare-legged creature in the T-shirt dress hovered around her. He would give a lot to see her like that again—preferably without Judy and a missionary in tow.

Now Shara was picking books out of an open carton. "I see you have an interest in ancient civilizations, Miss Blair."

"Call me Tracey, please. We don't stand on ceremony in the Kimberley. I've been interested in cave art for most of my life. Some of those books were left at the mission by my predecessors."

Shara flipped through pages. "I have some of these titles. I've made a study of the Uru people."

Tracey's eyebrows lifted. "You're Shara Najran who published an article in *Ancient Art?*"

Color sprang to Shara's face. "You read my article?"

"I saw some similarities between the art near the mission and the work attributed to the Uru. But I understood that the author was—"

"Not anxious to be recognized," Tom cut in before Shara could admit anything. As a missionary, Tracey had to be trustworthy, but it paid to be cautious.

Tracey began to fold the T-shirt dresses. "After reading the article, I followed the author's activities with some interest. On the Internet recently, there was something about an arranged marriage. But the bride had disappeared and there was concern for her well-being. I do hope she's safe."

"She's safe enough for now," Tom said shortly.

"If there's anything I can do to help—with your studies—you can call on me," Tracey offered, her tone making it clear she meant more than with Shara's work. Then she brightened. "Now I'm living in town, I hope to get out to Diamond Downs again and compare some of the cave art there."

Judy looked surprised. "You've visited the property before?"

Tracey smiled. "Many years ago, before I took up missionary work. Your grandfather had discovered some new cave systems on Diamond Downs, and your father was kind enough to show them to me. I didn't know much about rock art then, but thinking back. I'm sure the work I saw was in the Uru style."

A softening of Tracey's tone when she talked about Judy's father made Tom wonder if she'd been attracted to Des Logan. Tom pushed away the romantic notion. Shara was making him see hearts and flowers where, probably, none had existed.

"Would you be able to find those caves again?" he asked on a sudden impulse.

Tracey looked doubtful. "We're talking forty or more years ago. But I remember noting some distinctive landmarks." She lapsed into silence, thinking. "There was a rocky outcrop that looked like the heads of horses. At least I thought it did. And a grove of ancient trees, cycads, that was it. Your grandfather said they'd been growing in the area since the days of the dinosaurs."

Shara looked to Tom. "Do you know this place?"

"It could fit several cave systems I've been to on Diamond Downs. They may have nothing to do with Great-grandfather Logan."

"Some of those systems are deep and complex. It would be easy to lose your way in them," Tracey agreed. "It's sad that he was never found."

Judy nodded. "One day we'll find him and bring him home."

Provided Horvath's men didn't find him first, Tom thought. Their reasons for looking were a lot less sentimental than Judy's. The chances were high that Great-grandfather Logan's final resting place was close to his legendary diamond find. Assuming it existed at all, and Tom was far from convinced. But as long as Horvath believed it, greed would drive him to search, and that could only mean trouble for Tom's family.

"Are you interested in the caves for your research?" Tracey asked Shara.

The princess looked at Tom and he gave a slight shake of his head. "Something like that."

"Then I'll try to remember anything else that might be useful."

She wrapped the dresses in tissue paper and gave them to Shara. "I hope everything works out for you, dear."

Outside, Shara glared at Tom. "How could you lie to a missionary?"

"I didn't lie to her."

"You let her think you want to find those caves because of my research. But you think the diamonds are there, don't you?"

"That's not a lie. It's a sin of omission. Besides, if she knows the real reason, she could tell Max Horvath."

"She wouldn't do such a thing, would she?"

His gaze became shuttered. "Not willingly."

She looked horrified. "You make Horvath's people seem capable of anything."

"With what's at stake, I wouldn't put anything past him."

Judy frowned at them both. "It didn't take Tracey long to work out who Shara is. Doesn't that put her in danger, too?"

"Not for long. Before I got dragged into this shopping expedition, I was about to put her on the first plane to Derby. Whatever else you need, you can buy there," he said with a quelling look at the princess.

"I should go with you," Judy suggested, sounding worried.

Shara shook her head. "You can't leave your father. I'll be okay."

Judy looked unconvinced. "What will you do if Jamal follows you? From what you've told us, he isn't a man to give up easily, and he has a lot at stake."

"At least he'd be after me, not your family and friends. Enough people have taken risks on my account. I made a mistake staying in the Kimberley. I should have left as soon as I got away from Jamal."

Tom went cold inside. "Because of what you found out today?"

Judy looked puzzled, but Shara gave an emphatic shake of her head. "Never think that, Tom. No, my mistake was remaining in a small place where I stand out. In a bigger place, I can lose myself more readily until I can convince my father that Jamal is a traitor."

She would stand out wherever she went, Tom thought. He wasn't convinced that learning about his past hadn't changed her attitude toward him. It did for most people. But for now he was more worried about her. "What will you do if you never convince him?" he asked, emotion roughening his tone.

Judy gave him a speculative glance, but he wasn't about to enlighten her. Some things were not open to sisterly teasing.

"Then I may have to make a new life for myself here, under a different identity. Having an Australian grandmother entitles me to remain here if it comes to that."

Shara lifted herself on tiptoe and kissed Tom. She had intended to kiss his cheek but at the last second he turned his head and their lips met. Heat coiled through her. She battled down the rising desire. The regret.

She knew he thought she'd been turned off by what she'd learned about his parents. He expected people to judge him and find him wanting. Couldn't he see how similar their situations were? Her father, the king, may not be violent, but he was so used to his word being law that he couldn't conceive of Shara having a will of her own.

To her father, children were instruments of *his* will, just as Tom had been of his father's. The only difference was that Tom's father had used a real weapon, whereas King Awad used the power of his position to control other people.

A shiver shook her. She was not going to look back, remember? The thought of losing herself in yet another foreign place was terrifying, and she hoped it wouldn't come to that. But as long as she depended on others, she put them at risk from Jamal. It was time she stood on her own two feet.

She turned away from Tom and hugged Judy. "Thanks for introducing me to Tracey. Whenever I wear her handiwork, I'll think of your generosity."

Judy looked choked, and fumbled in her bag. "Here, take my cell phone so you can let me know you're okay."

By now Shara knew better than to argue with Judy. She tucked the compact phone into her satchel. "I'll call as soon as I get to Derby," she promised. "Give your father and Blake my love." She had hoped to meet their other foster brothers, Cade and Ryan, but it was not to be.

Forward, not back, she told herself. "What time does the flight to Derby leave?" she asked Tom, proud that her voice shook only a little. She didn't tell him she had no intention of contacting his friends once she was on her own.

He consulted his watch. "There's a flight in an hour. We'd better make tracks."

Back at the car, she stowed the T-shirt dresses in her satchel, intending to change after she landed at Derby. Her possessions were getting more meager by the day, she thought. Refusing to give in to self-pity, she squared her shoulders. "I'm ready."

He said nothing as he drove the short distance to the airport. Like most outback centers, the airport was barely worthy of the name, but the main terminal building was blissfully cool when they entered. People were milling around, most seemingly belonging to a tour group that a harried man with a clipboard was trying to organize.

She smiled at the chaos. No matter what their size or location, airports felt the same the world over. She looked around for a ticket counter, preparing to give Judy's credit card its first workout.

Beside her, she saw Tom's expression change. "What is it?" she asked.

He pulled her so the dozen or so people in the tour group were between them and the ticket counter. "Max Horvath is over there talking to another man."

Her blood turned to ice. The man wore dark trousers and a white, open-necked shirt instead of desert robes, but there was no mistaking his identity. Although he was too far away to hear her, she felt compelled to whisper, "It's Jamal."

Chapter 11

She saw Tom assess the man standing with Horvath. If ever the description tall, dark and dangerous fitted a man, it was Jamal. He'd been a champion runner in his youth, and he was still superbly fit. There wasn't an ounce of spare flesh on his six-foot, well-muscled frame. Not a man to be trifled with, and she saw Tom's expression harden as he reached that conclusion.

"He hasn't seen you yet," Tom said. "Stay put until this group moves out. When they do, we'll go with them."

It took all her courage to remain still, not a dozen yards away from Jamal, willing the tour group to move.

Glancing out of the airport, she saw what she had been unconsciously looking for, the private jet painted with the standard of the Q'aresh royal family standing on the runway. Hope sent her spirits soaring. If she could only get to the plane and find the tape, this might all be over. She might not be forced to leave Tom.

She couldn't remain still a moment longer. "Can you create some kind of diversion?"

Tom nodded, having no idea what was in her mind. "As soon as I do, you head for the car. I'll be right behind you. Got it?"

She had no intention of running for the car, but doubted if Tom would approve of her plan. So she inclined her head in apparent agreement. He approached the tour leader. "Tom McCullough, shire ranger," he said, offering his hand.

The man shook hands. "I didn't know anyone from ranger headquarters was meeting us."

"It isn't standard procedure," Tom said smoothly. "I've had a report that a rare snake was spotted around the bags belonging to this group. I'd like you all to check your belongings carefully. Or I can take a look if you're squeamish about snakes."

"What kind of snake is it?"

"A Jamal viper," Tom improvised. "A bite from one can be nasty."

"Can't say I've heard of it, but it's rare, as you say. We'd better all do as the ranger asks," the leader urged.

"You only need to worry about open bags," Tom said hastily. If he had to examine everything they carried, he'd be here all day.

The members of the group immediately dropped their belongings as if the bags themselves could bite. A few, mostly the men, began gingerly to examine their possessions. The rest flatly refused to touch anything without Tom's help. As he searched for the nonexistent snake, he made sure to spread the group out and create as much chaos as possible.

Out of the corner of his eye he saw Shara start to move. Then he suppressed a curse. Instead of heading for the parking lot, she ran out onto the tarmac where he saw her approaching a parked plane. As she reached it, she swept the ranger's hat off her head.

What the devil was she doing? Surely not surrendering to Jamal's people in some kind of misguided notion of self-sacrifice? The thought was like a knife in Tom's gut. She must know they wouldn't honor any agreement she tried to make with them.

He also saw the moment when Jamal recognized her. He spoke urgently to Horvath and they started to move. Tom's trick had left bags strewn everywhere, with members of the tour group still delving into them. When one man was roughly pushed aside, he pushed back, sending Horvath cannoning into Jamal.

This could get rough. He had to get these people out of harm's way. "My assistant just signaled to me that he's found the snake in the baggage-claim area, so I needn't detain you any longer. Thank you for your cooperation. Enjoy your visit," he said in a rush.

The tour members gathered up their possessions, some still handling their things reluctantly. Tom felt badly for worrying them unnecessarily, until he reminded himself what was at stake.

Looking even more bemused, the tour leader started to herd his group toward the entrance, right across the path of a fuming Jamal and Horvath. This time they didn't try to shoulder their way through, but Tom could see they were simmering with rage.

He had only minutes. Without hesitation he headed after Shara.

Shara's heart thundered and the fingers she wrapped around the strap of her satchel were white at the knuckles. Tom's offer to create a diversion had cemented the merest hint of a plan into reality.

She knew the guard standing at the foot of the steps. "Hello, Talib," she said in the Q'aresh language, sweeping the ranger's hat off her head so her raven hair cascaded past her shoulders.

The guard's jaw dropped a mile as he beheld his princess dressed in male clothing. She knew she couldn't have shocked him more if she'd appeared before him naked.

He recovered quickly and snapped to attention. "Forgive me, Your Highness. I was told you were ill."

"Or off my head," she said with a sweet smile. "Neither is true. I'm merely taking some time to myself before my wedding to Prince Jamal. The disguise is so I can move freely, without ceremony."

"Of course, Your Highness." His tone said whatever royalty did was fine with him, even if it made little sense.

Thanking her stars for loyal servants, she said, "Your service will be rewarded. Now kindly take a break."

"A break, but—Your Highness, I cannot leave the plane."

"Even if your princess orders it?" Her tone brooked no further argument.

"As you wish, Your Highness. Prince Jamal is inside the terminal. I will inform him of your presence."

"You will inform him of nothing. I wish to surprise him. Go now. Have some coffee and keep what you have seen to yourself for the moment."

The man reacted as if her father, the king, had spoken. Where did he think she'd learned the tone of royal command? "As Your Highness wishes," he said with a bow.

Suiting word to deed, the man hurried toward the airport building. Shara had already wasted enough time. She vaulted up the steps and straight into the cockpit of the plane.

She almost screamed as someone slid into the copilot's seat while she was trying to locate the switch that locked the door of the plane. Relief swept through her when she saw it was Tom.

"What do you think you're doing?" he demanded.

"Taking off," she said, not looking at him as she went through the motions. Behind her she heard the steps stow themselves in the body of the plane. Nothing could stop them now.

Tom watched her, his expression grim. "How many hours' flying time have you had?"

"Two," she said with scrupulous honesty.

"Two hundred?"

"No, two. My brother was the one taking lessons. I merely observed until the instructor saw how keen I was, and started to teach me himself. When my father found out, he put a stop to the lessons. He thought flying a plane was unfeminine."

Tom muttered an Australian colloquialism she was sure wasn't used in polite society. She wondered if he objected to her father's actions or her own inexperience. "I'm taking over."

Aware of her own limitations, she didn't argue. "Go ahead," she agreed, irked that he wasn't giving her a choice. "But I do know what I'm doing."

"You don't know how to do what you're told," he snapped, his hands busy with preflight routine. "I told you to head for the car."

"The plane was closer," she said mildly. And the tape incriminating Jamal was on board.

"Stealing it is going to put both our butts in a sling."

"I didn't ask you to follow me, and in any case, I'm not stealing it."

"What do you call it?" he demanded.

"Reclaiming my property," she said. "The plane was a gift from my father on my eighteenth birthday. Jamal is the one with no right to it."

Tom flipped switches and she heard him talk to the control tower. His use of her name and rank and her confirmation put an end to any objections the air traffic controller might have made, and they were quickly cleared to proceed.

Only as they headed for the runway, did she allow hope to bubble up. They were going to make it. Jamal was not only going to be cheated of his unwilling bride, he was also going to pay for his crimes.

Justice was sweet indeed.

She had allowed herself to hope too soon. Before they could reach takeoff speed, she saw a Jeep slam into a gate separating the runway from the surrounding land. The gate flew open. Without pausing, the Jeep headed right for them. "Jamal is trying to stop us," she warned.

Tom had seen the car, too. "Not if I can help it."

He got them airborne only seconds later. She looked down to see Jamal beside the Jeep. They were still close enough to the ground for her to see his twisted expression. He looked murderous.

"He's shooting at us," she said on a shocked gasp as bullets ripped through the air around them. She hadn't heard any explosions and thought the engine must have muffled the shots, until she saw the silencer on the gun in Jamal's hand.

Tom kept his attention on gaining altitude. "I noticed. Luckily he isn't the world's best shot."

"I could always beat him at trapshooting," she agreed, trying to match his calm demeanor.

He sent her a wry glance. "Is there anything you *can't* do, Princess?"

She couldn't resist. "What I'm told, evidently."

"We'll discuss that later. In the meantime—" he swore as the plane jolted under his hands "—your prince just hit something. We're out of range now, so you can breathe easier."

It would be a long time before she could do anything like breathing easier, she knew. Her heart thumped against her ribs, her pulse was erratic and she felt nauseous. As a child she had dreamed of escaping her sheltered life and having adventures, but the reality wasn't glamorous at all. It was downright terrifying.

"So you still intend to take me to Derby," she said, having heard him give the control tower that destination. If Jamal asked around the airport, he would soon learn where they had gone, but by then they'd be well away. She wished she could make herself feel better about it.

He nodded. "I would have preferred a less dramatic exit, but the result will be the same."

"You will be rid of me." Why was she surprised? He'd made no secret of his wish to wash his hands of her. But somehow she'd hoped, now she had access to the plane and it's precious evidence, things would change.

"Oddly enough, it's not a priority," he said. "In the last few days I've grown used to having you around."

The admission made her look at him in amazement. "I've endangered your life."

"When you have a crocodile hunter for a brother, your life is often in danger. You just don't think about it."

"So having me around is like hunting crocodiles?"

"Let's say it brings the same adrenaline rush, but for different reasons."

From what she knew of crocodiles, they were dirty, dangerous creatures who preferred their meals long dead. And they were unbelievably ugly. "I'm relieved to hear it."

"Thought you might be. Uh-oh."

Her heart missed another beat. "What's uh-oh?"

"From the look of these instruments, Jamal may have hit something vital after all."

"Will we make it to Derby?"

"We'll be lucky to make it over the next rise. Hang on, it's going to get bumpy."

Typical Australian understatement, she discovered a few minutes later as the plane bucked like an unbroken stallion. She was thankful Tom was at the controls, keeping them airborne. He seemed to be doing it by willpower alone.

The plane tilted and she fought the urge to scream, until she saw that Tom was steering them into a banking turn. Afraid to distract him, she chewed her lip, wondering where on earth he planned to set them down in this featureless wasteland.

Because they *were* going down. Despite his heroic efforts, she was aware that they were rapidly losing altitude. He informed her that he'd managed to get the landing gear down. Then she saw a group of buildings dotted beneath them. They looked familiar, and she recognized the old farmhouse at Diamond Downs where she'd spent her first nights in Australia. Tom steered for the cottage.

No, not for the building. For a barely discernible airstrip that must have served the farmhouse before the new homestead and larger airstrip were built. This landing strip was overgrown and looked as if it hadn't been used in years. She had time to follow Tom's instruction to brace herself, then they were down.

As landings went, it was hardly textbook but they made it, bouncing off rocks dotting the runway, and scraping against bushes until she was sure they must overturn in a fiery heap. But after what seemed an eternity, it was over. After their screaming progress out of the sky, the silence when Tom shut everything down was deafening.

She lifted her head from her arms and regarded him shakily. "We're alive."

He gave a shrug but she could see he was white to the eyes. "Piece of cake."

She unsnapped her seat belt, knowing she would have bruises where the straps had bitten into her body. "This cake of yours. I don't think I want the recipe."

"Makes two of us."

He freed himself and reached for her. Before their brush with death she might have hesitated. Now she went into his embrace willingly, needing to feel his heart beating in time with her own, needing to celebrate being alive.

He tasted of male sweat and heat. He tasted wonderful, she thought as his mouth moved over hers. When she parted her lips, she heard a small sound that might have been surprise, quickly overtaken by a hunger that more than matched her own.

Her heart thundered again, but with pleasure this time, as his tongue teased the corners of her mouth, then plunged deeper, taking her on a roller-coaster ride of sensation. The cheek he nuzzled against hers felt sandpapery, a new sensation to add to the dizzying assault.

Fire tore through her, more potent than Jamal's bullets, each heat-seeking missile of a kiss finding a target deep within her until she was a roiling mass of heat and need.

As her breasts were crushed against him, thought and reason deserted her. Through the cotton of the ranger's shirt, the slightly abrasive effect made her harden and ache. She yearned to tear the shirt away and feel him skin to skin, to have him caress her until she was his for the taking.

So close. So very close.

When he lifted his head, she almost wept with frustration. "Don't you want me?"

"More than you can possibly imagine," he groaned. "So much it hurts."

"Then why?"

"You know why."

"Because of some misguided idea that you aren't good enough for me?"

He gestured savagely. "I'm not good enough for you. If I'd had any doubts before, this plane would have convinced me we're worlds apart."

"It doesn't mean anything." Her father had a fleet of them in Q'aresh. He had given her the plane when she turned eighteen rather than give her what she desperately wanted, the freedom to attend university in another country. Her brother had been sent to America, to Yale. She'd had to be content with a tutor within the confines of the palace.

Tom's mouth thinned. "It may be nothing to you, but to me it represents the vast gulf between us."

"If I'd known you'd feel that way, I'd have run for the car instead."

He lifted her chin. "It wouldn't change reality. But it would have saved me having to put you over my knee for disobeying me."

Her gasp of shock changed to chagrin as she saw the sparkle in his eyes. "You wouldn't. No one lays a hand on a royal princess and lives."

"See?" he said, his expression sobering. "You turn back into the princess when it suits you."

"Is it any wonder, when you switch from romancing me to threatening to spank me when it suits *you?* I'd rather you refrained from both," she asserted.

"You tempt me to put you to the test," he said, smiling rue-fully. "But first I'd like to get some camouflage over this thing, so the plane won't be so obvious from the air."

She masked her disappointment. He was right. Jamal wouldn't know that one of his bullets had found its mark, or that they'd gotten no farther than Diamond Downs. When he made inquiries at the airport, he'd be told they were heading for Derby. They'd be safe from pursuit for the moment.

Tom had managed to steer the plane into the shelter of a group of trees. Now he snapped off branches and made a screen of them. She started to help but he lifted the branch out of her hands. "You'll hurt yourself doing this."

"I can help. You don't have to pamper me," she groused.

"Oh, no?" He took her hands in his and turned them palms upward. The contrast between her soft hands and his tanned, callused ones was immediately obvious.

He frowned over the scratches she'd already sustained while breaking off her sole branch. "These hands aren't made for rough work."

"Maybe it's time they were toughened up," she said in a strangled whisper as her eyes met his. "I want to earn my keep."

"You earn it by simply being," he murmured and lifted her hands to his mouth. The gallant touch of his mouth to her palm was so light, so unexpected and so arousing that heat arrowed through her.

When he released her she swayed, at first blaming his ef-fect on her. But the dizziness continued. She steadied herself by gripping his arm.

Concern darkened his gaze. "The heat is getting to you. Go inside the plane and splash some water on your face and wrists, then lie down and rest for a bit. You'll feel better."

Developing heat stroke wouldn't help him or her cause, so she nodded and made her way inside.

Out of the searing heat, her dizziness receded, although her thoughts were still in turmoil. Could she blame heat exposure for her response to Tom? Though sorely tempted, she settled for honesty. His every touch fired her with desire. If he stepped through the door now, her resistance would be zero.

What was she thinking? She was aboard the plane at last, and all she could do was mope about Tom. Later would do for that. Right now, the tape was what mattered.

She had chosen the interior décor herself, from the exotic wood paneling to the creamy leather upholstery on the armchair-like seats separated by marble-topped tables. Under the seats closest to the door was a compartment designed to hold valuables that didn't warrant being locked in the safe. She knelt on the thick Persian carpet and reached.

The compartment was empty.

Muttering, she felt around under the seat. A small object lay on the floor beside the compartment. The tape must have been jolted from its hiding place during flight. Her breath pumped as her fingers closed around it.

Sitting back on her heels to examine it, she almost wept. The tiny cartridge was splintered almost in two, the tape shredded where it had snagged on the jagged edges of the case.

A police laboratory might be able to salvage the contents but she'd have to get the tape to them before Jamal caught up with her. And did his best to convince the authorities to send her home to Q'aresh.

She pressed her knuckles against her temples, refusing to see herself as beaten. Think, she ordered herself. But the restless night and the strain of the day had taken a toll. Her mind treadmilled on the tape, as shattered as her hope of using it to expose Jamal's treachery.

This wouldn't do. She needed to think and formulate a plan, but her brain wouldn't cooperate. The heat must still be affecting her. Tom had recommended splashing water on her face and wrists. She could do better than that. The plane was equipped with a washroom where she could take a proper shower. Afterward she might be able to think straight again.

Stowing the damaged tape in her bag, she walked into the sleeping cabin.

She hadn't actually spent a night aboard the plane, but the designers had allowed for passengers to nap during a long flight, and had turned the limited space available into an inviting stateroom. The washroom opened off the stateroom.

After what she'd been through, the plane seemed almost decadent in its opulence. Living out of one satchel made a mockery of the vast closets filled with clothes at her father's palace.

She opened the door to a tiny closet. The clothes she kept aboard the plane were still there, pushed to one side to accommodate Jamal's things. She returned the favor, pushing his clothes aside to inspect the garments. Most were totally unsuitable for Outback conditions so she closed the door on them.

The cool shower went a long way to making her feel human again, dispelling the last of the dizziness, but leaving her feeling limp with exhaustion.

She looked out the plane window. Below her, Tom had removed a panel and was tinkering with something mechanical. By the time she'd dried her hair, he still hadn't finished his task.

Enjoying feeling really cool for the first time in days, she pulled on a terrycloth robe and padded to the stateroom, the carpet soft under her bare feet. Tom had also prescribed rest. Only a few minutes, long enough to be sure she was recovered enough to face the dangers ahead.

Chapter 12

"The damage isn't too serious, but I'll need some tools I don't…" Tom's voice tapered off as he entered the main cabin and found it empty. A strange sensation clutched at his chest. Where was Shara? For a moment he couldn't deal with her absence, until common sense told him she couldn't have left the plane without him knowing.

Then he saw a door leading to another cabin. A bedroom, he saw when he pushed the door open. He stopped in his tracks. Like the embodiment of Sleeping Beauty, she lay on her side on the bed. One hand was tucked under her cheek, the other rested in front of her.

He felt the impact like a fist slamming into him. With her hair fanned out on the pillow, she looked like every man's fantasy. *His* fantasy. Her lovely features were serene, long lashes sweeping over dusky cheeks. Her terrycloth robe quivered ever so slightly with each breath.

The plane must run to a bathroom, because she looked

freshly showered. Her hair shone like satin, and the cabin smelled of enough female potions to overload his senses.

She looked breathtaking, but then, he hadn't found her hard to look at when she'd been wearing his shirt. If anything, the hint of shapeliness under the ranger's shirt had given his imagination more of a workout than the little she had on now.

Not that he had any problem with now.

As if becoming aware of his scrutiny, she stirred, lashes fluttering then eyes widening. She sat up, clutching the edges of the robe to keep it from slipping open. "How long was I asleep?"

"Not for long. I've inspected the damage and it's fixable as soon as I can borrow the proper tools from Judy's mechanic."

"I found the tape," she said.

He drew his own conclusions from her tone. "I gather the news isn't good."

She nodded. "It's useless until we can find an expert to re-trieve the data on it. It must have been shaken out of the com-partment when we dodged Jamal's bullets."

"He really is a piece of work."

Her shaky smile rewarded him. "The difficulty is in prov-ing it."

"We'll manage it somehow."

"Yes, we will." She uncoiled her long legs, shortening his breathing by a considerable margin. "I'll get dressed and we can go to Judy's mechanic."

He felt a really bad mistake coming on, and wondered if he had the strength to keep from making it. Almost immedi-ately, he knew the answer. "It's too hot to go anywhere for a couple of hours. If there's enough water on board, I'll follow your example and clean up first," he said.

She licked her lips, destroying his last hope of resistance. "And second?" she asked.

If the shower was cold enough, they might not get to sec-ond, he thought, doubting if the plane's water supply could ever be that frigid.

"We'll worry about second when things cool down," he said, carefully not being more specific. As much for himself as her, he said, "When Jamal finds out we're not in Derby, he'll come looking for his plane."

"My plane," she corrected. "He's not likely to look for us for a few hours, is he?"

"Probably not."

Her gaze held steady on his. *She knew what was in his mind,* he thought. Dare he hope the same thought was in hers? "Then we can take these hours as a gift," she said, leaving him in no doubt.

Could he? She was certainly a gift he'd never hoped to receive, and she seemed to want him as much as he wanted her. She also knew the truth about his past, and claimed not to care. What more did he need? An engraved invitation?

"Where's the bathroom?" he asked, his voice betrayingly husky.

When he came out she was in the same spot, apparently relaxed against the banked pillows, her expression composed. Then he saw that her hands trembled ever so slightly.

She might think she was ready for him, but she wasn't. Tom didn't want to entertain second thoughts. Not when his first were so appealing. But he couldn't follow his impulses in good conscience unless she felt the same.

He hitched the towel more securely around his hips, appreciating the thickness of the fabric hiding his growing arousal. His shower had only made his blood run hotter as he pictured her waiting for him.

Had she ever been with a man? She'd certainly been kissed before, but as a princess, she'd led a sheltered life. If her experience ended at kissing, was it fair of him to take advantage of her present vulnerability, knowing that he couldn't give her the happily-ever-after ending she deserved?

When had he become a saint? he asked himself. She might be a princess but she was a grown woman, a free agent, as he was. Her life couldn't have been so sheltered that she didn't know what she was inviting.

He eased himself onto the edge of the bed and took her hand, feeling a slight shudder. Anticipation or apprehension? He wished he knew.

He grazed the back of her hand with his mouth. "I'm sorry about the tape."

She swallowed hard, but didn't pull free. "Me, too. But Jamal is bound to betray himself some other way. He's totally unprincipled."

Right now, Tom didn't feel too principled himself. "I should go to the old farmhouse," he said, not moving.

"Yes, you should." But she leaned closer and kissed him lightly, making nonsense of her denial.

Already feeling himself swell, he kept from groaning by the slimmest margin. He had nothing to offer her, no future. Without hard evidence they were no closer to eliminating Jamal's threat. For now, he couldn't make anything matter except a hunger for her, as unstoppable as a bushfire raging through him.

She cupped the back of his neck. "When Jamal shot at us, I thought it was all over."

"So did I." He'd fought the damaged plane to a safe landing not only because he wanted to live but to save her. For himself? *For her,* he amended the thought. He couldn't imagine a world without her in it. Desire swept through him, so powerful it eclipsed everything but the rightness of being with her. "Second chances are rare. I don't want to waste ours."

"Nor I," she said.

He nuzzled the soft skin between her shoulder and chin and heard her groan of surrender. Her palms slid over his chest, tracing the marks of his initiation. His need felt like an inferno inside him.

This time he did groan. But with the pleasure of fastening his mouth on hers. He slid his hands under her wonderful hair and pulled her against him, letting her feel exactly what she was doing to him. His mind became hazy and he forgot all the reasons why he shouldn't do this. Forgot everything but how sensational she felt in his arms.

Her hands linked around his neck. The nip of her teeth at his lower lip sent sensation spearing through him. He kissed his way along her shoulder to her throat, feeling her pulse flutter like a trapped bird. It was a reminder to go slowly, to teach as well as take.

Easier said than done, he thought as her lips parted. Unable to stop himself, he plunged deeper, hearing her dragging intake of breath. He teased, he tasted, he nipped, feeling her shudders of response. When he tried to pull back, telling himself he should go slowly, she followed, taking the lead this time, until he was the one driven to the brink.

Feeling the power of his arousal, Shara was almost scared by what she had unleashed. Tom was no undergraduate, as inexperienced as Shara herself. He was a man in every sense, as capable of wrestling crocodiles as he was of making love to a woman. His air of danger and power both fascinated and frightened her.

Fascination won and she gave herself up to his kisses with a passion that surprised and elated her. Her awareness spiraled until there was nothing but his roughness against her smoothness, the feel of his sure hands exploring, touching, arousing until she wanted to cry out with excitement.

She had never suspected it could be like this between two people. Nothing in her experience had warned her what heights of unimaginable delight a simple touch could elicit. Nor how powerful she would feel in her turn, as her seeking, stroking hands carried him to the edge with her.

He trapped her hands between his. Sliding a hand under her sweetly rounded bottom, he lifted her with him as he stood. Given his state of arousal it was no mean feat, but he was determined to treat her like the princess she was.

Setting her beside the bed, he swept the covers and tasseled pillows aside then reached to bring her closer, parting his legs so she stood between them, her lithe body aligned with his.

Insatiable hunger gripped him. He burned, he ached, he wanted as he had never wanted before. Lifting her, he lay back and took her with him onto the bed, rolling until he was stretched out beside her, one leg covering hers. Somewhere during the maneuver he'd lost the towel. He began to ease the robe off. "Uniform of the day," he pointed out.

Breathing hard through her mouth, she sat up and shrugged the robe off her shoulders. As it fell away he drew a deep breath of admiration. She looked exactly as he'd dreamed she would, all dusky flesh, the roseate peaks of her breasts hardening as he caressed them. "You're so beautiful, I can't believe you're real," he whispered.

"I've never felt so real, so alive," she admitted. "I feel as if I'm balanced on the edge of a cliff, and if I step off I'll soar like an eagle."

"We can soar together."

Only then, she pulled away a little. "Tom, I haven't—"

He touched a finger to her lips. "It's all right."

"How *can* it be? I don't know anything. What to do. How to make you happy."

"You make me happy simply by being who you are. Everything else can be learned."

"You make it sound simple."

"It is simple," he assured her. "You have to admit, you haven't done badly so far, for an amateur." He guided her hand down to his erection so she could gauge for herself how well she was doing.

Her eyes danced as she stroked him, testing his control to the limit all over again. "Such power."

He didn't know whether she referred to him or herself. His ego wanted to claim the compliment, but he suspected the power was mostly in her hands. She'd made him want her more than he'd ever wanted any woman. Made him break every rule he'd ever set for himself.

She knew the worst about him and yet she was here, her long limbs tangled with his as she befuddled his senses with her jasmine scent, and the softness that made him so very, very hard.

Still he held himself in check, wanting to do all he could to make this glorious for her. Levering himself onto one arm, he used his free hand to slide along her creamy flank. When she reached to pull up the covers, he stayed her hand. "You have no need to hide from me. You're perfect."

"Oh, Tom." Having him see her as perfect was a gift. Always she had been aware of her imperfections, starting with being born female. Her tutor had been an opportunist. Even Jamal wanted to marry her for her royal status, not because he worshipped her as Tom was doing now.

His fevered mouth was exploring places she had never imagined could be tasted by a man. The result was a mindless, dizzying onslaught of pleasure almost beyond bearing. She sucked in a panting breath, pressing her hands to his head and arching her back. "Tom, I can't stand it. I can't…"

She couldn't help it. Overwhelmed by feelings she could scarcely begin to name, she screamed his name. Time stopped, then started again as every part of her throbbed in time with the rush of blood through her veins. Most of all she was aware of a sense of euphoria washing over her in waves that slowed and slowed until her mind caught up with her body again.

Mustering her voice with an effort, she said shakily, "I had no idea anything could feel like that."

He gave her a heavy-lidded look. "We haven't even begun."

She laughed lightly. Surely he wasn't serious? "How can anything be better than that?"

He touched a hand to the side of her face. "Give me a moment, then I'll show you."

Still held in passion's thrall, she could barely lie still as he left her to pad into the bathroom. His absence, brief though it was, chilled her. Aching, heating, yearning, she wanted him back.

She wasn't so much of an innocent that she didn't recognize the condom in his hand. Frantic for his return, she resented the seconds he took to cover himself, although she should be thankful one of them had given protection a thought. It should have been her, but it hadn't.

If Tom had wanted to make love to her without it, she would have let him without thinking of possible consequences. At the same time, she couldn't help imagining the joy of bearing his child. A boy as fearless as Tom himself. Or a beautiful little girl they could spoil. How could she regret that?

Would he?

She felt a twinge of fear. Was he protecting her or himself? Surely he meant this to be a beginning for them? She refused to believe she was the only one.

Then he was taking her in his arms again, his hungry mouth banishing her fears. He ran a hand over her flat stomach and she trembled. It was the first teasing step in a game that seemed designed to make her mindless with desire.

Tom felt her tremors in his own body, and recognized them for excitement. When he'd brought her to ecstasy before, he'd almost lost his own tightly leashed control. Only his determination to make her first time wonderful had kept him from tumbling over the edge.

Now the precipice reopened in front of him as she closed her eyes and arched like a bow under his questing hands. He took shallow breaths until he felt steadier, then opened them to drink in the sight of her. Could a man ever have enough of such beauty?

Knowing he was playing with fire, he lowered his head and worshipped her breasts in turn with his mouth, hearing her breath catch as her nipples hardened. He let his fingers play over her silken skin, lower and lower, until he eased her legs apart and slid one of his between them.

His blood sang with the need to take and ravage, negating thousands of years of civilization. Feeling anything but civilized, he struggled to keep his touch gentle, to give her time to be ready for him.

Her eyes turned glassy and she shook from head to foot. "Tom, please."

Willing himself to go slowly, he lifted his aching body over her and into her, slowly until the first resistance was past, then more completely, fighting the urge to plunge deeper and deeper. Finding himself more aroused than he had ever been, as he fought to hold back for her sake.

At the intrusion, her fingers bit into his shoulders, but her hips lifted to meet his first tentative thrusts. He heard her breath hiss between her teeth, although she didn't cry out. The thought of hurting her was more than he could stand, so he stilled for a moment, giving her time to catch her breath.

Then as he moved carefully, she began to move in rhythm with him. He saw delighted surprise on her lovely face as she absorbed that the fleeting pain was over, and the pleasure only beginning.

What seemed like an eternity later, but couldn't have been more than minutes, she came down to earth with a rush, trembling and weak, but happier than she had known it was possible to be.

Gradually her breathing returned to normal and she turned her head to smile at Tom, lying as limply as she, his body pressed tightly against her. They had tumbled over the edge at almost the same moment. She'd thought she cried out his name, but she couldn't be sure. At the time, her world had been spinning too fast for conscious thought.

"Are you okay?" he asked as his heated gaze met hers.

She suspected her own gaze was as hot. "Why wouldn't I be?"

"I was afraid I was being too rough with you."

"I'm not as fragile as I look."

His mouth slanted into a smile. "Consider me convinced."

She pretended an embarrassment she didn't feel, although part of her wondered if she should. "Now you'll think I'm a wanton woman."

He cupped her chin and lifted himself to kiss her firmly. "If it's always as good as this, you can be as wanton as you like."

"You're teasing me."

"No, I'm stating a fact. In Australia, provided you're both consenting adults, there are far worse sins than making love out of wedlock."

"Such as?"

"Running out of beer or money."

She smiled. "Then I should be grateful we got our priorities right."

He levered himself over her to kiss her again. When he lifted his head, he said, "Our priorities are perfect. In fact, I'm inclined to test them again."

Feeling the pressure of his burgeoning arousal against her, she widened her gaze. "Already?"

A small frown wrinkled his forehead. "Unless it's too soon for you."

She linked her arms around his neck and pressed herself against him. "I told you, I'm not as fragile as I look."

He nuzzled her cheek. "You're also a fast learner."

"Is that a compliment?"

He shook his head. "It's a statement of fact. There can't be another woman in the world like you."

"Now, *that* must be a compliment."

"Nope, another fact. Along with how much I want you right now."

She was already well aware of it, and this time she didn't allow him to go slowly. As soon as he came to her, she wrapped her legs around him, making sure he wasn't going anywhere for the longest time.

When the world finally stopped spinning again, she looked at Tom, sleeping peacefully, his limbs entwined with hers. She wondered if he knew how boyish he looked when he relaxed completely.

A lock of dark hair fell across his face and he stirred as she brushed it out of his eyes. She looked down at the marks of initiation standing proud on his chest. He was a desert warrior, *her* desert warrior, responsible for initiating her into his own kind of tribalism. She felt drained of energy, and every muscle ached, including a few she hadn't known she possessed, but she also felt elated. Whatever happened between them after this, she would never regret making love with him.

He opened his eyes and caught her studying him. "What?"

"I was thinking how cute you look when you're asleep."

He groaned. "No man likes to be called cute."

"Virile, then."

"After today I may never feel virile again."

"Maybe I should have been gentler with *you.*"

He laughed. "Princess, you're really getting the hang of this. The man who marries you will be one lucky devil."

Her insides constricted in protest. She'd thought—

No, she'd been *sure* he was the man for her. Was she wrong? Her joy evaporated, leaving confusion in its wake. "I thought by sharing your bed, I was also committing to sharing your future," she said, keeping her voice carefully emotionless when what she really wanted to do was hurl something heavy and breakable at a wall.

"We made love not wedding plans," he said, sounding strained.

"And in Australia, that isn't a sin," she parroted, adding, "even so, I thought you cared about me."

He sat up and swung his legs over the side of the bed. "I do care about you, enough not to let you make plans that include me."

"Do you think I care that your father's in prison?" she shouted. "That's what this is about, isn't it? Talk to me, don't turn your back on me."

She grabbed his shoulder, desperate to have him look at her, and was stunned when he swung around and caught her hand, forcing her arm down. Her elbow screamed in protest but she kept her cry to a faint whimper.

He heard it and stared in horror at his hand clamped around her wrist. When he freed her, the marks of his fingers remained. She saw the blood drain from his features. "This was a mistake," he said.

His raw tone flayed her. "What part? The lovemaking, or my expectations?"

"All of it."

She lifted a shaking hand. "For pity's sake, don't apologize. What we shared was wonderful and beautiful. I won't believe it was wrong."

He passed a hand across his eyes. "You're right, it was wonderful. But it's still a mistake and I made it."

"No," she denied angrily. "You didn't force me into anything I didn't want to do willingly." Remembering how willingly, she felt heat flood into her neck and face until she drove it down. "This isn't about me at all. Whatever you think I'd find unacceptable in you is really something you can't accept about yourself, isn't it?"

His angry gaze raked her. "Didn't you see what I just did? I almost broke your wrist."

Her heart was in far greater danger, she suspected. "You stopped," she pointed out. What was this all about?

He stood up and reached for his clothes. "Yes, I stopped, this time. Next time you might not get off so lightly."

"Why, Tom? What is it you think you might do?" she asked, but the bathroom door slammed between them, cutting her off.

Chapter 13

Next time you might not get off so lightly.

His words resonated through her as she clutched a sheet around herself. What made him think she'd gotten off lightly this time? Her body ached, both from him and for him, but her thoughts were in the greatest turmoil.

No regrets whatever the outcome, she'd vowed. She hadn't counted on Tom simply walking away. She knew she was reacting from her own history. In many countries these days, lovemaking was regarded almost as a recreation. It was different in Q'aresh. There, physical love was sanctioned only between two people who were committed to each other.

Clearly Tom wasn't committed to her. It would help if he told her the reason. She'd made it clear she didn't hold his father's record against him. Was it her position? He'd called her princess with affection, and it hadn't stopped him from taking her to bed.

Perhaps it was simply the wrong time. The specter of Jamal hovered over them both. And Tom had many concerns with his foster father's illness and the threat to his home from their neighbor. In her country, men usually put their affairs above personal matters, so there was no reason to feel so slighted.

She could be grown-up about this, she decided. If time was the problem, it would also be the solution. Above all, women of her desert clan knew how to be patient. She would wait until their other problems were resolved, then she would talk to Tom and make him tell her why he considered this an ending rather than a beginning.

In the meantime, she wouldn't let anger sully what they'd shared. She now knew the great secret between men and women, and she understood why it was celebrated in story and song. With the right man—and Tom had been more right than she'd imagined—the experience was incomparable.

After the first few awkward moments, having him undress her and touch her had felt as natural as breathing. Her skin still felt flushed and her body tender. But they were good feelings. She refused to condemn herself for something she knew in her heart was right.

Tom cared for her and she cared for him. What the future held, she didn't know, but somehow he would be a part of her future. She knew it as surely as she knew the sun would rise every morning. All she had to do was convince him.

She pulled on one of the T-shirt dresses over her jeans for maximum protection from the sun. Her explorations turned up several pairs of shoes, and she smiled at the impracticality of wearing the strappy confections in the outback. Rejecting them, she retrieved the dusty sports shoes and put them back on. She could almost see her father's frown of disapproval. Not that he would approve of anything she'd done lately, she thought with a pang. Would she ever see her home and family again?

Dismissing the sadness, she rummaged through the closet for the most practical clothes to take with her. She stopped as Tom emerged from the bathroom dressed in his ranger's uniform. He seemed to have reached a similar decision to hers, for he made no reference to their lovemaking, although she saw his glance go to the chaos of the double bed.

He looked at the cotton shirt and pants in her hands. "Is that all you're packing?"

She was foolishly pleased to hear him sounding less than steady. She thought of the designer clothes in the closet. Most were unsuitable for the outback. The makeup would slide off her face as soon as she applied it. There was no sign of the jewelry case she usually kept aboard. Jamal must have it. "We could take some of the food supplies," she suggested.

Tom slanted her an odd look, and she felt elated. Had he expected her to act the shrew, ranting over his lack of promises? He'd made promises, she'd decided, only he didn't know it yet. With his body, he'd shown her a future she was determined to have. She wanted his children. She wanted him.

All in good time.

In the main cabin he filled a bag with food and drink then went around shutting everything off. "No sense wasting the generator. We won't be back here until Jamal is dealt with," he said. "Once the plane is repaired, you can use it to return home."

She met his gaze unflinchingly. "I intend to ask my grandmother to send me the title deeds and put the plane up for sale. When I find a buyer, there will be enough money to repay your family's kindness, including your foster father's medical care."

"Money doesn't solve everything," Tom replied, his tone rough. "Horvath has big ambitions. Even a share of the proceeds of this plane might not be enough to satisfy them. Assuming you can establish clear title to it."

Worry furrowed her forehead. "You think I might not?"

"I think Jamal is more devious than you're giving him credit for. He isn't the type to leave you such an easy way out."

"I should have considered that. He's already taken the jewels I usually keep aboard." Then she had another thought. "There's a supply of cash in various currencies kept in the safe."

She went to the framed etching that concealed a small safe, slid it aside and keyed in the combination. "The cash is gone, too," she said. An envelope was all that remained inside. She took it out and opened it, feeling herself turn pale. "This is a letter from my father to Jamal, confirming his ownership of the plane."

"You mean like a dowry?" Tom asked.

She clasped her hands together. "Not precisely. In my country, a woman's wealth is held in trust by her parents until she marries and has a man to help her manage her affairs." Bitterness colored her tone. "My father is so sure I'll soon be Jamal's wife that he has already started handing my life over to him."

Tom raked a hand through his hair. "What happens if the marriage plan falls through?"

"To avoid that, every couple goes through a traditional two hundred-day engagement steeped in rituals."

"And you and Jamal had already started this ritual engagement?" Tom surmised.

"One hundred and eighty days to be exact. That's how I got close enough to Jamal to discover his evil plan." Then a new thought occurred to her. "Do you think Jamal wanted us to gain access to the plane?"

Tom's thumbnail worried at his lower lip. "It was convenient. He may have set it up as bait, hoping that you'd try to get on board. I should have thought of the possibility long before."

But she had distracted him. She had also led them both into the trap, if such it was. She pushed the guilt away. If she let herself feel badly about what she and Tom had shared, she gave Jamal power over her. "If it is a trap, why did he shoot at the plane?" she asked.

"It may have been for show. His aim was suspiciously bad. Maybe he didn't intend to hit anything."

"Then his plan has already gone awry. He may track me down through the plane but he can't fly it anywhere until it is repaired."

"By which time you'll be well away from here," Tom assured her.

"I'm not leaving," she said quietly.

He stared at her. "What?"

"We're in this fix because you insisted on sending me away to safety," she said. "As long as Jamal stalks me, nowhere is safe. I intend to stay until I have the evidence to condemn him."

Tom's mouth twitched. "Very noble, but it won't take him long to find someone who saw the plane heading this way. As soon as it's repaired, he'll have the means to drag you back to Q'aresh."

"Assuming he still wants me. I'm—" she chose her words with care "—no longer pure."

Tom's gaze grew heated. "He'll want you. Men may say they want to marry virgins, but the truth is sometimes different. Experience has its advantages."

Thinking of what kind of experience he meant, she fought to keep from blushing. The woman Tom would marry had been a virgin when she came to him. Nothing else mattered. "In any case, my body is not all that Jamal wants," she stated, untroubled by the truth of it. Being desired by a man like him was no compliment. "I am only his passport to my country's crown."

"Nice guy," Tom agreed. He picked up the bag and her satchel. "We'll go to the farmhouse first and retrieve your notes. Then we'll go in your car to Des's place. I want to see how he is. I'd rather you didn't tell Des your theory that a vanished tribe may have lived on Diamond Downs. In his present condition, it's better not to get his hopes up."

"I understand. I want to be certain, too."

He made no more reference to taking her to the airport and putting her on a plane to Derby. The likelihood was that Jamal's men, or Horvath's, would be watching the airport. It wouldn't make any difference. She meant what she'd said. She wasn't leaving Tom.

Tom might be right about Des not accepting her help, but she intended to try anyway. First she had to recover ownership of the plane, then she could look into selling it. She could worry later about convincing the Logans to share the proceeds. After she had resolved the question of what she and Tom would share.

The only way to the farmhouse was on foot. In the midday heat, even a short walk was enervating, but they agreed they weren't safe near the plane. They had already spent more time there than was prudent, and not only because of the threat from Jamal and Horvath.

Tom knew that if he was alone with Shara for much longer, he would take her back to bed and damn the consequences. Knowing how dire they could be didn't stop his blood from heating at the thought. She had surprised him today. Expecting a trembling virgin, he'd found a fiery, passionate woman who'd fulfilled his every dream.

But they'd shared more than sex aboard the plane. He'd begun to care. Realizing how close he was to falling in love with her, he had to step back, to think this through. The stronger his feelings, the more he owed it to her not to give in to them. He knew better than most that strong passions could hurt as well as heal. They could kill.

His father had loved his mother. Yet he'd stabbed her in a drunken rage, claiming she'd been with another man. Her frantic denials hadn't saved her. After what he'd shared with Shara, Tom fully understood the drive to keep what was his. Primitive it may be, but his whole body sang with the urge to challenge any male who so much as looked at her.

Pity help Jamal if he showed up now.

Shaken by the power of his feelings, Tom widened the space between him and Shara. If he didn't, he would crush her to him, then they'd both be lost. The instinctive way he'd grabbed her wrist, almost breaking it, was a warning. In his genes, love and violence were entwined. She deserved better.

"Someone has been here," she said, breaking into his thoughts.

He inspected the footprints in the dust outside the old farmhouse. "We knew Jamal would head straight here. He's probably long gone, but to be on the safe side, you wait here while I check inside."

Her chin lifted. "You do not command me. I'm coming with you."

Stubborn woman. Beautiful, strong-willed, he added to himself, the urge to possess her surfacing again. He pushed it down. "As you wish, Your Highness."

She gave him a sharp look but said no more as they approached the door. The lock had been forced. Carefully, every sense on alert, he pushed the door open.

The cottage was deserted. "Looks like nothing's been touched," he said.

Her gaze was fixed on the coffee table in the living room. "My tape about the Uru people is gone. Jamal must have taken it."

"You had the player with you, so Jamal couldn't check what was on the tape. He probably took it in case it incriminates him."

"If he only knew I now have the recording of his traitorous meeting, for all the good it will do us."

At her ragged tone, Tom turned to her. "Science can do wonders these days. We'll find an expert to retrieve the data off the tape."

"Not soon enough."

To stop her from being forced into marrying Jamal, Tom read between the lines.

"Jamal and Horvath probably won't understand the potential value of the rock art," she said. "I'm sure Jamal only took the tape in case I'd recorded something on it about his activities."

"But Horvath will know we're up to something, and is likely to step up his campaign to foreclose on Des's mortgage. We're going to run out of time to help you or Des."

She eased the hair off her nape with both hands. "Losing the information will make it more difficult to compare the rock art in my country to the examples on your land. I can reconstruct the research, even from here, using the Internet, but not with Jamal breathing down my neck."

"Then we'll have to find a way to stop him."

Tom was mainly interested in how her work could help his foster father, Shara recognized, but she felt a frisson of pleasure. Hearing Tom ally himself with her was enough for the moment.

"Jamal would not have taken the tape and tipped us off that they'd been here, without good reason," she observed, thinking of the plane. She'd taken his bait once.

"They probably expect us to try and get your tape back," he agreed. "Jamal is wily enough to consider an exchange— the record of his meeting for your research tape."

"It's reasonable," she said slowly. "At least one of us gets what we want."

Tom's grip tightened on her shoulders. "You're not sacrificing yourself for Des. He wouldn't want it, and I won't permit it."

She drew herself up. "I remind you again that I am not yours to command."

"Are you sure?"

Before she could guess his intent, he lowered his head and claimed her mouth so possessively that her knees softened, and his grip became the only thing holding her up.

Instantly her thoughts swirled like windblown clouds. The heat inside the cottage had nothing on the furnace roaring to life inside her. She couldn't do a thing to prevent it. Telling herself not to return the kiss was futile. Without conscious volition, her lips parted and hunger swelled through her, craving release.

Helpless to do anything but kiss him back, she felt the need growing until she would have done anything to have this sweet torment last forever.

Such was not Tom's intent, she knew, when he lifted his head and she saw triumph glittering in his gaze. "In Australia there's a saying about putty in one's hands."

In his hands, she wasn't only putty. She was a mess of needs and desires only he could satisfy, she thought, her anger rising. Unnerved by her weakness, she tried to move away but he held her close. "I'm waiting for your promise not to barter your freedom for Des's land," he reminded her. "Haven't I just demonstrated who commands here? Do I have to do it again?"

Torn between wishing he would, and anger at her inability to resist him, she shook her head. "I believe you have made your point."

"Good."

Was she imagining it, or did he release her with a reluctance that spoke of her effect on him? Perhaps he wasn't as much in control as he wanted her to think. She subdued the rush of satisfaction accompanying the thought. Hadn't he made it clear that any influence she possessed over him was limited to the bedroom?

Wanting him was futile. Even if he took her to bed again, and her whole body tingled at the very prospect, it wouldn't solve anything. They had far more pressing problems to resolve.

She was bitterly disappointed at the loss of the plane to Jamal, who had completely deceived her father. How typical of Jamal to use her father's indebtedness to him to benefit himself. If Jamal took her back to Q'aresh now, she'd have no chance of evading their marriage. Thinking he was acting in her best interests, her father would gladly give control of her life to Jamal.

Tom didn't seem to have noticed that she hadn't given her word not to follow Jamal's trail, and that was exactly what she intended to do. She was tired of the cat-and-mouse game, and especially of being the mouse. With the private plane disabled, Jamal would have to take her back on a commercial flight. The scene she would create would make him think twice, although she hoped it wouldn't come to that. She had to find a way to incriminate him. Running and hiding wasn't going to help.

"You're plotting something," Tom said, watching her.

Years of royal training enabled her to blank her expression. "If I am, you have a most effective means of ensuring my compliance."

He colored hotly, distracted as she'd intended. "*Compliance* is not the word I'd use to describe what we shared, Princess."

It was her turn to flush, but she met his gaze squarely. "Nor I."

He looked as if he would like to say more, then turned aside as if as aware as she that this wasn't the time or place for them. "If there's nothing you need here, I want to see how Des is doing," he said.

She picked up her satchel. "Everything of value I brought with me is now with Jamal." Surprising how little one could manage with if one had to, she thought.

Tom placed the bag on the back seat of the car Des had loaned her. "Not everything," he said. "He doesn't have you, and to get to you, he'll have to go through me first."

She knew he spoke out of the chivalry that came so naturally to him, but her heart swelled with joy. He cared enough to defend her against Jamal. As a spark could be fanned into a roaring flame, caring could be nurtured into love. All it required was time.

Would they be granted time? They had to be, she thought, refusing to countenance anything else.

Chapter 14

A dirt road ran from the old cottage to the homestead, wide in areas where cattle mustering had taken place, and a mere bush track in others. The trees ranged from white gums standing out from the black soil plains, to towering paperburks and pandanus growing along the riverbank. The bush of the Kimberley was so varied and beautiful, and so crowded with animal and bird life, that Shara managed to forget her worries for whole minutes at a time, until Tom's muttered curse brought her crashing back to earth.

"What is it?"

"We're being followed."

She slewed around. A cloud of dust masked their pursuer. "Could it be one of Des's stockmen?"

"Possibly, but I don't think so." Tom tapped the radio between them. "They would have contacted me on the two-way."

"Should you try to contact them?"

"Not if it's who I think it is."

Her heart seized. "Jamal?"

Tom wrestled with the gears. "If we'd been in the Jeep, we could have given them a run for their money."

She heard what he didn't say. In the old work car it was only a matter of time before they were overtaken. Tom drove like a rally driver, negotiating the bumpy terrain with all the skill at his command, but she could see that the other car was gaining steadily. "They're going to catch us, aren't they?"

"Not if I can help it."

She didn't mind putting her own life at risk, but she refused to risk Tom's. "Stop the car. I'll try to talk to Jamal. Maybe I can bluff him into thinking the record of his meeting is still playable but hidden somewhere."

Their speed didn't slacken. "You're more likely to get yourself dragged back to an arranged marriage."

"It isn't the worst thing in the world." The thought of harm coming to Tom was more terrifying.

"Then why are you here?"

He already knew. "If he takes me back, I could still try to convince my father to see reason."

Tom shook his head. "After this little escapade, your father will have you married off so fast your head will spin."

His tone suggested he agreed with the tactic. "You can't want me to marry Jamal?"

He slanted her a quick look. "If you were mine, I'd want to make sure you weren't going anywhere."

If you were mine. He didn't mean anything by it, but the words taunted Shara and she knew why. She was dangerously close to falling in love with him. It was madness. Just because they'd *made* love didn't mean he wanted her love. But she suspected she couldn't stop herself any more than she could stop their pursuers' progress by willpower alone.

She looked back. A car was following them, its outline becoming clearer through the dust as they closed the gap. "We can't outrun them," she stated.

They traded looks. She felt as if she could read his thoughts. "Nudge?" she asked.

He nodded. "I'll try and get us out of sight of Jamal's car."

Could she pull this off? "Won't they follow our tracks?"

"Yes, so you'll have to make this fast."

Tom didn't waste time. He knew as well as she did that they had run out of other options for the moment. He swung the wheel and the car careened off the track into a thicket of tall trees and undergrowth. Branches slapped at the windows but he didn't slow until they were deep in the greenery, the car settling at a steep angle so it looked as if they were stuck fast. Hopefully it wouldn't turn out to be true.

Then he turned to her. "They don't know this area as well as I do, so I should have bought us a few minutes. Make them count."

She was already delving in her bag for the ranger's shirt. Swiftly she dragged the T-shirt dress over her head and tugged on the shirt. Her fingers shook too much to fasten the buttons.

Tom took over, speedily completing the task. She tried not to think of the touch of his fingers against her skin, arousing vivid memories and desires. He handed her a wrench. "Get under the car."

She hadn't thought beyond repeating this morning's trick, of lowering her head and pretending to be Tom's schoolboy protégé. Evidently he had something more in mind. "What do you want me to do?"

"Hit the wrench against the bodywork as if you're making repairs. Don't damage anything we're going to need later. And don't come out until I give the all clear, no matter what you hear. Understood?"

"I understand." Heart pounding, she slid as far as she could under the car, being careful not to touch any steaming metal. The smell of hot oil clogged her nostrils as she followed Tom's instructions.

Above the clang of the wrench against the bodywork, she heard Tom put the hood up and poke around in the engine. Moments later, their pursuers' car plowed into the grove. She held her breath.

From her limited vantage point, she saw Tom stride around the car and stand near her. "Great timing, mates. We could use a winch out of here."

"Tell us where to find the woman." She recognized Jamal's voice.

She heard Tom force a laugh. "If it's a woman you want, you're in the wrong place. Isn't he, Nudge?"

She felt him kick her shoe. She hammered at the car body to avoid the need to reply.

Jamal's boots came closer. "Who is that? Come out from there."

The wrench almost slipped from her clammy fingers as she pounded again and heard Max Horvath say, "I ran into them in town this morning. He's a skinny schoolkid who thinks he can learn something from this clown."

She could only see Jamal's legs but she knew he would have his head lifted slightly as if to scent a bad smell. It was his habitual expression and made his features seem hawklike and arrogant. She thought of his deep-set eyes, their ice-blue color rare in her country. They would have been striking if they hadn't been as cold and devoid of feeling. "The boy may learn more than he expects if the woman isn't handed over. She belongs to me."

His arrogant tone made Shara feel sick. Even if she was forced to marry him, she would never belong to him.

"You're not from around here, or you'd know you're trespassing on Logan land," Tom said, steel in his tone. "I'm prepared to overlook it if you and your lapdog leave now."

"You're a real comedian, McCullough," Horvath said. "You won't be laughing when I take over here as mortgage holder."

"You'll have to go through me first," Tom snapped.

She could almost see Horvath shrug. "It would be a pleasure."

"Enough," Jamal thundered. "We know you are sheltering the woman. Where is she?"

"Australia's a free country. If she doesn't want to go back

with you, that's good enough for me. We outlawed slavery centuries ago."

"Princess Shara is not a slave. She is my bride-to-be."

"Not according to her."

There was a groan of pain and she saw Tom's legs start to buckle as if he'd been punched. Anger on his behalf almost made her betray herself, until she realized she could get them both killed by revealing herself now. All she could do was stick to the plan and hope he wasn't too badly hurt. She slammed the wrench against the bodywork in frustration.

Tom's legs straightened. "I wouldn't do that again."

At the sound of his voice, strained but coldly defiant, relief swept through her.

"Tell me where you're hiding the princess, and it won't be necessary."

"Go to hell."

She tightened her hold on the wrench, bracing herself to come out fighting if Jamal attacked Tom again. Stupid, heroic fool. Didn't he know it was dangerous to provoke a man who considered himself above the law? Jamal had killed men for less.

Max Horvath came between Jamal and Tom. "We'll be quicker finding her ourselves, Prince Jamal. If she isn't at the plane, we can deal with the ranger and his halfwit assistant later. Without a winch, they aren't going anywhere in a hurry."

"She had better be with the plane," Jamal snarled at Tom, "or you will live to regret your part in this."

Praying that Tom wouldn't respond to the taunt, she almost sobbed with relief when he didn't. It was exactly what Jamal would want, giving him an excuse to take out his anger and frustration on Tom. She was sure that only the thought that Jamal would then turn his attention to Nudge kept Tom from retaliating.

"Get off this land," he growled.

She wasn't the only one hearing the warning in his tone, because Horvath said, "Please, Your Highness, this isn't getting us anywhere."

Weasel, she thought, wishing she could smash her own fist into the neighbor's toadying face. It was agony to lie under the car, unable to take action. She slammed the wrench against the bodywork again.

The metallic sound rang in her ears as Jamal said, "If you have touched the princess, I will kill you, McCullough."

"She's a free woman. You can't dictate what she does. Why don't you go back where you came from and leave her alone. She'll never marry you."

"She will be mine. And you will pay for keeping her from me."

The conviction in Jamal's voice made her flesh crawl. But the thought of what he would do to Tom was far worse. She almost slithered out from under the car and confronted Jamal then and there.

Tom somehow sensed her intention and positioned himself so she couldn't slide out from under the car. "Don't get cute now, Nudge. Just do what I told you."

"Good advice. I suggest you take it yourself," Jamal said. A few minutes later the other car screamed away, spraying gravel.

Tom moved aside so she could crawl out from under the car. He looked murderous. One hand splayed across his midsection, and movement made him wince. "Did he hurt you?" she asked, reaching to open his shirt and see for herself.

He ducked away from her hand. "It's nothing compared to what I'll do to him if he lays a hand on me again."

"You shouldn't have stopped me from confronting him."

"He had a gun. We can both be thankful he only slugged me with the butt. If you'd shown yourself, he'd have killed me then kidnapped you."

And if he'd married her and learned that she was no longer pure, Jamal would kill her too. By letting Tom make love to her, she had placed them both in terrible danger. She couldn't undo what was done. But she could help him keep Horvath from claiming his family's land, she resolved.

If she said as much to Tom, he'd try to stop her, so she didn't tell him. "Would you like me to drive?" she asked.

"He only winded me, I'm fine." Then he read the fear in her gaze and his arms closed around her. "I'm glad you didn't play into his hands."

Pulling his head down, she let her mouth tell him how much she'd wanted to help. Heat tore through her, ignited by desire, until she remembered that it was precisely this desperate hunger that had put Tom at risk. She forced herself to step back. "Now you know why I despise him so."

"He may be royal, but he's an ignorant son of a—"

Her finger against his mouth silenced him. "We both know what he is, and royal isn't part of it. His is a courtesy title, accepted because of his service to my father. In truth, he is the son of a palace guard, a far more pleasant man than Jamal himself."

"Pity he didn't take after his father."

"Not everyone does," she said, loading her tone with meaning.

He ignored it. "We'd better get moving. It won't take Jamal and Horvath long to find out you're not at the plane or the old cottage, and hightail it back here. We won't linger at the homestead in case they follow us there."

"We're running out of options," she said.

He lifted her chin and touched his mouth to hers, kindling fresh fires. "We're going to get that tape repaired and bring Jamal to justice. Now I've seen for myself what he's like, he'll have to kill me before I let him take you."

Because she feared it was exactly what Jamal intended, she suppressed a shiver. "Let's pray it won't come to that."

The flight had taken mere minutes. The drive was longer and bumpier, and by the time they reached the homestead, her throat was clogged with the red dust seeping into every crevice.

Judy flung herself out of the house and hugged Tom then Shara. "I saw the plane go over, and I thought maybe Jamal and Horvath…"

"They were watching the airport," Shara informed her. "We took the plane and got away, setting down at the old airstrip near the cottage."

Judy lasered Tom with a look. "You took your sweet time getting back here."

He shifted awkwardly. "We had things to do."

Seeing Judy reach her own conclusion, Shara fought the inclination to blush. She was doing too much of that lately, thanks to Tom's effect on her. Now his foster sister would have a fair idea how they'd spent the hours since they landed.

"Jamal shot at us as we took off," she said, wanting to distract Judy.

The other woman paled. "Did he hit anything?"

"Neither of us," Tom assured her. "But he damaged the plane. I'll need your help to get it airworthy again."

"Are you both okay?"

"We're fine," Shara insisted. "Although Jamal punched Tom."

Tom gave her a "did you have to tell her that" look, but Shara was defiant. If he'd been seriously hurt, she'd never have forgiven herself.

To Shara's surprise, Judy's smile widened. "Which hospital?"

Perplexed, Shara asked, "What do you mean?"

"If Jamal slugged Tom, he must be in the hospital by now."

Shara lowered her head. "Tom couldn't fight back without betraying me."

Judy's attention swung to Tom. "Who are you and what have you done with my foster brother?"

"Very funny. I don't always argue with my fists."

"And Christmas doesn't come once a year."

Shara was perplexed. It sounded as if Judy had expected Tom to fight. Yet Shara had seen a different side of him. Was he putting on an act for her sake? She had trouble believing that he was a violent man. If he'd been given to responding with force, he would never have stood for Jamal hitting him without retaliating. Perhaps Tom was stronger-willed than Judy knew.

Perhaps stronger than Tom himself knew.

"Did he do any damage?" Judy asked him as they climbed the steps into the homestead.

"I'll live," he said shortly, but Shara saw discomfort flash across his face when he lowered himself into a chair. When she moved toward him, he waved her away, his frown closing the subject.

Crazy man, she thought. The men in her family loved being babied at the slightest excuse. Jamal could turn a common cold into pneumonia, requiring nurses in constant attendance, the more nubile the better. She couldn't imagine him shrugging off any hurt the way Tom did.

Crazy, but heroic. She was in deeper trouble here than she'd known, because she grew hot as she imagined ministering to him. She resisted the thought. He didn't want her attention.

But he would, as soon as this was over.

A plate of sandwiches and an open book told Shara that Judy had been eating lunch when they arrived. Now she gestured toward the food. "Help yourselves. I made plenty in case Dad was hungry, but he doesn't want anything."

Tom helped himself to a sandwich. "How is he?"

Judy chewed her lip. "He had a rough night after the visit from Horvath and Jamal. The doctor came out to see him an hour ago and gave him something, so he's resting now."

"Did our arrival disturb him?" Shara asked.

"His room's at the other end of the house. He won't hear us if we keep our voices down." Judy balled her hands into fists. "This stupid mortgage business isn't helping his condition."

Tom gestured with his sandwich. "Shara has an idea that may help."

The other woman's eyebrows lifted. "He could sure use some good news."

Shara looked down. "It may not be much. You remember the ancient tribe I was researching in Q'aresh?"

"The one you wrote to me about? The Uru?"

Shara nodded. "I've seen what could be proof that the same tribe once lived on your land."

"When you accidentally hurt your leg," Judy said with a sharp look at Tom. When he didn't rise to the bait, she continued, "How does that help Dad with his mortgage?"

"If I'm right, visitors would come from all over the world to see the paintings. Not the ones in the taboo gorge," she said with a quick look at Tom. "Tom thinks there are other caves with rock art from the same period on Diamond Downs."

A smile lit Judy's face. "My Lord, that would be perfect."

"Except that Jamal took the information I need to be certain. He may not understand the significance of the discovery, but if he thinks it's important to me, he'll try to use the information against me."

"Bait to tempt you out of hiding," Judy surmised.

Tom nodded. "I'm trying to figure out how to get the tape back without risking Shara."

Shara's stomach knotted with fear. "You heard Jamal's warning. If you cross him again, he'll kill you."

Judy put out glasses and a carafe of water clinking with ice. "Dad won't want either of you taking crazy risks on his account. Horvath had his sights on Dad's land long before you got here, Shara."

Shara poured water into the nearest glass. "Tom told me Jamal offered to repay the mortgage if you turned me over to him."

Judy's expression darkened. "I hope you don't think we'd consider any such thing."

"No. Tom explained the code of the outback."

"Then you know we stand by our mates."

The feeling of having her friends try to help her gave her a rush of warmth.

"And judging from the Cheshire cat grin on my foster brother's face, you more than qualify as a mate," Judy said. "And don't tell me it's because he was pleased to see me."

Tom's face flushed. "This seems like a good time for me to check on Des."

When he'd left the room, Judy leaned toward Shara. "Whatever's between the two of you is your own business, but Tom has had a hard life. He isn't the easiest person to love."

Shara had found him disturbingly easy to love, but knew that wasn't what Judy meant. "I know why. We met up with Max Horvath in town this morning. He thought I was one of Tom's trainees, and he flung Tom's history in his face in my hearing."

Judy helped herself to ice water. "How did Tom react?"

"He refused to talk about it." She leaned forward. "Does he fear he'll end up like his father?"

"You've made more progress with Tom than you know," Judy observed. "The therapist took months to dig that fear out of him, but you've worked it out in only a few days."

It was the only possible explanation for why Tom had been so aghast when he'd grabbed her wrist, Shara thought. And who was to say he wasn't right, that blood would out? Just because she believed Tom was a compassionate man at heart didn't mean the violence he'd learned as a boy wouldn't surface under provocation. Was she willing to chance it?

It wouldn't come to a choice. Because of Jamal, she was a much greater risk to Tom than he could be to her.

It didn't stop her heart from skipping painfully when he came into the room. Judy offered him ice water but he shook his head, and took a light beer from the refrigerator, opening it with a pop and hiss.

"How's Dad?" Judy asked.

"Not good. He needs that transplant soon, if he's to have a chance of making it."

Judy frowned. "Even if a donor is found, as long as Diamond Downs is at risk, wild horses won't get him into the hospital."

If only the plane had still been in her name, Shara could have done something to help. Surely Des wasn't so stubborn that he'd chance death before accepting money from her?

Yes, he probably would. Australian men were so stubborn and prideful, she thought with a rueful glance at Tom. She would just have to help the family by proving that the Uru had left their mark on Diamond Downs.

Since she couldn't retrieve her research tape from Jamal without risking being dragged back to her country as his unwilling bride, she would have to use other means to prove her case, starting with the Internet. And she would have to work fast, before Max Horvath could foreclose on Des's mortgage.

Her head lifted. She could do this. Stubborn pride wasn't exclusive to the Logans, as Tom was about to discover.

Chapter 15

Judy encouraged them to stay for dinner, but Tom declined. "This is the first place Jamal and Horvath will come once they find out that Shara isn't at the plane."

"Don't worry. I can handle them if they turn up here," Judy said confidently.

He squeezed her shoulder. "They're the ones I should be worried about."

His foster sister grinned. "Now you're getting the idea."

"Doesn't stop me worrying anyway."

Judy rolled her eyes. "How brothers do fuss."

"I know. I have one of my own." *Had,* Shara amended silently, wondering if she would ever see Sadiq again. "Our relationship was far more formal," she added.

"I know a few men who could take lessons from him," Judy said with a pointed look at Tom.

He dropped a kiss on her forehead. "Just as well you love me anyway."

Shara felt a surge of envy. How wonderful to have such an

easy relationship with a sibling. Sadiq had always been conscious of his position as heir to the throne, insisting she use his title in public, and discouraging displays of sisterly affection in private. Their father had approved, although Shara wondered if he would have been more relaxed if their mother had lived.

She would never know, and now wasn't the time to ponder. Suddenly she felt achingly weary. The day's tensions and the near miss with Jamal were taking a toll. She stifled a yawn.

Tom noticed. "Time we headed off. It occurred to me that Tracey Blair might be able to help you prove the Uru were here, since you share the same interests."

"I'm sure she'll do whatever she can," Judy agreed. "But not today. Shara looks all in. Why don't you take her home to bed."

Shara's tiredness vanished in the quiver of anticipation Judy's comment elicited. The other woman might not have meant the suggestion literally, but Shara's body responded instantly. She shuddered and not with fear, as heat and hunger shot through her. Suddenly his home seemed very far away.

Tom had seen the naked need leap into Shara's expression, and its twin gripped him as he drove back to town. He wanted nothing so much as to stop the car and roll her into the back seat, tear off her clothes and make love with her like a teenager in heat.

She deserved better. Not only as a princess, but as the incredible woman she was. For her he wanted candles and soft music. A room scented with roses and a bed made with the finest linens. Slow and careful lovemaking, building and building until they scorched the sheets with their passion.

And not tonight.

First she needed time to rebound from the harrowing encounter with Jamal and the upheaval in her life.

Tom wasn't proud of giving in to his desires on the plane, although he knew she'd wanted him as much as he'd wanted her. And he couldn't suppress a feeling of insufferable pleasure at knowing he'd been her first lover. Had she any notion of how much that meant to a man?

Keeping her safe had become much more than a duty.

How unsafe they were came crashing back when Tom saw his front door hanging drunkenly from one hinge. "Looks like we've had visitors," he said grimly.

She wouldn't hear of remaining in the car, and shadowed him to the house and through it, muttering in her own language at the wanton destruction they found in every room.

If Q'aresh had swearwords stronger than his own, he could use them right now, he thought, picking his way across a debris field of shredded paper and shattered glass. His couch had been slashed with a knife until the stuffing oozed out. His large-screen TV was a wreck. In his office, the computer hemorrhaged circuitry. Every file had been pulled out of his cabinets and dumped on the floor, then ink from the printer cartridges ground into the pages. His bed was wrecked, his clothes dragged from the closet and dumped on the floor.

"This wasn't a search. This was revenge," he said.

"Jamal," she said, her shocked gaze meeting his.

He hated having to say it. "Yes. Not him personally. Even if he'd lower himself, he wouldn't have had time, but he or Horvath could have sent one of their henchmen to turn the place over." Before she could say it, he cupped her face. "It isn't your fault."

She trembled under his hands. "I brought Jamal into your life."

"You brought *you* into my life. I can't regret that, no matter what the cost. Everything here is replaceable. I can't begin to put a price on what you gave me today."

Had Jamal suspected that Tom had slept with Shara? It seemed possible, judging by the viciousness of the attack. He couldn't have known for sure, or Tom doubted he'd have been left alive in the clearing. What Jamal would have done to Shara if they were found out didn't bear thinking about.

She picked up a bark painting that had been broken in two. "This is terrible."

He looked at the mess. Not as terrible as what was going through his mind. If she'd been here when they came—he drove the thought down, refusing to let himself see her as anything but whole and warm and alive in his arms.

"He's going to pay for this," he vowed. His anger toward Horvath and Jamal before had nothing on the cold fury consuming him now.

"Shouldn't you call the police?"

"I'll have to, for all the good it will do. Our friends will have made sure they left nothing to be pinned on them."

She heard what he didn't say. "You can't mean to go after them yourself?"

He righted a bedside lamp, the head swinging by its wires. "There's no longer a choice. This is a declaration of war."

"Or a cover-up," she suggested.

He followed her train of thought. "They were looking for your tape of the meeting." Taking her hand, he helped her pick her way through the debris toward the door. There he paused. "When they didn't find it here, they must have moved on to the old cottage."

"Did they have to be so destructive?"

Surveying the wreckage of his living room, Tom nodded grimly. Whoever it was, and he had a feeling one of them was named Eddy Gilgai—had had a personal grudge against Tom. "There's more to this than a few notes about a vanished tribe, or a tape that's already half destroyed."

She picked her way gingerly through the littered room. "You said Max Horvath wants to find your great-grandfather's lost diamond mine. Could there be a connection between the Uru sites and the location of the mine?"

Just then, Tom pressed his mouth to hers, the kiss hot and sweet, and not nearly satisfying enough. He forced himself to step back. "In his journals, my great-grandfather recorded sighting some cave paintings that were completely different from those done by the present-day groups living on Logan land. He described the art in detail."

"Identifying those paintings might lead you to the mine," she speculated.

"And it might not. As kids, we spent a lot of time looking without success, imagining what we'd do with all our riches if we ever found Great-Granddad's mine. We boys used to scare the hell out of Judy with tales of how his ghost haunts the site."

Shara gave a slight shiver. "You'd mentioned that some people still believe the site is haunted."

Tom frowned. "Too bad Eddy Gilgai isn't one of them. He must have promised to help Horvath find the mine as payback for being exiled from Diamond Downs."

"Eddy Gilgai was the man your foster father dismissed for stealing, wasn't he?"

Tom nodded. "He'd been cautioned several times, until Des had no choice but to let him go. He would have been allowed to remain on his traditional land, but his own elders voted to banish him. Evidently he'd stolen from them, too, and messed around with girls who were taboo to him. Tribal law takes such transgressions very seriously."

She rubbed her calf. "As I learned to my cost."

His conscience twinged. "Does it still hurt?"

"Seeing the destruction of your home hurts more."

He rested his hands on her shoulders and turned her gently into his arms. "They're only things. My insurance will replace them. The main thing is you weren't here when they came." Everything in him chilled at the thought.

His mouth hovered over hers and he saw her lashes flutter closed. A sigh escaped her parted lips. Rattled by what could have happened, he had to taste her again. Only taste.

"What the blazes happened here? I don't remember a cyclone warning being issued for today."

Tom wrenched himself away from her as if stung. His foster brother stood in the doorway. "Blake, come in. Sorry I can't offer you somewhere to sit."

Blake surveyed the chaos. "Or anything else for that matter. Are you okay?"

"We're fine. Whoever did this came while we were at the homestead."

Blake scrubbed a hand over his face. "Any suspects?"

"The obvious ones—Max Horvath and Jamal Sayed. We ran into them near Bowen Creek this morning."

Blake's eyebrows lifted. "They didn't see Shara?"

"She was disguised as Nudge, my current work-experience schoolkid. And she was lying under the car, apparently working on it at the time."

"That's about the only way you'd fool anybody into thinking you were a schoolboy," Blake said to her.

If Blake made just one more untoward comment about Shara, Tom would have to flatten him, he thought, alarmed at the urge to do violence surging through him. His hands were tight fists until he made himself relax them. Blake was only stating the obvious. No call to act like a bull buffalo confronted by a rival.

But he wanted to.

The attack on his home had roused his fighting instincts, he knew. Right now caveman hormones were pouring through him, setting his reflexes to hair trigger. He felt as if he could strangle a tiger with his bare hands if it threatened his woman.

His woman. Now, where had that come from? Just because they'd made love didn't make her his property. With his family history, he was the last man who could claim her. This fight-or-flight thing was skewing his thought processes worse than he'd allowed for.

He'd instinctively moved between her and Blake, and now he made himself step away. "Shara recorded a meeting between Jamal and his henchmen. Before Jamal caught her, she hid the tape on the plane that brought them here. This morning we were able to retrieve it."

"Unfortunately, the tape is badly damaged," she contributed.

Blake quickly put two and two together. "But Jamal

doesn't know that." He surveyed the devastation. "Did he get what he was looking for?"

"The tape is still with us, until we can find a way to make it playable."

Tom thrust a hand through his hair. "That may not be our only worry. Shara has a theory about what else they were looking for." He didn't voice his own theory about why the destruction was so total. That was between him and Shara.

"I've been researching an ancient tribe called the Uru who may have lived on what is now Diamond Downs," she explained. "Tom thinks their rock art could lead us to your great-grandfather's diamond mine."

"When we got to the cottage this morning, a research tape on the Uru that Shara had had with her was gone. If Horvath heard that tape, he'd want to find out why it was so important to us. He probably had this place ransacked hoping to discover more clues," Tom contributed.

"Is the cottage in the same condition as this?" Blake asked.

Tom felt his mouth thin. "No, this was personal."

To his credit, his foster brother didn't ask why, although Tom felt sure he'd made that connection as well.

Blake righted a fallen chair and braced his hands on the back. "Horvath won't be very happy about us finding a lead to the mine before he can foreclose on Des's mortgage. My guess is he'll either try to destroy the evidence of an earlier tribe…"

"Or destroy the witnesses," Tom finished for him, having reached the same unwelcome conclusion.

Shara frowned. "Others like Tracey Blair have made similar studies."

"With any luck, Horvath doesn't know about her. I didn't even know she'd moved into the town until we met this morning." Had it only been hours before? It felt more like days. "She should be safe enough, but when the police come to sort this out, I'll let them know they should keep an eye on her."

"You can't stay here tonight," Blake insisted. "Apart from

the mess, you can't make this place secure in case you're right about witnesses being inconvenient."

Shara looked at Tom. "Where will we go?"

Before Tom could answer, Blake smiled at her. "I hope you like crocodiles."

By the time Tom had called the police, had the damage inspected and given them what little information he could, a couple of hours had passed. Shara was trying ineffectually to restore order in the office when he came in and lifted a bundle of ink-stained files out of her arms. "There's no point trying to do this tonight. I'll probably heave the whole lot out and start again."

"I feel so responsible."

He touched the back of his hand to her cheek. "We've already been through this once. You're not responsible for Jamal's cruelty or Horvath's greed. They're to blame for this, not you." He lifted her chin. "I'll make sure they pay."

Anger flared in her gaze, eclipsing the despair. "You won't do it alone."

He smiled gently. "I'm counting on it."

Since there was nothing more to be done that night, Tom had accepted Blake's invitation to spend the night at his crocodile farm. It was the first time Shara had seen crocodiles up close, and she stared in awe as Blake led the way past a pen of what he called subadult breeders.

They looked to be five or six feet long, and she could see several lying in the mud or floating like logs in the pond, only their eyes protruding above the water.

"Normally I'd take you through the gate leading from the car park into my quarters, but I thought you'd like to see my saltwater friends first," Blake explained.

She was fascinated and repelled all at once. "They look so primitive."

"They've hardly changed since the time of the dinosaurs. They come from the same family, Sauria, and retain lots of prehistoric qualities like the scaly horned tail and back, and a skull as hard as flint," Blake told her.

"And you make pets of them?"

Tom laughed. "Not if you know what's good for you. If you start when they're hatchlings, crocodiles can be conditioned to behave predictably around humans, but they can never be tamed."

"Then what do you do with them?"

Blake shrugged. "As well as doing research into crocodiles, we breed them and show them to the public."

"Make handbags and steaks from them," Tom contributed.

She turned wide eyes to him. "Are you serious?"

"Think of them as a kind of cattle," he suggested helpfully.

"The man-eating kind," his foster brother added.

Since she couldn't tell whether they were teasing her, she fell silent, thinking guiltily of a crocodile-skin handbag and shoes her grandmother owned. There were Nile crocodiles in Q'aresh but they were not farmed and were shy creatures, with a far less fearsome reputation than the Australian saltwater crocodiles.

She had a feeling she wasn't going to get much sleep, staying so close to these primitive monsters. On the other hand, they were a powerful deterrent against a late-night visit by Jamal, Horvath or their men, she thought, liking the idea more.

Blake's house was in the center of the thirty-acre park, fenced off from it for privacy, with the living room overlooking an area of wetlands Blake explained was used for nesting. Looking out the window, she saw the setting sun glinting off a series of ponds and wondered how many big crocodiles they held.

Blake read the unease in her posture. "Relax, Shara, the house is crocproof. Tom lived here for a couple of years and he still has all his fingers and toes. You tell her, Tom, while I organize a meal."

Blake left the room, and Tom held out his hands palms down, curling his thumbs out of sight. "See?"

She batted his hands away. "With you, I never know what to believe."

"Believe this. You're safe here."

For how long? she wanted to ask, but rejected the question as unfair. Tom and his family had already done more for her than she had any right to expect. Now it was time to start earning her own way. "Tomorrow, as soon as I can get on the Internet, I'll start establishing the Uru connection with Diamond Downs."

Tom leaned forward and kissed her forehead gently, letting his own rest against hers for a moment. "Tomorrow is soon enough to worry about tomorrow. This has been one hell of a day," he said when he lifted his head.

It had included her masquerading as a schoolboy, appropriating a plane, hoodwinking Jamal and losing her virginity, she cataloged mentally. Without a doubt, the most amazing day of her life.

Apart from the wreckage of Tom's home, she wouldn't change a thing, especially the part where he'd made love to her. He'd made the experience so special and memorable that she would treasure it forever.

They could reminisce about it when they were old and gray and surrounded by grandchildren, she thought, knowing better than to speak her mind. Tom would find out soon enough how she intended things to be between them. As soon as they were out of danger.

Blake reappeared and announced that he had steaks "on the barbie"—which she knew by now was short for barbecue—telling them to hurry if they wanted to freshen up before eating.

When they'd arrived he'd shown Shara where she was to sleep. The bathroom was next door. For one giddy moment when Blake had opened a door onto a room containing twin beds, she'd thought she and Tom were to share it, until she was shown the single room opposite. To her chagrin, she'd felt disappointed. What a long way she'd fallen from the gently bred princess of Q'aresh, she mused.

No, not fallen, risen. Tom's making love to her had lifted her up. She would never feel ashamed of giving herself to him. She'd do it again in a heartbeat, and only prayed they would have the chance.

The sun was setting by the time she joined the men on a covered terrace overlooking the wetlands. She had washed her face and hands, brushed the dust out of her hair and changed into one of the shirts and a pair of pants she'd brought from the plane. Wanting Tom to look at her as appreciatively as he'd done when they'd made love, she left the top buttons undone and tied the ends of the shirt into a knot at her waist.

Blake was turning steaks on the barbecue, while Tom added dressing to salad vegetables in a bowl. When he saw her his jaw dropped.

She felt a flush start. "I think that's plenty of oil," she commented, pleased to be the cause of his distraction.

He jerked the bottle upright, saving the salad from drowning barely in time. "I don't…I meant…you look…"

"Croc got your tongue?" Blake asked, sounding amused. He'd also given Shara a glance of frank appreciation, but seemed more fascinated by his foster brother's discomfiture. Shara hoped it meant Tom wasn't in the habit of becoming tongue-tied at the sight of a woman. Good, she liked being the one to have that effect on him.

"Go to the devil," Tom muttered, pulling himself together visibly.

"Can't. Steaks are nearly done," Blake rejoined.

To her the meat looked like a close cousin to charcoal. "The salad and bread are enough for me," she said.

A bottle of verdelho labeled as being from the Margaret River wine region near Perth stood uncorked on the redwood table. Shara allowed herself half a glass and was content to let the men drink the rest. Also to let them carry the conversation. In her country, it wasn't unusual for women to listen quietly while their men settled the world's affairs, but she knew it was far from the norm in Australia. However, she was too tired to do anything else. Besides, she liked watching Tom.

Blake waved a forkful of meat in the air. "If Shara's right and the Uru people inhabited Diamond Downs before the present tribes, why haven't we heard of them before?"

Tom toyed with his wineglass. "Perhaps we have. Remember the cave we played in as kids?"

Blake grinned at Shara. "Tom discovered the cave one day while running away from home after a fight over chores. I was following him at a safe distance, and saw him disappear into what looked like solid rock. Checking it out, I found him in a cave that none of us knew was there."

"The rock walls of that particular escarpment are honeycombed with them," Tom said. "After I changed my mind about running away, we kids adopted the cave as our secret hideout. We moved in some old furniture, blankets and supplies and made it a home away from home. I can show you where it is."

He went inside and came back with a crumpled map of the area, tracing Bowen Creek with his finger to a body of water she remembered seeing when they'd tried to get away from Jamal. "This is Cotton Tree Gorge, with Wolf Lake at the tip. The cave entrance is in this wall, almost directly above a paperbark tree that's had its trunk cleaved in two by lightning. It's been a while but I could find the cave with my eyes closed."

"Remember how Judy tracked us one day and threatened to tell Des if we didn't let her hang out with us?" Blake said, sounding as excited by the memory as his foster brother. Tom nodded.

"What does this have to do with the Uru people?" she asked, curiosity overcoming some of her torpor.

"The cave roof was decorated with paintings in a style we hadn't seen before. We didn't tell anyone in case it was taboo for us to have see them, and they made us stop going there.

Then we realized that the paintings were ancient and hadn't been touched up by the elders like the ones in the gorge, so nobody cared about them," Tom said.

Her excitement rose. "Or they were done by someone other than the present indigenous people. Someone like the Uru. How soon can we go there?"

Tom held up a hand. "You're staying right here. Jamal might be staking out the plane, and it isn't too far from there to the cave. You might be seen."

She felt an urge to stamp her foot. "I can't hide here forever. You've spent most of your vacation baby-sitting me instead of trying to help your family fight Horvath. Now I want to do something to repay you."

"There's no debt and no need for repayment," Tom said huskily. "That's not how we do things here."

She knew what he meant. "According to the code of the outback."

Blake shifted uncomfortably. "You told her about that?"

"Most of it," Tom said.

What part hadn't he shared with her? She told herself it hardly mattered now. He'd told her what was important. "Tom says that under the code, you don't back down, you don't give up and you stand by your mates. That's what I want to do."

Tom refolded the map. "You'll get your chance as soon as Jamal is out of the way."

"He has his own code, too," she pointed out. "He also doesn't believe in backing down or giving up." And he had as much, if not more, to lose than Tom and Blake and their family.

Tom skimmed a hand down her hair, sending a ripple of sensation through her. "But he doesn't have mates like us."

No, Jamal didn't have mates. He had hirelings and those who did his bidding because they were afraid of him. He didn't have anyone like Tom and his family, who would stand by their mates to the gates of hell and beyond if necessary. It felt good to be included in their company.

But she had learned something else about mates, too. In order to have them, you had to be one. It wasn't all take and no give. Somehow, she had to show Tom she was a mate to him. If he wouldn't give her the chance, she'd have to do it her way.

Chapter 16

Next morning, dawn was staining the sky vermilion when Tom joined Blake in the kitchen. Shara's door had been closed when he'd passed it, so he'd showered and dressed as quietly as he could, and she hadn't stirred. She needed the rest, he thought. So did he, but images of the wreck of his home had disturbed his sleep. He knew if he got his hands on whoever had done the damage, they'd be suffering some painful damage of their own.

At the breakfast table, he dumped cereal into a bowl and began to slice a banana on top. At the stove, Blake was tossing bacon in a pan.

"Still risking your arteries?" Tom joked.

"My arteries, my business. You're a fine one to talk about risk."

"Because I don't want to wrangle crocodiles for a living?"

"Because you can't see what's right under your nose. Shara's in love with you."

Tom almost sliced his finger instead of the banana. "She's

scared and confused. Her whole life's been turned upside down. I've been there for her. You're mistaking Stockholm syndrome for love."

Blake flipped toast out of the toaster and piled it on top of the bacon. He brought the plate to the table and sat down opposite Tom. "Stockholm syndrome is what happens when hostages start sympathizing with their captors. I don't see you holding Shara at gunpoint, but I do see her making goo-goo eyes at you whenever she thinks you aren't looking."

"You've been around prehistoric animals too long. They've reduced your perceptions of human need to food, shelter and procreation."

Blake picked up a piece of bacon and stripped the rind off it with his teeth. "We'll get to procreation in a minute. You know the saying, 'First comes love, then comes marriage.'"

Tom suppressed a pang. "Judy chanted it at us often enough when we were kids, before we'd bonded as brothers and sisters. She thought one of us should marry her when we grew up. Love and marriage have nothing to do with Shara and me."

Blake's eyes gleamed. "So you agree there is a 'Shara and you'?"

"So what? It doesn't mean you're going to be best man any time soon," Tom said.

Blake grinned. "I can wait."

"Hope you're prepared for a long one."

"I'm a patient man. And you have to agree, she's worth it."

This time Tom couldn't think of a single reason to argue. "She's pretty special. It doesn't mean I'm in love with her," he added quickly.

Blake made a sandwich of his toast and bacon and bit into it appreciatively. Around a mouthful he said, "I don't recall saying anything about you. I was talking about Shara's feelings. Does she know what a basket case you are?"

Inside, Tom was slowly coming to the boil, but he kept his tone mild. "How'd you like to have that sandwich rammed down your throat?"

"So she does know?"

"Horvath blurted out my life story in her hearing in town yesterday when he thought she was a work-experience kid."

Blake's eyebrow lifted. "So she knows about your dad being in prison. And she's still hanging around with you. Hmm."

"What's 'hmm' supposed to mean?"

"It means I'll start dusting off my tuxedo."

Tom concentrated on eating, refusing to be provoked any further. Even if his foster brother was right, and Shara did have feelings for him, it didn't mean anything could come of them. In the first place, she *was* vulnerable right now. And in the second, nothing had changed for Tom. Bad blood still ran in his veins. One woman he'd cared about had already left him, saying she couldn't be sure that normal anger wouldn't erupt into violence. Since he wouldn't know the answer until a crunch came, he'd agreed, figuring she was safer apart from him. He wasn't sure he could let Shara go so readily. He only knew he had to, for her own safety.

He glanced at the clock. "Do you think I should wake her?"

Blake made smooching noises. "There's always the traditional way, with a kiss."

Tom got up and put his breakfast things into the sink, thinking of how much he'd enjoy kissing Shara awake. He imagined her long lashes slowly lifting over eyes fogged with sleep, her glorious hair fanned across the pillow. First he'd kiss her forehead, then her full lips. Thinking of yesterday aboard the plane, his groin tightened at what he'd want to do next.

He settled for getting another cup out of the cupboard and pouring coffee into it to take to her. "Your love life isn't exactly the stuff of movies right now," he flung at Blake.

"I'm keeping my options open."

That made two of them, Tom thought on an inward sigh. Like himself, Blake's start in life hadn't predisposed him to close relationships. As a baby, his foster brother had been left on someone's doorstep and taken in by strangers. Not surprisingly, he'd run wild and finally come into Des Logan's care, where Blake had done a more spectacular job of straightening himself out than anyone in authority had expected. Knowing him, Tom hadn't been as surprised. Whatever Blake set his mind to do, he would achieve, whatever the cost.

"This love stuff isn't easy, is it?" he asked, not really expecting Blake to answer.

He did anyway. "Frankly, I'd rather wrestle crocodiles. I gather you didn't tell her about the last part of our code of the outback, the bit about no mushy stuff?"

Tom felt his face heat. "Of course I didn't. Anyway, we were kids when we wrote that. What did we know?"

Blake grinned. "We sure didn't understand how our attitude toward mushy stuff would change as we grew up." He looked at the cup in Tom's hand. "Would you like me to take that to Shara?"

"I'll do it. You're wrong about her making eyes at me." Even as he said it, Tom wondered which of them he was trying to convince.

Blake sighed. "I'm not wrong, mate. I wish I was."

At the door, Tom paused. "Because?"

"Because I'm afraid if you let her slip through your fingers out of fear, you'll regret it for the rest of your life."

His foster brother's words rang in Tom's ears as he carried the coffee to Shara's room. His fears were valid, weren't they? His temper was every bit as quick as his father's, and there were times when he'd had to struggle against the urge to lash out. That he hadn't hurt anyone so far didn't mean he never would. The more he cared about Shara—and he suspected Blake was right about how deep his feelings went—the more Tom wanted to protect her, even from himself.

There was no answer to his knock and the bathroom door stood open, so she wasn't in there. He hated to wake her after their eventful day yesterday, but she wanted to make a start on reconstructing her research, and Tom knew it was time he got back to work, too.

He hadn't counted on finding her bed empty. The room was

small enough that he could check it with a glance. Her clothes and her bag were gone. He put the coffee cup down on the bedside and hunted for a note, or some clue to where she'd gone. A sinking feeling in the pit of his stomach forewarned him that it wasn't for a walk around the wildlife park.

When Shara awoke she hadn't had any real plan in mind, except to find the cave Tom and Blake had talked about at dinner the night before. She could have waited until Tom awoke then talked him into taking her to the cave, but she didn't need a nursemaid. She wanted to do this alone.

What was she trying to prove? That as a princess she wasn't as mollycoddled as everyone thought? As she tried to dress quietly in the dark, fumbling and mismatching buttons, she grimaced at herself. She still wasn't used to getting herself ready for the day, having had servants assisting her for most of her life, even down to choosing what she should wear each day.

Not a dilemma that troubled her now, she thought. With only a few outfits to her name, she didn't have much choice. The white cotton shirt and pants she had worn to dinner last night would have to do. This time she tucked the shirt into the pants. Thinking of Tom's openmouthed reaction when she'd appeared with the shirt tied beneath her breasts and her midriff bare, she felt her mouth lift into a smile. Knowing the effect she'd had on him made her early-morning foray all the more worthwhile.

She might tell herself she wanted to repay the Logan family for helping her, but deep down, she knew Tom was the reason. He had been her first and only lover, but somehow she knew he had made it special for her. If she never knew any other man in her lifetime, she would be content. Now all she had to do was convince Tom.

Helping to solve Des's money worries would be a start. After the older man was relieved of the worry of the mortgage, he could concentrate on staying well until a transplant became an option. After that, she and Tom would be free to focus on themselves.

His bedroom door was firmly closed when she slipped out into the hall, only a sliver of predawn radiance lighting her way. She had willed herself to awaken early, sure that both men would be early risers. Carefully she felt her way along the hall to the kitchen where she collected some oranges for breakfast and a bottle of water. She found the keys to the old work car where Tom had dropped them on the hall stand, near the door she remembered led to the front entrance Blake had pointed out last night.

Although they hadn't come that way yesterday, he'd said there was a gate that avoided the need to go through the crocodile park. Just as well. She didn't think she'd have had the courage to find her way between the pens of monster crocodiles.

The gate was locked, but not from the inside, she saw as she let herself out quietly. A security light burned in the car park, illuminating the car she'd driven since coming to Diamond Downs. It would take Tom some time to work out where she'd gone, and follow her. By then she hoped to have some useful evidence to show him.

She had to concentrate on finding her way along the unfamiliar roads. By the time she crossed onto Logan land and began to navigate the network of cattle tracks leading to Cotton Tree Gorge, dawn had broken.

This was where things became tricky. In her bag was the map on which Tom had shown her the cave where they'd hidden out as children. He'd mentioned a tree split by lightning as a landmark. By daylight, however, she saw there were many such trees. Every rocky escarpment looked similar.

Exploring on foot was the only way she had any hope of finding the right cave. She stopped the car in the shade, ate an orange and drank some water, then put the bottle in her bag and got out. Screwing up her eyes, she squinted upward. Where should she start?

A twinge in her calf reminded her of the penalty for a wrong decision. When Tom's friend aimed the spear at her leg, she had never suspected Tom had also been firing an arrow into her heart. She was doing this for him, she reminded herself, and for the future she was determined they would share.

Shouldering her bag, she began to climb.

Two hours later she was no closer to finding the fissure leading into the secret cave. Once, she'd located an opening in the rock, and her heart had begun to pound, but the cleft hadn't been deep enough to be called a cave, and was open to the sky. Ancient rock art adorned a few of the crevices she explored, but none was in the style she remembered as belonging to the Uru people.

"Coo-eee! Coo-eee!"

At the sound of the traditional Australian bushman's call, she lifted her head from a petra glyph she'd been examining. Could Jamal have somehow found her? Apart from the shallow cleft there was nowhere she could hide, and in any case, they'd have seen her car by now. Whoever was calling knew she was up here.

"Coo-eee! Coo-eee!"

As the call echoed around the canyon again, she recognized the voice. It was Tom and he was alone. Her heart sank. By the time he'd found her, she'd hoped to have some progress to report, but she'd achieved nothing except to make him angry with her for going off on her own.

Shara Najran might be many things, but she wasn't a coward. Squaring her shoulders, she stepped out of the shadows.

Moments later he bounded up to her, his face flushed. "What the devil do you think you're doing?"

"Looking for the entrance to your cave."

"Out here alone? You could have gotten yourself lost or killed."

"Would you have cared?" she asked quietly.

"You know bloody well I would."

"Why, Tom?" *Admit that you care for me,* her heart implored silently.

"It's my job to care."

"Only your job?"

His dark gaze bored into her. "It can't be anything else, Shara."

"Yesterday it was a lot more."

He pushed his hat back on his head. "Yesterday was a mistake."

"I don't believe you."

"It doesn't matter what you believe. You don't know what you're risking with me."

She thought of how sublime she'd felt when he'd made love to her. "Surely the risk is mine to take?"

"Not in this," he said harshly. "Yesterday I was thinking with my glands instead of my brain."

A pang shot through her. "You regret making love to me?"

His hands dropped to her arms. "Never that. I'll take the memory of what we shared to my grave. But I shouldn't have let it happen. There's too much danger of you coming to harm because of me."

"I know you would never harm me," she stated, believing it with all her heart.

His gaze turned bleak. "Do you, Shara? Because it's more than I know for sure."

"Just because your father was a violent man doesn't mean you take after him."

Her shot in the dark had hit home, she saw when his eyes widened. "Don't you realize," he said in a tone barely above a whisper, "the only way I can be sure is if I'm put to the test."

"You were willing to take a spear meant for me," she pointed out. "They're hardly the actions of a violent man."

He turned away from her. "My mother said much the same thing to my dad. In one of his sober moments, my father begged her to take me and get away. She thought that meant he could change, so she stayed. Wishful thinking cost my mother her life."

"And you've been paying the price for her decision ever since. It's not fair."

He slammed a fist against the rock wall. "No, it isn't." He

swung around, his eyes blazing. "I'd accepted my lot in life, until you came into it. Damn you, Shara, you make me wish I was anybody but the man I am."

Her spirits lifted. No matter what he said, he did care for her. There was hope for them. "In my country, there is a saying—the sword is nothing without the fire. If you hadn't been tempered by the fire of your experiences, you wouldn't be the man you are."

"And that's supposed to be a good thing?"

"It is, to me."

"Then you're a bigger fool than I took you for."

She couldn't conceal her hurt. "Believing in you doesn't make me a fool."

"You're right, Your Highness. My apologies. It merely makes you misguided."

"It's your task to set me straight, I suppose?"

He nodded tautly. "Somebody has to, before you get hurt."

She would get hurt no matter what happened, she knew. It had become unavoidable the moment she gave herself to him. But there was no going back. "My father has the same attitude. His solution is for me to marry Jamal. Are you suggesting I should do so?"

Tom's fingers flexed as if he would like to feel them around Jamal's throat. "You know me better."

"I'm beginning to think I don't know you at all."

He made an angry sound of dismissal. "Let's find the cave."

She concealed her satisfaction. Tom might be convinced he had nothing to offer her, but she knew differently. She wasn't afraid of him, or of what he might do in a fit of temper. Maybe she was the fool he'd accused her of being, but she trusted her instincts and the love he'd shown her. If he could only learn to trust himself, there could be a chance for them.

First, they had to locate the entrance. "I've been trying for ages with no luck," she said.

At last he smiled, and her heart almost cracked open. "You've been looking in the wrong places. Des did the same thing whenever we kids pulled our disappearing act, and he never found the cave either."

She took some small comfort from that. "I looked in line with the lightning-blasted tree, but there are so many of them."

He gestured toward a tree not far below them. "Only one has a trunk like an arrow. You were closer than you think. Give me your hand."

The touch of his fingers sent fire tearing along her veins. He might think yesterday had been a mistake, but she couldn't make herself believe it for a second. In her country, one's fate was supposed to be written before you were born. If it was true, she had been meant to come to Australia and find Tom. Everything in her life, even her quirky interest in rock art, had led her directly to where she was now, and the man at her side.

Especially the man at her side.

He guided her along the ledge to where it seemed to taper to nothing. "I've already explored along here," she protested, gasping as gravel spilled into the air under Tom's feet.

Suddenly he tugged his hand free and disappeared, seemingly melting into the solid rock.

If he could do it, so could she. Like a sight-impaired person, she felt her way along the rock face until her fingers closed around a jagged edge that was invisible until she was right on top of it. Closing her hand around it, and her mind to the conviction that at any moment she would plunge off the narrowing ledge to her death, she forced herself to take another step.

Moments later she swung around the jagged edge through an opening like the eye of a needle, into Tom's waiting arms.

"Why didn't you tell me this was here? I thought I was about to plunge off the cliff," she protested. Her heart slammed against her ribs so hard that she could hardly breathe, although whether from falling into the hidden cave, or from finding Tom's arms around her, she didn't know.

He took her bag and dropped it on the sandy floor. "Amazing, isn't it?"

She couldn't argue. Being held tight against him certainly

fit the description. So did the way his mouth was roving hungrily over her face and eyebrows. His hands were warm on the back of her neck. She dropped her head back and let him feast.

When her own need became too great, she fastened her lips to his and took in her turn, feeling heat pool deep inside her, igniting the core of her womanhood. Oh, how she wanted him. Was this how it was supposed to be? First the discovery of what a man could give a woman, then the all-consuming desire to revisit that sacred place? To create love and children and a future there?

In Tom's arms, she had found her spiritual home, she thought, wishing this moment didn't have to end. The thought of Jamal's pursuit weighed heavily on her, along with what Horvath might be planning against Tom's family. Was there never to be a time when she could simply follow the dictates of her heart?

Tom let his hands slide down her body to her waist, the touch thrilling of itself, until he put her carefully away from him. His breathing was shallow and his face was flushed. He sounded unsteady as he said, "I should have known better than to bring you here."

Her own voice felt less than reliable. "It wouldn't matter where we were. I would still feel the same."

"Me, too, damn it to hell," he said.

She shook her head. "I hardly think hell is where we were headed."

He dragged his hat off and placed it on a ledge, then raked his fingers through his hair. "I didn't bring you here for that."

Her whole body throbbed with the need for him to totally possess her. She felt like a tuning fork struck at precisely the right note, vibrant and strong and sure. And just as certain that it wouldn't end here. "Wherever we are, it seems to come down to *that*," she said.

"All the more reason to focus on what we came to do," he rasped.

He was right, as she'd already reminded herself, but she'd

already learned that the expectation verged on the impossible. He felt it, too, she saw from the fire in his gaze and the unsteadiness of his hands. He might not share her people's belief in predestination, but her belief was strong enough for them both. It told her as surely as if their fate had been carved on the cave walls, that she and Tom were destined to be one.

She suspected he also felt that, but meant to fight it as hard as he could.

For both their sakes, and the children she believed with all her heart were already written in her and Tom's stars, this was one fight she was determined not to let him win.

Chapter 17

Despite knowing he should get out of here before he gave in to the desire to kiss Shara again, Tom stood his ground. He felt a tug of nostalgia as he looked around the cave. As a boy he'd been able to stand up in every part of it. Now he had to bend to access the farthest reaches. "Everything's just the way we left it," he said.

Shara followed his gaze. A pair of camp stretchers stood at right angles to each other in a corner. A large rock had been manhandled between them to serve as a table. An assortment of chipped enameled mugs and plates still stood on it. Tom sat on one of the cots and picked up an adventure novel he last recalled seeing when he was about fourteen. He dusted off the cover with his sleeve and sneezed. "Guess it's been a while."

She coughed to chase the dust from her throat. "It's a wonderful hideout, but I don't see any unusual cave paintings."

"There's a gallery opening off this one." He stood up. "You have to crouch to get through the access tunnel to reach it."

He wasn't wrong, she soon discovered. The tunnel was barely her height in places, and Tom had to stoop to pass through the lowest section. But the effort was worth it when she emerged into a high-ceilinged cavern. Tom had gone ahead of her and was already standing in the middle, hands on his hips.

During the course of her research, Shara had seen many pictures of rock art, aeons old. Her father's reluctance to allow her to travel meant she had been unable to visit most of the sites she'd researched, other than those in Q'aresh. It was hard to believe she was actually standing in this one. She had never seen anything so breathtaking.

A natural fissure opened at the cavern's highest point, allowing light to filter in through a mesh of tree roots. At this time of day the cave was gently illuminated, and she looked around in wonder.

As her eyes adjusted, she saw that every surface was covered in figures of people, fish and kangaroo formed from hundreds of fine lines drawn in natural ochre. She had read that the ochre had been carried north, sometimes for more than a thousand miles, until it was pulped and kneaded by the tribal artist, and painted onto the wall. Barely perceptible depressions on the rock floor would have served as an artist's palette.

Some of the figures were drawn on overhanging rocks sixty feet from the ground and many feet from the closest wall. "It's remarkable how they managed to paint up there," she said, pointing. "The cave entrance isn't wide enough to bring in lengths of timber."

"The local people say they were put there by an ancient tribe existing thousands of years before the present inhabitants."

"The Uru," she said, awe coloring her tone. "The style is identical to the work I've studied elsewhere. Perhaps they had another means of access then, higher than where we came in."

"It's possible. The land formations would have changed over the centuries since the Uru lived here."

Looking at the figures, she could almost hear the click of the rhythm sticks and the throb of the didgeridoo, that ancient instrument made from a hollowed-out log that had accompanied tribal rituals since the Stone Age. The sounds reached out to her from across time, sighing to her from a spiritual meeting of ancestral clans like a tribal séance.

Tom was watching her. "You hear it, too, don't you?"

She shook off a vision of black figures daubed with white lime clay and adorned with goose feathers, carrying spears and stamping their bare feet to the haunting music. "There's nothing to hear."

"Liar," he said softly. "You hear it, and you feel the presence of the song men."

"Song men?"

"That's what Andy's clan call the custodians of their tribal history. The stories are told and retold through song, rather than being written down. The rock art is the only tangible record."

A sigh rippled past her lips. "What is it we think we hear?"

"Echoes of the past stored in the cave walls? Maybe nothing outside our imagination. Who knows?"

"It doesn't matter as long as we're witness to their legacy."

He hadn't noticed, or didn't mind that he had dropped his arm around her shoulders as they talked. A frisson of pleasure feathered through her at the closeness. Then she felt a frown gather. She had dreamed of confirming the travels of the Uru around the world. Now the finest examples she could imagine surrounded her, some of the drawings close enough to touch. And where was her attention focused? On the wish that Tom would sweep her into his arms and make her forget everything but him.

She forced her attention back to the rock art. "Are there more caverns like this in this system?"

"Almost certainly, but as children, we were afraid to explore any farther for fear of getting lost."

Hard to imagine him being afraid of anything. "Why didn't you come back as an adult?"

"Until you raised the question of this site belonging to the Uru people, I had no reason to. Diamond Downs has hundreds of rock art sites. As far as we knew, this one was no different from the others. And you have to agree, it isn't the easiest place to get into."

Thinking of her leap of faith off the end of the ledge, she nodded, "Probably why it was chosen in the first place, and almost certainly why it has remained untouched for so long."

"We'll have to take care that any access we allow doesn't harm the paintings," Tom observed.

She tilted her head back to admire the painted roof. "Would Andy and his people consider creating replicas that can be opened to visitors? Then the original caverns could be restricted to scholars who know how to protect the work."

Tom rubbed his chin thoughtfully. "It's possible, not unlike making prints of the works of the old masters in our culture. We could even set up a touring exhibition for people unable to travel to Diamond Downs."

"Your father's home will become world famous," she observed. She switched her gaze to the closest of the drawings, an elongated figure of a man, his head haloed. "Unlike the paintings in the taboo gorge, these don't look as if they've been retouched."

"According to the local clan, the drawings were done by spirit people, so the spirits are expected to maintain them."

"Except that the Uru people died out many thousands of years ago." Her excitement grew, and she gripped his hand. "Tom, do you realize what this means?"

His fingers curled around hers. "You'll be famous for discovering the link?"

She fought to ignore the tingling sensation his touch created. "You and your foster brothers and Judy discovered it. All I've done is put a name to the artists."

Tom slanted her a grin of triumph. "If it brings the kind of acclaim you expect, it will save Des from ruin and keep the land out of Horvath's hands."

Sharing his excitement, she slid her arms up around his neck and kissed him.

It may not have been the first time she'd kissed him of her own volition. In his arms she had trouble remembering anything. But Tom seemed startled and she wondered if she'd been too forward.

On the point of pulling back, she reminded herself that this was Australia. Men and women were equal here. If she wanted to kiss him—and she wanted to about as much as she wanted to keep on breathing—she had a perfect right.

He didn't seem to mind. After his first jolt of reaction, his mouth softened under hers and he allowed her to explore to her heart's content. Kissing was different from being kissed, she decided, her scientific mind eagerly soaking up the sensations.

Up to her whether to tease around the edges of his mouth with the tip of her tongue, or to plunge deeper. She did both, eliciting a groan from him that made her senses sparkle. So much for his determination to resist her.

"For pity's sake, Shara," he said around her kisses. "Do you know what you're doing to me?"

She knew because the echo was in every part of her, too. In the dimly lit cave, surrounded by evidence of a prehistoric civilization, she felt prehistoric herself. The thought filled her with awe. Yesterday she'd been a virgin princess. Today she was a cavewoman, wise to the ways of love, arousing her caveman with her kisses until there was only one place left for them to go.

Without speaking, Tom grasped her hand and led her back through the labyrinth to the hideout cave. Over the centuries, leaves had drifted through the narrow entrance onto the cave floor, making a soft carpet underfoot. Tom lowered her to the cot in the corner, his mouth never leaving hers. Subtly he had shifted from letting her kiss him, to kissing her with an ardor that left her breathless.

He was doing much more than kiss her. His hands were busy at the buttons of her shirt, worrying them until he got them open and plunged inside, exploring her body with almost worshipful care.

As he caressed her breasts the virgin princess in her knew a moment's resistance, until the cavewoman remembered that this was Tom. Her Tom. She leaned closer, letting him hold and surround her, touch her until desire clouded her mind to everything but how much she cared about him.

Would she ever have enough of his touch? Of his mouth? Of his love? She burned with the wanting. The clothes she'd retrieved from the plane were soft and finely woven, but they created an unwelcome barrier between her and her heart's desire. Frantically she placed her palms against his chest. He moved away long enough for her to shrug the shirt off her shoulders and reach both hands behind her to undo her bra.

Breathing hard, he took the garment from her. "You're the most beautiful woman I've ever known."

She touched her hand to his face. "And you're the most beautiful man."

"Men aren't beautiful."

"You are, to me. You have an amazing body and a beautiful mind. The work you do is selfless. Even your concern for your foster father is beautiful. What more can a woman want?"

He didn't see himself the way she did, she realized, when he blinked in surprise. He opened his mouth as if to argue and she pressed her fingers against his lips. "Don't say anything. Just love me."

He didn't need a second invitation.

With swift, careless movements he stripped off his shirt. Balling it into a pillow, he placed it under her head. His delicious man scent rose from the fabric when she filled her lungs with air. Emboldened, she slid the zipper of her pants down and eased them off over her hips, kicking them away. A narrow band of black lace was her only remaining cover.

Kneeling beside her, he started to ease her panties down. Suddenly shy, she moved to prevent it and he grasped her hands between his, kissing her fingertips. "It's all right," he soothed. "We can stop anytime you want to."

Feeling the unbelievably erotic pull of his mouth around her fingers, she dragged in a shallow breath. "Do you want to stop?"

"It may well kill me, but I will for your sake. I'll do anything you want me to, Shara."

Anything but promise her forever, she thought. All because he didn't trust himself to do what he was doing—sacrifice his own desires for her sake. Couldn't he see the illogic? He was already holding himself back. He would never hurt her in this or any other way.

Logic was for later. Now was for the two of them. "I don't want you to stop," she whispered.

He peeled her panties off and stood up. Giddy with anticipation, she crooked an arm behind her head and watched him finish undressing. He was more than beautiful. Naked, almost fully aroused, he was magnificent.

He knelt again but didn't touch her. The waiting was almost intolerable. "Is something wrong?" she asked. How could she bear it if he'd changed his mind about wanting her?

The truth was in his heated gaze. "I'm taking my time, looking at you. Princesses aren't the only ones capable of appreciating beauty."

A glow stole over her. "I'm not a princess right now."

He leaned over her and traced a line of kisses from her neck to her navel, making her shiver with delight. "To me you're always a princess. A pagan princess in this setting, perhaps, but always special."

His kisses traveled lower and she arched her back, her fingers scrabbling among the bed of leaves. He skimmed the gentle curve of her stomach and she let out a long, unsteady breath. "Oh, Tom."

"The way you say my name, you make me want to give you the moon."

"The moon isn't what I want right now." Couldn't he see that the waiting was killing her? Not to mention the white-hot sensations bombarding her as his hand began a new voyage of exploration.

He sat back on his heels. "Yesterday, this was all new to you. Today, you're making demands."

She blinked hard. Had she misunderstood how things were in Australia? "Have I done something wrong?"

He circled her nipple with his finger. Fresh heat tore through her. "Hardly."

He teased the other nipple and she writhed beneath his hand. "Then why do you make me suffer so?"

His eyes gleamed with wicked intent. "Because I can."

Then she knew. He was building the tension to make the release so much more wonderful. She linked her arms around his neck and pulled him down to her. "You're a hard man."

He unhooked one of her hands, kissing the palm before guiding her fingers down to cup him, showing her just how hard she'd made him. Instinct took over and she began to stroke him.

It was his turn to squirm. "Have a little pity, woman."

"I'm having as little as I can," she teased, her fingers moving. No amount of biology lessons had prepared her for this. For the silk and steel and volcanic heat of him. Or for the heady discovery that she was the cause.

She couldn't resist. "Do you know why I'm doing this?"

With a groan, he raised his head. "It's a form of torture unique to Q'aresh?"

"No. Because I can."

His gaze darkened. "You think so?"

"Mmm-hmm."

"You think you're the boss?"

She kneaded gently and thought he was about to explode. "For the moment, since you're in my hands, so to speak."

He scissored her legs between his, forestalling further exploration. "We'll soon see about that."

He moved away from her long enough to grab his discarded pants and reach into a pocket. He retrieved a small packet and tore it open with his teeth.

"Do you have an inexhaustible supply of those?" she asked.

"This is the only one. We'd better make it count."

He sheathed himself and came back to her almost in the same movement. She was more than ready.

"In all my studies, I never imagined making love in a cave," she murmured much later as she lay in the crook of his arm. She felt exhausted but sated, and happier than she had ever dreamed was possible. "Do you think the spirits of the cave approve?"

His free hand splayed across her stomach. "I know I do."

"What about the Uru?"

"Oh, definitely. Why is it important?"

"Do you believe in reincarnation?"

"I believe there are many things in life we can't explain." She drew a deep breath. "I feel as if I've been here before."

He chuckled. "Me too, aboard your plane."

She swatted at him. "Don't you believe in déjà vu?"

"I've never experienced it myself, but if you say you've been in the cave before, I'm willing to go along. I just wish you'd have let me know."

"Do all men have such one-track minds?" she asked.

"Only when lying beside beautiful women they've just made passionate love to," he explained. Then he kissed her lightly. "I love that you have to ask."

"Because I'm such a novice at this?"

"For a novice, you catch on pretty fast. For a while there, I was afraid I might not last the distance."

"I'll try to be more considerate in future," she said primly.

"Shara…"

His hesitation notched the fear higher. "It's all right," she said, striving to sound as if she meant it. "I haven't asked for any promises. Nor will I."

"You deserve them. You deserve better than me."

"Shouldn't I be the judge of that?"

"So far, you haven't shown much judgment where I'm concerned."

She sat up and pulled her legs close to her body, hugging her arms around them. The sun was no longer spilling through the entrance, but she hadn't felt cold until this moment. "As you just reminded me, I haven't had much experience with men, but I'm not stupid. If I thought you were a danger to me, I wouldn't be here."

"How can you be so positive, when I'm not?"

"Because I know you. Not the small details of your life," she said before he could interrupt, "but the kind of man you are."

He reached for his clothes. "Whenever I'm with you, you make me wish I could be that man."

"You already are. I love you," she said on impulse.

He had stood up to pull on his pants. Now he froze, his expression appalled. "Don't, Shara. What we've shared was more wonderful than anything I've ever known, but it isn't love. It can't be. Not with me."

She stood up and began to dress. "Perhaps it's me who didn't satisfy you, and you're trying to let me down lightly."

He pulled up his zipper, then thrust his hands into his pockets as if to stop himself from reaching for her. "You must know that's not true. Maybe if we give this some time—no." He cut off whatever he'd been about to say. "No, I won't risk it. I won't risk you."

"And that's an end to it?"

"It has to be."

She put on her bra then slid her arms into her shirtsleeves and began to button it, trying not to think of Tom's fingers undoing those same buttons. "I haven't been brought up to beg, but I will if you leave me no choice."

He'd pulled on his shirt and boots. As he tucked the shirt into his pants, he said, "You could be begging for the love of a monster."

Before she could utter the cry of denial welling inside her, he'd moved to the entrance and disappeared through it.

Chapter 18

She took her time finishing dressing, needing to think. Her whole body throbbed with the effect of his lovemaking but her mind was clear. He wasn't the monster he imagined himself to be, she would stake her life on it. Yet as long as he believed it, there was no hope for them.

One thing was certain. If she persisted in trying, she would drive him away from her for good. Play it cool, she believed was the Australian expression. Pretend she was happy with the status quo until his own need for her brought him back to her.

What if it didn't? What if all they really shared was physical? She didn't believe that either.

Time to put it to the test.

When she finished dressing, he still hadn't returned. Her heart raced at the thought of confronting the frightening climb, but she steeled herself and followed him.

Going out from the cave wasn't as bad as going in, she discovered. From this angle, the way back to the ledge was obvious. It only looked like a dead end from the other approach.

If scholars were to come to the caverns, the access would have to be made as safe as possible without harm to the surroundings, she thought.

She found Tom hunkered down at the lower end of the ledge, his cell phone in hand. Everything in her yearned to touch and stroke, but she held back, knowing nothing else was going to work.

"What is it, a message?" she asked.

He nodded. "Judy couldn't contact me while we were in the cave. She left a text message to say that Des has collapsed."

She couldn't stop herself from touching him in mute support. "Is he in the hospital?"

He shook his head. "He should be but Judy couldn't persuade him to go, and the doctor's away delivering a baby, so he can't get there for some time. And Blake's chasing after a rogue croc that's threatening a settlement."

"You must go to your foster father."

He stood up. "Judy's message warns that Jamal has been seen in the area. He's probably waiting for you to show up."

"It doesn't matter," she said firmly. "Des's life may be in danger if you can't convince him to go to the hospital."

"I can't risk you either."

He sounded so ragged that her heart turned over. "Leave me here. Go to him. You and your brothers spent many hours here. I'll be fine until you return. Call Judy back and tell her you're on the way."

He nodded and pressed numbers on the keypad. "The number's engaged. She could be talking to the doctor."

"Then don't waste time. Go."

"Are you sure?"

"I'm sure. My tape recorder is still in my bag. I can start making a record of the rock art in the cavern."

He pressed his lips hard against hers, sending her temperature soaring. "I'll tell Des what you're doing. If it gives him hope, he may agree to get help."

"Do it."

Still, he hesitated. "Do you still have Judy's cell phone?" When she inclined her head in agreement, he said, "Good. I'll let you know what's happening when I get to the homestead. Call me if there's any sign of trouble in the meantime. You'll find food and drink and a torch in my bag. Use whatever you need. There's no telling how long I'll be gone."

She drew herself up. "My people come from the desert. I'm as at home here as you are. This cave sheltered you when you were a boy. It will do the same for me until you return."

"Don't try anything heroic. Promise me you'll stay here until I get back?"

"You have my word. Now go."

He wasted no further time. She watched him climb down to his car and heard the engine fire moments later, then waited until he was a speck on the horizon before turning back to the cave.

Documenting the Uru paintings kept her occupied until she was too tired to think anymore. Turning off the compact recorder, she made her way back through the tunnel to the entrance cave.

Wearily she dragged one of the stretcher beds into the open air and beat the dust out of it, then took it back inside and settled on it to eat some of the sandwiches from Tom's pack. The bread was thicker and the filling more generous than she was accustomed to, but when she removed the meat, the bread and salad was more than enough to satisfy her hunger. Washed down with water, it was all she required.

She wished she could say the same for her mental state. Jamal had been seen around the homestead. Was he the reason for Des Logan's collapse? She couldn't help blaming herself and wishing there was more she could do to help Tom. This relentless stalking couldn't go on. Not if the cost could end up being Des's life.

Even now she would have followed Tom. Her car was parked in the bush below the cave and she was fairly sure she could find her way to the homestead. But she had given Tom her word she would wait.

She pulled Judy's cell phone out of her satchel. It was fully charged and the reception, sometimes patchy in the Kimberley according to Tom, was good as long as she was near the cave entrance. But the instrument remained stubbornly silent.

She debated calling him. If he was taking care of Des, he didn't need her distracting him. She decided to lie down for a while, and hope he called.

Tom should never have left Shara alone, he told himself as he drove back to the homestead. Instinct told him something was wrong with all this. What was Jamal doing at the homestead? And why wouldn't Des let Judy take him to the hospital if his condition was so bad? He was a stubborn man, but he wasn't an idiot. He wouldn't put such a burden on his daughter.

If this was a trap set by Jamal, had Tom played into his hands by abandoning Shara? The only way to find out was to get to the homestead, assure himself Des was all right, then get back to the cave as fast as he could. Until then he'd have to trust her word she'd stay put where she was safe.

He left the car in a thicket of trees and approached the homestead on foot. The house looked deserted, but that was normal at this time of day. The stockmen would be scattered around the property, leaving only the elderly clan members drowsing in the sun outside their cottages, their dogs lolling in the dust at their feet.

Then he saw it. The door to the living room was closed. Des and Judy only closed that door during a cyclone or a dust storm. She must have intended it as a warning to him.

Keeping to the shadows, he padded around the back and nodded in grim satisfaction at the sight of two strange vehicles parked behind the house. One was the Jeep Jamal had been driving when he followed Tom's car. Two men were smoking a short distance away. One was Eddy Gilgai. The other was the man who had been with Horvath and Jamal yesterday. He looked big and ugly enough to be Jamal's bodyguard.

Moving silently, Tom slid between the cars until he stood beneath an open window. Judy's voice reached him clearly. "Tom will never fall for your message. If he comes, he won't have Shara with him. She's miles away from here by now."

"Then he will lead me to my fiancée, or he will watch you and your father die," a heavily accented voice responded.

Tom risked glancing over the sill. Judy and Des were seated on a couch. Jamal stood over them, the silhouette of a gun barrel protruding from his arms, a bulky silencer at its tip. He had his back to the window. Horvath was at the opposite window, no doubt expecting Tom to arrive from the front.

Four against one, two if Judy pitched in, and Tom didn't know of any way to stop her. Hardly good odds, considering Jamal's weapon. Keeping out of sight of the smokers, Tom returned to the front of the house where he heaved a good-size rock at the door. He was on his way to the back again before the door had fully opened.

As he'd hoped, shouts sent the smokers racing around to the front, giving Tom his chance. He slipped in through the window, only to come up short at the sight of Jamal's gun aimed at his heart. "Did you think I'd fall for such a childish trick?"

Tom slowly lifted his hands. "It was worth a try."

Jamal gestured to his bodyguard who'd come in the front way, followed by Eddy Gilgai. "Take him."

The larger man pulled Tom's arms roughly behind him. Judy's face fell. "You shouldn't have come."

Tom tried unsuccessfully to shake off his captor. "I got your message about Des being ill."

Her shoulders slumped. "Jamal sent it to lure you here."

"Evidently your brother is not as smart as you thought," Jamal said, stepping between them. He pressed the gun against Tom's temple. "Where is my fiancée?"

"No idea," Tom said, then the air rushed out of him as Jamal cuffed the side of his head with the gun barrel. Head ringing, he slumped in the bodyguard's grip. Through a haze he saw Judy start to jump up, but Des pulled her back down.

"Look, son," Des said to Jamal. "This is Australia. If the princess doesn't want to go with you, you can't force her. Beating up Tom is not going to change her mind."

Jamal swung the weapon back to Des. "I am not your son. Under *our* laws, Shara became my property when King Awad promised her to me in marriage. I am only claiming what is mine."

Making sure to appear groggier than he was, Tom stayed on his knees, feeling gratified as the guard's grip loosened. This time he was ready. When Jamal swung the gun around, Tom grabbed the barrel and yanked, sending the man crashing into his bodyguard. Before either could recover, Tom pulled Jamal to the floor and pressed the gun into the back of his head. "One move by any of you, and Prince Jamal dies," he stated, his tone steely with purpose.

They froze in place. Tom lifted the barrel slightly and dug his boot into Jamal's side, knowing that to touch someone with your foot was a deadly insult in the other man's culture. "Get up."

Jamal moved slowly to his knees, then shouted something in his own language. Everything happened in slow motion. A gun appeared in the bodyguard's hand and stuttered almost at the same second. Tom only knew he'd been hit when pain like white-hot needles flamed across his wrist. He dropped Jamal's gun.

He saw Judy spring at the bodyguard, who knocked her aside.

Jamal picked up the gun and swung it in a wide arc. "Everybody back off," he ordered. Horvath seemed immobilized by the gunplay.

Judy picked herself up and rejoined her father. At a signal from Jamal, Eddy and the bodyguard moved to stand over them.

Jamal's eyes blazed. "I will kill you," he growled at Tom.

"You've already disabled him," Horvath insisted, sounding petrified. "Let's get them secured and go after your fiancée. Now the plane's fixed, you can settle up with me, and take Shara back where she belongs. I didn't agree to be a party to murder."

Tom pulled off his bandanna and wrapped it around his throbbing wrist. "You'll never find her."

"I think we will." Jamal snatched the bloodied cloth from him. "Eddy's people are famously able to track anyone anywhere. When they do, your blood on this should convince her to give herself up."

Tom's heart became a lump of stone in his chest as the bodyguard herded them at gunpoint into the main storeroom. Intended as a shelter in the event of a cyclone, it was the most secure room in the house. The walls and floor were concrete, with only a tiny window set high in the wall, and a low-wattage electric bulb for light. The solid door slammed shut and they heard the key being turned in the lock on the outside.

Judy snapped on the light and came to inspect his hand. "How bad is it?"

"It's only a graze. Looks worse than it is." Felt worse, too, but Tom kept that to himself. "How about you?"

She rotated her shoulders experimentally. "A few bruises, nothing serious."

Knowing Judy wouldn't thank him for fussing, he nodded. "We have to get out of here before Jamal finds Shara."

Des rummaged through boxes, coming up with a supply of cotton wadding and surgical tape. He handed them to Judy, who began to bind Tom's wrist. The pain had him grinding his teeth, but when she finished he felt better and the bleeding had stopped. "Now can we get out of here?" he demanded.

Judy shot her father a knowing look. "You were right, he's in love."

Pain and worry had considerably shortened Tom's fuse. "Will you stow it?"

Des's face was drawn with illness and strain, but he summoned a wan smile. "Calm down, son. I know you're worried, but if Shara's where I think she is, she's safe for now."

"You took her to our cave, didn't you?" Judy said.

Tom nodded. "She wanted to check out her theory that the

people who did the paintings are from an ancient race called the Uru."

Des massaged his chin. "I've heard of them. If she's right, it means we might have a valuable site on our land."

"She's right. And once Horvath finds out, she'll have him as well as Jamal to contend with."

He paced to the door and rattled it to no avail. In frustration, he thumped on the wood with his good hand. "I shouldn't have left her alone."

"You didn't know the message was a fake."

Tom spun around. "The message. I am such an idiot."

They thought he meant for falling for Jamal's lie, he saw, until he fumbled one-handed in his pocket and fished out his cell phone. "They didn't think to frisk me before locking us in. The battery's low but should last for one call."

"There's only one place you'll get a signal in here," Des said, looking pointedly at the window above their heads. "Neither of us is in any condition for climbing."

Judy's jaw firmed. "You may not be, but I am."

Voices woke her. Sleepily she lifted her head from the pillow she'd made out of her satchel. She felt chilled to the bone. Something was wrong.

She sat up with a start. Through the needle-eye entrance of the cave she could see the sun hanging low in the sky. How long had she been asleep? She went to the entrance and peered out cautiously, then felt her heart seize. In the clearing below the cave were two Jeeps. Beside them stood Jamal, Horvath and a couple of their men.

With shaking fingers, she pulled the cell phone out of her bag and punched in Tom's number, only to be told by a recorded voice that she should try again later. Frustration gripped her. Later might be too late.

Shara withdrew into the cave, her thoughts whirling. Perhaps it was just as well she couldn't contact Tom. If he came now, he would be outnumbered. Better to wait it out and hope Jamal had no better luck finding the cave than she had earlier.

She had reckoned without the tracking skills of the man with him. Another cautious glance out of the cave saw them gesturing upward. They seemed to be looking right at the cave entrance.

Moments later, Jamal's voice rang out. "You may as well show yourself, Shara. We've found the car and tracked your footprints to the bottom of the rock wall."

Then why didn't they come up and get her? Perhaps Horvath's man was superstitious about approaching the cave. She stayed where she was.

Silence. Then, "If you don't show yourself, I will have the entire escarpment blown up."

She was sure Jamal would have no compunction about destroying the ancient gallery. If he did, his friend Horvath would succeed in claiming Tom's family's land, and it would be her fault for bringing Jamal here. She couldn't let him wreak havoc on her country. Neither could she let him destroy the cave.

Her only hope was to pretend to cooperate, and buy some time. And hope it would be enough. She checked the tape recorder, returned it to her bag and shouldered it. "I'm coming out," she called.

When she stood on level ground in front of him, Jamal took the bag from her hand and touched the side of her face almost gently. "My beautiful Shara. We are together at last."

"We will never be together," she spat back. "I'm only here because I won't let you help Horvath destroy Tom and his family."

"Ah, but we've already destroyed them," Jamal said. He pulled out a bloodstained cloth. "I'm sure you recognize this."

Tom's bandanna. Her heart almost stopped. "What have you done to him?"

"It was self-defense. He tried to kill me."

"So you killed him." She hadn't thought it was possible to

feel such pain and still function. If Tom was gone, she had no reason to go on. Jamal could do what he liked with her and it wouldn't matter. She was already dead in every way that counted. All she could do was make sure Tom hadn't died for nothing.

"You'll have plenty of time to grieve when we're back in Q'aresh," Jamal said. "Our plane is waiting. We can take off immediately."

Horvath looked shocked. "You can't leave yet." He scrabbled in his pocket and came up with a small handful of crystals the size of rice grains. "What about the mine? These diamonds Eddy found in the river leading out of this escarpment prove it can't be very far from here. You told me we'd be partners as soon as I have control of the land."

Jamal gave him an icy look. "My plans have changed. You'll be paid for accommodating me, like any good innkeeper."

She saw Horvath flinch. "You can't treat me like a servant. I did everything you wanted, helped you take care of the Logans. We're in this together."

"Do you have diplomatic immunity?"

"Of course not."

"I do. Therefore I am not accountable under your law, unlike you." He caught Shara's arm. "Don't try to stop us from leaving."

His meaning was clear. If Horvath got in his way, he would meet Tom's fate.

"Your immunity has limits," Horvath said viciously. "I'll find those diamonds with or without you, then I'll have the resources to bring you to justice."

Jamal laughed. "I wish you luck prosecuting the king of Q'aresh."

"You'll never be king while my family and I are alive to stop you," she vowed.

He looked unperturbed. "But my dear, none of you will be alive to stop me. Your life ends as soon as we're legally married and I have access to the contents of the royal treasury."

The cold-blooded assertion made Horvath fall silent. He must have known what manner of man he had teamed up with, but his appalled expression suggested he hadn't grasped the full extent of Jamal's villainy. Horvath and his man were still standing in the clearing when she was hustled into the car. Jamal's bodyguard got behind the wheel and they drove off.

Her look of hatred should have seared Jamal as he sat beside her. "You won't get away with this."

He gave her a pitying look. "I already have."

"I'll tell my father everything."

"Who will believe the ravings of someone exposed too long to the Australian sun? I'll tell him you were found wandering lost in the outback, and your reason was affected. He'll be so grateful to me for bringing you home, he won't question anything I tell him."

"Not even why you'd marry a supposed madwoman?"

"The king will respect my wish to take care of you for the rest of your life. Short though that may be."

He had everything worked out. Unfortunately her father was likely to believe Jamal's outrageous story, she knew. Easier for the king to accept that Shara had suffered sunstroke while lost in the outback than that he had driven her to desperate measures to avoid marrying Jamal.

The plane was still parked under the trees where Tom had steered it, she saw when Jamal drove up to it. Signs of recent work suggested that the repairs had been completed.

He really meant to take her back to Q'aresh.

Her mind worked furiously as she boarded, apparently quietly. She didn't contradict Jamal when he recounted his story about sunstroke to the guard, Talib, who looked at her in concern as she sat down.

Only the two men were on board besides herself and Jamal. The bodyguard, acting as pilot, was in the cockpit, she saw through the open door. The guard readied the cabin for takeoff. Jamal settled into the copilot's seat.

Was she really calculating the odds of putting up a fight?

With Tom gone, there was nothing in Australia for her now. Her last hope was to convince her father that not only was she rational, but Jamal was the one whose sanity King Awad should question. She had to make him believe her.

If she couldn't, she was dead anyway and Tom had died in vain.

Talib closed the door to the cockpit and strapped himself into the window seat in front of Shara. Hearing the engines start up, she turned to the window for a last glimpse of the outback she had come to love. "Goodbye, my darling," she whispered, her vision blurring.

She must have conjured the vision out of her own desperate need, because through the veil of tears, she thought she saw a Jeep racing toward the plane. She blinked hard. If she hadn't known better, she would have sworn that Blake and Tom were in the front seat, with Judy in the back, leaning between them as if urging Blake to drive faster.

Shara closed her eyes. She refused to let Jamal have the last laugh by giving in to hallucinations. Tom was dead. She was returning to Q'aresh to marry Jamal. Time she faced reality.

She opened her eyes expecting to see nothing but empty bush. The Jeep was still there and gaining on the plane. Her heart almost exploded with joy. It *was* Tom in the front seat. They were close enough for her to see the bandage on his wrist. Jamal hadn't killed him after all. Bad enough that he'd been injured, but he was alive. Merciful stars, he was alive.

They were trying to stop the plane from moving, she saw as Tom's gesture made Blake swerve to put the Jeep across their path. Frantically she looked around for something she could do to help. There wasn't much. But waiting for rescue didn't appeal. So she used the only weapon at her disposal.

Chapter 19

She began to scream.

Talib came out of his seat in an instant. He hadn't seen the Jeep racing toward the plane, and was focused on calming his princess, as she'd intended. When she wouldn't be calmed, he opened the cockpit door and spoke urgently to Jamal, who looked back in alarm.

Her throat felt raw. Surreptitiously she undid her seat belt but kept it tucked under her so it still appeared to be fastened. As Jamal came back into the cabin, she subsided into desperate sobbing.

"Stop this display, it won't change your fate," he ordered.

He turned to the guard. "Fetch me the medical kit."

This was where her plan became risky. The kit contained sedatives intended for fearful flyers. Her plan didn't include letting Jamal administer one to her, so she made a show of pulling herself together. "I'll be calm," she promised, flinching as she saw Talib approach with the kit in his hand.

"I want no more of these outbursts. Prepare a sedative for Her Highness," Jamal ordered.

Like all the key royal attendants, the man was trained in first-aid procedures. He did as bidden. She knew him well enough to regret what she had to do next, but couldn't let the feeling stop her. Waiting until he was within touching distance, she leaped up and twisted his arm so the syringe plunged into his own body. With a startled look, he pulled the needle out and looked at it, then started to slump. Jamal caught him, and while he was lowering the man into a seat, Shara acted.

Diving for the main cabin door, she wrestled with the opening mechanism. Although she had seen the operation performed dozens of times, she had never needed to do it herself, and her movements were clumsy.

Jamal had divested himself of his burden and sprang forward to stop her. "You should have made it easy on yourself and let Talib sedate you," he said, fastening his arm around her chest from behind.

She held on to the door mechanism with everything in her. One more clamp and she would have it open, or she would die trying. "You'd have to sedate me for the rest of my life to make me stay with you."

"It can be arranged."

Hooking his arm around her throat, he started to drag her backward. With her oxygen supply curtailed, she began to see stars. She released her hold on the clamp and dug her fingers into his arm, trying to get air.

Her knees jellied and she felt herself pulled toward a seat. With his free hand, Jamal was groping in the open medical kit for another syringe of sedative. Realizing the danger, she clawed at his face with her fingernails. They weren't as long as they would have been in Q'aresh, but they did the job. He yelled in fury as she drew blood.

His hold slackened long enough for her to gulp air, then tightened again as he got his legs back under him. The pressure on her windpipe increased and blackness fringed her vision. "I should kill you now and take your body back to your father. You'd be a lot less trouble."

"Go—to—hell."

The words used the last of her air and her knees buckled, despair filling her. Jamal was going to win, and her country would pay the price. Whether she lived or died, he would use her as a stepping stone to the throne. She would never see Tom again.

"No."

Desperation lent her the strength to jab a stiffened elbow backward, seeking a vulnerable target. She only succeeded in ramming her elbow low into Jamal's stomach. He swore but didn't let go.

A few inches lower and she'd have threatened his chance of providing heirs to his usurped throne, she thought in agonized frustration. She heard hammering on the door of the plane and voices yelling.

"Give up or you'll force me to really hurt you," Jamal said into her ear. He sounded sadistically pleased at the prospect. In horror she realized he was aroused by the fight with her. He was turned on by her resistance, and his power over her.

Well, to the devil with that.

With the last of her strength she dragged Jamal with her toward the medical kit, her fingers closing around cool metal. With no time to aim, she lifted the object over her head and pressed the trigger.

Jamal screamed and the weight on her windpipe eased abruptly. She sucked in air and spun around. He was staggering and clutching his eyes. Her aim had been better than she knew. The anesthetic spray had caught him in the face. Roaring, he blundered to the back of the cabin.

Air rushed over her and daylight blinded her momentarily as the cabin door was wrenched open and Tom vaulted through the opening. "Are you all right?"

Joy at seeing him again, alive, shrilled through her. "I'm okay. We're not moving."

"Blake and Judy stopped the plane while I played super-hero and climbed aboard. Where's Jamal?"

She jerked her head at the man who was frantically scrubbing his eyes, and handed Tom the spray can. "I hit him in the face with this."

Tom looked at the sleeping attendant then at the can, before dropping it onto a seat. "You've been busy."

"Not quite busy enough. Both of you sit down."

Red-eyed but otherwise unhurt, Jamal loomed over them. In his hand was a gun leveled at them. Shara cursed herself for not checking that he was genuinely disabled.

Tom stepped in front of her. "It's over, Jamal. I'm taking Shara with me."

Jamal shook his head. "In a few minutes we'll be airborne. There's nothing you can do to stop me now."

Tom glanced out the window. "Then what do you call that?"

It was the oldest trick in the book, but amazingly, Jamal fell for it. He looked.

The split second was all Tom needed to launch himself in a flat dive that carried both of them to the back of the compartment. The gun skidded under a seat. She heard a grunt of pain but couldn't tell who'd made it. Please, not Tom.

The aisle was too narrow for her to intervene. The gun was somewhere under the seats. If she could get to it, she could end this.

With his upbringing, Tom knew how to handle himself, but he was hardly in fighting trim with one wrist bandaged. The punch he threw at Jamal's jaw snapped the other man's head back, but at the cost of a burst of agony Tom felt all the way to his shoulder.

When Jamal came up, there was murder in his eyes and an evil-looking stiletto in his hand. He waved the blade in front of Tom's face, almost laughing as Tom was forced back down the aisle toward where Shara was groping under the seats.

Tom knew what she was looking for. He'd been keeping an

eye out for the gun himself, without success. Letting Jamal get anywhere near Shara wasn't on his agenda. He launched a flying kick that knocked the blade out of his adversary's hand. It clattered somewhere between the seats. Tom feinted with his damaged hand, saw Jamal's gaze follow the move, and used a foot to hook the other man's legs out from under him.

As soon as Jamal hit the deck, Tom leaped on him, landing a blow to his kidneys and another to the side of his head. It should have put most men down for the count, but Jamal had the strength of desperation. Taking Tom with him, he rolled until they were both hard up against a pair of seats. Then Tom saw the glint of metal and knew they'd seen the gun at the same time.

Shara dived for it at the same moment. Everything in him made him want to order her to stay back, but he didn't want to distract her. She held the gun steady while Tom yanked Jamal to his feet.

"Shoe's on the other foot now," he snapped. "Let's see how you like facing your own death."

Staring sullenly at the gun in Shara's hands, Jamal came to his feet and placed his hands on the tops of the seats on either side of him. With great care, Shara lowered the weapon so it was aimed at Jamal's groin.

The man's breath hissed. "You would not."

"It would ensure you never terrorize an innocent woman again."

Sweat beaded Jamal's forehead. "I can make you both wealthy beyond your dreams."

She tossed her head. "How? I have enough wealth for Tom and me. You'll never get your hands on it now."

"Give me the gun, Shara," Tom said quietly. The glazed look in her eyes had him worried. She was entitled to want revenge, but he didn't want her doing anything she'd regret for the rest of her days.

Slowly she passed the weapon to Tom and he leveled it at Jamal. Seeing the other man reduced to a puddle of terror in front of him, Tom understood her need for revenge. This was the man who had tried to hurt the woman Tom loved. Castration by bullet was no more than he deserved, more satisfying even than killing him. This way, he'd have a lifetime to repent the day he'd crossed Tom's path and put Shara's life in jeopardy.

Tom tightened his grip on the weapon. Adrenaline poured through him. He felt powerful, the gun in his hand an instrument of justice. All he had to do was pull the trigger and the world would be a better place.

Would it?

Had his father felt this sense of power as he approached Tom's mother with a knife in his hand? Tom's father had been equally convinced of the rightness of his cause. He'd truly believed she was seeing another man, and that her infidelity gave him the right to be her judge and executioner. He hadn't hesitated, stabbing her over and over until she stopped screaming. Stopped everything.

Tom's father had been drunk. What was Tom's excuse?

He wanted to protect the woman he loved. But could he do it from a prison cell? Could he even look her in the eye after taking the law into his own hands? He remembered the judge's words before sentencing his father—no one has the right to kill, no matter what the provocation. Tom couldn't even claim self-defense because Jamal was unarmed, carefully not making any threatening moves. If he did, there might be some justification for pulling the trigger.

Tom knew he would still hesitate. At long, long last he had his answer. When faced with the opportunity to kill, the provocation even, he wouldn't do it because it wasn't in him to do.

Jamal watched him intently, unaware of the great gift he'd just given Tom. "You're too much of a coward to shoot me," he said.

Read like a book, Tom nodded. He knew that pulling the trigger would have been the more cowardly act. What Jamal thought no longer mattered. "I don't intend to shoot you, not because you don't deserve it, but because you aren't worth the bullet. I'll let the Q'aresh authorities take care of you. Move toward the door," Tom ordered.

Jamal started to obey then seemed to stumble into one of the seats. As he righted himself, he came up with the spray can of anesthetic clutched in his hand. In a lightning move, he threw the can so it struck Tom's injured wrist, sending the gun flying.

With a howl of pain, Tom clutched his bandaged wrist. Before he could recover, Jamal knocked Shara aside and slammed into the cockpit, pulling the door shut behind him. She threw herself at the door. It was locked.

She ran to Tom. "He's barricaded himself in the cockpit."

Tom straightened, still nursing his injured wrist. Fresh blood bloomed on the bandage but he shrugged her off. "They're getting ready for takeoff."

Through the open door she saw the ground start to roll past.

"Come on." He hooked his arm around her waist and steered her to the entry.

Had he lost his mind? Surely he didn't intend for them to jump? They'd be killed. Then she saw Blake racing to bring the Jeep alongside. Terror threatened to pin her feet to the floor. She knew what Tom expected of her and she feared she couldn't do it.

Tom's hold tightened. He pressed his mouth to hers in a quick, hot kiss. "For luck," he said. "As soon as they're alongside, you go. I'll be right behind you."

The wind whipped her hair into a satin banner. Her heart rate jumped as fear lodged in her throat, and her chest tightened with terror. Tom thought she could do this, she told herself, clinging to her love for him as a lifeline.

The Jeep was almost alongside. Judy had pressed herself against the far side of the back seat to give Shara as much room as possible. Taking a deep breath, she released Tom's hand and jumped.

The landing drove all the breath out of her, and she would

have bruises on bruises where she collided with the back of the seat, but unbelievably, she'd made it.

Exhilaration poured through her. She had never felt more alive. Judy was tugging at her to get her attention. "I'm climbing into the front. When I do, scrunch as far to this side as you can. They're going faster. Tom will land a lot harder than you did."

Like a stunt actor straddling a pair of runaway horses, Judy balanced between the seats before dropping into the front passenger seat beside Blake. Immediately Shara backed against the far door, clearing as much space as she could. The plane had gathered speed since her jump. Tom was already injured. Could he make it?

He had to, she wouldn't let herself believe anything else.

A split second later he slammed into her, driving all the air out of her body. Blake didn't stop. Gravel spat from the tires as he spun the Jeep around and into the cover of the bush edging the airstrip.

Did Blake expect Jamal to shoot at them from the plane? As the engine roar grew louder, Shara shuddered, unconsciously braced for the sound of gunfire. Why hadn't Tom killed Jamal when he'd had the chance? She'd seen him warring with himself, readied herself for the explosion and the blood. No one would have blamed Tom for pulling the trigger.

Except Tom himself.

She looked over her shoulder, seeing the plane's nose come up as the jet climbed skyward, taking Jamal out of their lives, she hoped for good. Her breath rushed out in a huge sigh of relief. Tom had wanted to shoot Jamal but he'd stopped himself, and she thought she knew why. He hadn't wanted closeness because he feared becoming a murderer like his father. Now he knew it wasn't going to happen, what did it mean for them?

She had her answer when his arms came around her, tightening as his gaze followed hers to where the plane was becoming a dot in the clear blue sky. "I was a heartbeat away from killing him."

"But you didn't."

"No, I didn't."

"Why not?"

He brushed a strand of hair out of her eyes. "I couldn't take a life, not even one as deserving as his."

"Don't you see, Tom? You're not a killer. It isn't in you. You proved that today."

His eyes shone with moisture before he blinked hard and he squeezed her hand. "For a princess, you're pretty smart, you know that?"

"Not smart enough to think of grabbing my bag before we jumped out of the plane," she said soberly.

He hunted around near his feet and came up grinning. "You mean this? I thought you might need your papers or whatever else you have in here, so I grabbed it before I jumped."

She fastened a hand either side of his face and planted a kiss on his half-open mouth. Heat ran riot through her as she lifted her head. "My papers can be replaced, but not the tape recorder I had running while Jamal boasted about killing my family and usurping the throne. Once my father hears that, Jamal is finished."

"As I said, a smart woman."

The careful way he held his bandaged hand against his chest wasn't lost on her. "You're in pain. You must have struck your wrist when you landed."

"Jamal lobbing the spray can at me didn't do it much good."

She felt his suffering inside herself, and tapped Blake on the shoulder. "Tom's hurt. We have to get him to a doctor."

Blake and Judy had been scrupulously keeping their eyes front, giving Tom and Shara what privacy they could. Now Judy looked back. "Do you need a doctor?" she asked.

Tom favored Shara with a long look. "What I need, a doctor can't give me. The bleeding's stopped for now. I'll live." He flexed his fingers by way of demonstration.

Blake spoke over his shoulder. "Then you don't mind if we take a detour to the cave?"

"Feeling nostalgic?" Tom asked.

"I'd like to check out Shara's cave paintings," Blake said.

"Horvath and his men might still be there," Shara said. "He wasn't very happy when Jamal told him he was leaving with me. Horvath seemed to think they were partners."

In the mirror she saw Blake's mouth tighten. "All the more reason to find out what he's up to."

Chapter 20

Bruised, battered and tired though she was, Shara had never felt so happy. She hardly noticed the jolting of the Jeep as Blake drove back across the corrugated landscape to the hideout cave. At last she had the means to end Jamal's plotting. She could now prove his evil plan to her father. She wouldn't be forced to marry him—she was free.

She hardly dared think what that might mean to her and Tom. Would his interest be as strong, his passion as fierce without the spur of another man's involvement? Forbidden fruit was always the sweetest.

Her own feelings were in no doubt. She loved Tom and wanted him more than she had dreamed it was possible to want a man. Giving up royal life to make her home in Australia would be a sacrifice, but she would make it willingly for him. Her experience of life in the outback had whetted her appetite for more, and she'd proved to herself that she could manage without servants and a palace around her.

What would Tom be prepared to give up for her?

This afternoon he'd given up the horror of turning into his father. She'd seen the moment when he could have shot Jamal but stopped himself. Seen the awareness of what the decision meant dawn on him, and the invisible shackles fall away.

As a reason to avoid close relationships, it no longer applied. If he had other reasons, she could only hope what shimmered between them was strong enough to overcome them.

Judy and Blake were talking together. Shara stole a glance at Tom. "How do you feel?"

He lowered his tone to match hers. "As if I've gone a dozen rounds with a prize-fighter who doesn't mind fighting dirty as long as he wins."

"Jamal hasn't won," she denied. "He may have gotten away for the moment, but as soon as we get the tape proving his guilt to my father, Jamal will be arrested for treason."

Tom smiled. "King Awad will be proud of you."

"I doubt it. He may be grateful, but he'll never feel the same way about me as he does about his son and heir."

A little awkwardly with only one good hand, Tom reached across and lifted her hand, grazing the back with his lips. She trembled as she hadn't done when he'd asked her to jump out of the plane. He kept his fingers in hers as he said, "More fool the king if he can't see what a treasure he has in you."

Could Tom? What did he see in her now, after laying to rest his greatest fear? A runaway royal who belonged back in her own world, or a woman he was finally able to love?

Wrong time and place to ask, she told herself. Until they'd dealt with Max Horvath, they didn't have the luxury of focusing on themselves.

She let out a long breath. Putting her concerns on hold while she solved someone else's was becoming a habit. A cop-out, Judy would call it. Would she be right?

Not sure of the answer, Shara let her hand rest in Tom's as she savored the warmth of his touch. Deliberately she blanked her mind to everything but how good it felt to be with him.

To feel safe. How long had it been since she'd been able to stop looking over her shoulder?

Too long, she thought. Peace of mind had been at a premium ever since she'd overheard Jamal scheming to usurp her father's throne. Her mind still wasn't entirely peaceful, but this was turmoil of a pleasurable kind. She saw it reflected on Tom's angular features, and her spirits rose.

For the first time in her life, she felt glad she was a woman. Tom had made her feel valued and desirable. He didn't treat her interests as frivolous, or expect her to elevate his concerns above her own. Strange, the effect that had. She found herself wanting to put his needs first.

Was that how it worked? If each person in a relationship made the other their priority, both of you got your needs met. Jamal would never have understood, but she was sure Tom did. They would have a lot to discuss when they were finally alone.

She kept her fingers in his as her heart fluttered. They were nearing the base of the escarpment where Jamal had left Horvath. The car Des had loaned her was where she'd left it in the shade of some bushes. Horvath's vehicle stood out in the open, deserted for the moment. Then she saw why. He and another man were exploring the rock wall, searching for the hidden cave entrance. They didn't appear to be having much luck.

They looked down as Blake, Judy, Tom and Shara pulled up and got out of the car. Tom cupped his hands to his mouth. "Give it up and come down, Horvath. There's nothing up there to interest you."

"You're trespassing on our land," Judy added.

With surprising agility, considering his bulk, Horvath jumped from ledge to ledge until he stood beside them. The other man followed, hovering a few feet away.

Horvath grinned nastily. "It may be your land now, but all this will be mine as soon as I foreclose on Des Logan's loan."

Blake folded his arms. "It hasn't happened yet."

"If we have anything to do with it, it never will," Tom agreed.

Horvath looked surprised to see Shara at Tom's side. "Where's Prince Jamal?"

She narrowed her eyes. "On his way to prison."

Horvath's shock was obvious, although he tried to hide it. "I take it the marriage is off?"

"It was never on," she asserted.

Tom moved closer. "Unfortunately, there's nothing we can charge you with yet, except choosing your houseguests unwisely."

"If you don't get out of here, we might think of something," Blake added.

Judy looked up at the cliff then back to Horvath. "Since when are you interested in rock art?"

"Is that the cover story you hatched between you?"

Shara looked at Tom in puzzlement. "What does he mean by cover story?"

Horvath shifted his attention to her. "This whole area is riddled with rock paintings. But they aren't what your new boyfriend is interested in." He pulled a cloth bag out of his pocket and spilled a dozen tiny, clear crystals into his hand. "The creek where I found these runs into this cave system. The lost mine has to be here somewhere. I know it."

Tom's patience snapped. "You don't know beans. There's no diamond mine, only a collection of ancient rock paintings that will attract enough international interest to let Des pay back what he owes you."

"Why bother with a few daubings on cave walls, when there's a fortune practically under our feet?"

Tom grabbed the man by the shirtfront. "Haven't you worked it out yet?" He jerked his thumb at Horvath's man. "Eddy here is stringing you along. He wants revenge against us for firing him. He doesn't care whether the mine even exists."

Blake came between Tom and Horvath. "Easy, mate. He isn't worth getting your hands dirty."

Horvath made a show of dusting himself off. "The mine is real. Just like the money your father owes me."

Tom's mouth thinned. "He didn't borrow it from you. He borrowed it from Clive, who'd be ashamed of the way you're hounding his old friend."

Horvath's eyes turned cold. "My father was a fool who preferred to work himself into an early grave running cattle, when there are easier ways to make a fortune."

"Your father was no fool. He bred some of the best cattle in the world," Blake argued. "No wonder you two didn't get along."

"Well, now the land's mine, so I got the last laugh. And I get Diamond Downs into the bargain if the loan isn't repaid within the time Des Logan agreed *in writing*."

"Des was the one who insisted Clive take his promissory note. Clive never wanted repayment. He meant to tear the paper up."

"But he didn't, and it's a legal contract with only a few months left to run. Time's almost up, folks. You'll need more than a few cave paintings to make this place profitable before I foreclose."

"We're not beaten yet," Blake stated confidently. "From what Shara and Tom tell me about the gallery they discovered, scholars will flock to see it."

"Not if they're too scared to set foot on Diamond Downs."

Tom loomed closer. "What the hell's that supposed to mean?"

Instinctively, Horvath moved back, almost running into Shara. "I'm only saying, the outback is a dangerous place. You never know what might happen to visitors."

Blake shaded his eyes. "That sounds suspiciously like a threat."

"Take it how you like. Just don't be surprised if your venture falls flat on its face."

"If it does, we'll know where to look for an explanation," Tom vowed. "So whatever you're planning, you'll forget it if you know what's good for you."

Shoulders lifting, Horvath affected an innocent expression. "Who says I'm planning anything? This is wild, dangerous country. Lots of things can go wrong that have nothing to do with me."

Blake's jaw firmed. "If there's as much as a monsoon out here and somebody gets wet, we'll hold you responsible."

"Don't you have better things to do?"

Judy stepped forward. "You just made yourself our priority, Max."

"Pity you didn't think of that when I proposed to you."

"Is that what this is about? You're still brooding because I turned you down?"

Their neighbor's face twisted. "You flatter yourself. You were only a means to an end. Inheriting your father's promissory note gives me the land without the need to saddle myself with you."

This time it was Blake's turn to restrain Judy, who would have launched herself at Max if she hadn't been held back. At Judy's livid expression, Shara had to fight the urge to laugh. Tom had feared he was violent because of his genes, but he and his foster siblings were a matched set, she thought. Any one of them would defend the family's honor to the death. They weren't so different from her own family whose motto was, "My name and my country," the two elements the royal family was dutybound to preserve.

King Awad would approve of them, she decided.

Horvath gestured toward the other man. "Let's get out of here, Eddy. But I'll be back—as the new owner."

As Blake surged forward, Tom grabbed his arm. "Let him go. You said yourself he isn't worth it. He's all talk."

"Since when did you become Mr. Nice Guy?"

Tom's gaze met Shara's. "Since I had the right incentive." He lowered his head and found her lips in a gentle kiss filled with promise.

She felt herself redden but kept her head high. Shame was for the inexperienced person she'd been when she arrived in the outback. Now she was Tom's lover and proud of it. In a perfect world, she'd be his wife. Even in an imperfect world, she'd be at his side in whatever role was open to her. Unthinkable for her to be anywhere else now.

Blake was grinning from ear to ear. "If I'd known a kiss was all it would take to straighten you out, I'd have kissed you myself long ago."

Judy punched Blake on the arm, but Tom grinned. "Sorry, you're not my type."

When he transferred the gaze to Shara, making it clear she *was,* a pleasurable ache gripped her. A longing to have him all to herself. He came with a package, she reminded herself. Des, Judy and his foster brothers, even the legacy of a father in prison. The code of the outback demanded she accept everything he was. She knew she'd already taken the first giant steps, and his heavy-lidded look told her he knew it, too.

They waited until a cloud of dust followed Horvath's progress in the direction of his own boundary. "Do you think he'll try anything to sabotage our efforts here?" Judy mused out loud.

Tom massaged his chin. "Hard to see what he can do."

"Especially after shooting his mouth off in front of all of us," Judy observed. "He knows we'll be watching his every move."

Blake shifted restlessly. "Speaking of moves, how about showing us this new gallery you discovered, Shara?" Then he shot Judy an accusing look. "What did you kick me for?"

"Sorry, accident," she said, sounding not at all repentant. "We can see the gallery later, after Tom and Shara have had time to discuss their plans for it. Alone."

Blake finally caught on. "Oh, *their* plans. Of course."

This time Shara did blush as she understood what Judy was trying to do. "You don't have to rush away on our account."

"Yes, they do," Tom said, sounding impatient. "You and I have plans to make."

She studiously avoided meeting his gaze. "For the gallery?"

"Naturally, for the gallery."

Judy was trying not to laugh as she steered Blake back into the Jeep. "Let Shara drive you back. Your hand still needs medical attention," she said over her shoulder. "So don't take too long discussing the—cave."

Tom didn't dignify this with an answer. Holding tight to Shara, he waited until Blake and Judy were on their way. Then he helped her to climb the escarpment to the rock ledge. With one injured hand it wasn't the easiest climb, but Shara had a feeling nothing was going to stop him, least of all her.

Inside the shadowy coolness of the hideout cave, surrounded by reminders of some of the happiest times of his boyhood, he steered her to the folding cot where she sat down and waited. She wasn't usually patient, but today she could wait as long as he needed her to. She felt surprisingly calm. Surely when your future hung in the balance, you should feel more turbulent? The serenity filling her felt strange.

Then she knew it was because she was prepared for whatever Tom had to say. If he wanted to propose marriage, there was only one answer. If he wanted her as a lover, she'd already give the answer. No other possibility existed.

Folding her hands in her lap, she said, "Yes."

He looked startled. "I haven't asked you anything yet."

"It doesn't matter. Whatever your question, my answer is yes."

His breath rushed out. "I'm not like Jamal. I don't ever want to take you for granted."

"You can, *because* you're not like Jamal," she explained. "I'm yours, Tom, however and whenever you want me. You can't change that fact."

"I don't want to change it," he said quietly. "When I thought Jamal had taken you away from me for good, I realized how much I love you."

Thinking of what she'd believed to be her own loss, symbolized by the bloodied bandanna, she felt herself sway. "I thought I'd lost you today, too, and it almost killed me. I love you, Tom, more than I have words to tell you."

He dropped to one knee and took her in his arms. "You don't need words. I can see the honesty in your eyes. That's as rare as it is wonderful. You know the worst about me, and still you can look me in the eye and tell me you love me."

Pleasure shivered through her at his touch. "I also know the best about you. The man who fought back from despair to make a new life for himself, accepted into another culture for his courage and integrity, helping teenagers find their way…"

He pressed a finger to her lips. "I love seeing myself through your eyes. It's way better than the reality."

Silenced, she let her eyes tell him what she saw *was* reality. Seeing the look, he took her mouth in a burning kiss, making her shudder with desire, with love. Distantly she heard the throbbing chant of the ancient people who had painted the rock art. It called to her, tugged at her, sang in her veins. She was where she belonged, perhaps where she had always belonged in some far past.

Her trembling stopped and she put into her kiss the joy of homecoming, of being at peace in the arms of the man she loved.

Looking dazed, he lifted his head. He heard the music too, she saw. Heard and understood what it meant to them and for them. *"Habibi, ya ghabein. Behebbak,"* he said.

Joy bubbled through her. "When did you learn to speak the language of Q'aresh?"

"I looked up some phrases on the Internet, although I told myself I was wasting my time because I'd never have the right to say them to you. How did I do?"

"Perfectly." Any woman would rejoice to hear, *Beloved, you are the light of my eye. I love you,* and her tone told him so.

"I can say them in a couple of Aboriginal dialects, too," he offered, proceeding to demonstrate.

Then he said them again in the timeless language of a kiss, the most eloquent and passionate of all. "I'll never tire of hearing you say you love me," she promised as warmth flooded through her.

"Then you'll marry me?"

"I already said yes."

He smiled. "And I'll never tire of hearing you say it."

Her mouth curved. "Then yes, yes and yes. A thousand times, yes."

"Do you think your father will approve of me?"

"How could he not, when I do?"

"Then I'd better practice the proper way to ask him for your hand in Q'aresh."

"English will do nicely. He speaks several languages," she assured him. "I suspect after he sees us together, you won't even need to ask."

"What about when we have children? Won't he want them raised as members of the royal family?"

Dazzled by the thought, she slid her arms around his neck. "They'll share our two worlds. Royal when we visit Q'aresh, and Australian when we're at home in the outback."

"At home in the outback. I like the sound of that."

So did she, and she let her embrace show him just how much. Covering her body with his, Tom swept her back onto the cot and possessed her mouth utterly. Her heart leaped. She hoped Blake and Judy didn't expect them back too soon, because they hadn't even started discussing the rock art.

First things first, she thought as she surrendered to the purest happiness she'd ever known. Above their heads, the figures painted on the rock looked as if they were dancing.

Epilogue

Des passed Tom a few more feet of colored lights from the string looped over his arm. "After tonight, you'll be an officially engaged man. Still not too late to make a dash for freedom."

Halfway up a ladder, Tom took the nails out of his mouth and grinned at his foster father. "Better not let Shara hear you say that after our hard work convincing King Awad I'm the man for her."

"I wondered if you'd decide to stay in Q'aresh. Royal life can be pretty seductive, I imagine."

"Too cushy for me. For her, too, now she's fallen in love with the Aussie outback."

Blake passed them carrying a long trestle table he proceeded to set up in the courtyard ready for the engagement party that evening. "Somehow, I don't think it was the outback she fell in love with," he observed. "Although what she sees in you, I still don't know."

Tom arched his eyebrows. "You mean when there's a virile Aussie bloke like you around? Mate, it's your pets she can't handle."

Blake grinned. "Leave my crocodiles out of this."

"Boys," Des chided as he'd done when they were teenagers. "If she had any sense, she'd pick a handsome, eligible widower with a bit of gray in his hair as a sign of his great wisdom."

Blake laughed. "I thought that bristle-haired British anthropologist in the tour group was going to race you off first."

Strictly speaking, the group from a leading British university weren't tourists, but had come to Diamond Downs to document the Uru site. They'd paid handsomely for the privilege, and that was enough for Tom. A sign of things to come, he hoped. Their fees had already put a dent in the money Des owed Max Horvath. Their neighbor hadn't been pleased to receive the check, Tom recalled, and had reminded them the whole amount had to be paid within six months, or he'd still be entitled to foreclose.

That left them four more months, Tom thought as he fastened the last of the lights to the side of the house facing the courtyard. They'd make it. Andy and the elders of his clan had already begun to paint a replica of the ancient rock art at a place where visitors could see it. Since the media broke the news about the discovery, bookings to stay at the homestead and hear the stories of the Uru were coming in. Tom could see an improvement in Des already. While hope couldn't provide him with the new heart he needed, it might keep him alive until a transplant was available.

Six weeks had gone by in which Tom and Shara had traveled to Q'aresh. He couldn't remember when he'd been more nervous. King Awad had greeted him warily, the welcome only thawing in the face of Tom's obvious love for Shara and hers for him.

Tom's case hadn't been harmed by Shara's explanation of his role in saving her from Jamal. The king hadn't dismissed Shara's concerns, as she'd believed, but had sent Jamal to Australia while he conducted an investigation. Shocked to learn she had traveled with Jamal, the king hadn't known what was going on. Once King Awad heard the tape of evidence against Jamal and his co-conspirators, their fate had been sealed.

Finally, King Awad had given Shara and Tom his blessing, insisting on giving them a royal wedding in Q'aresh and decreeing the traditional two hundred days of ritual engagement underway.

A royal wedding for the boy from the wrong side of the tracks still seemed like a dream, although Tom wasn't sure how he'd cope with all the pomp and circumstance. Blake hadn't gotten over the king wanting to make Tom a prince. He was afraid he'd never hear the end of that. Or from Judy, who'd called him Your Highness for days, until he'd threatened to feed her to one of Blake's crocs.

The object of his thoughts came out with a cloth she proceeded to spread across the trestle table. "Typical," Judy mumbled. "The men get the easy jobs while Shara and I slave over a hot stove."

Tom injected mock horror into his tone. "You're letting her cook?"

"I heard that," Shara said, coming out to join them. "I'll have you know my second attempt at making sponge cake turned out perfectly."

Love for her twined around his heart so tightly he had trouble breathing. "What happened to the first attempt?"

She screwed up her face. "Don't ask."

He came down the ladder to her. "I wish you didn't have to work at all."

Her expression softened. "When I had servants, I wasn't nearly as happy as I am now. All I want is you, and our children growing up in this wide brown land."

He pulled her against him. "How did I get so lucky, finding you?"

She shook her head. "I'm the lucky one."

Blake maneuvered a trestle table past them. "Pardon me,

Your Highnesses, but the peasants need to get this set up before the guests arrive." He turned to Des. "Is that journalist of yours joining us tonight?"

Des shook his head. "Under the terms of our agreement, she's only supposed to come near the homestead in a life-or-death emergency."

Judy shook out a large checkered tablecloth for the second table. "An engagement party hardly qualifies. How long does she have to spend living off the land to get her story?"

"Two months," Blake contributed. The magazine's editor had approached Des with the idea for a survivor-type story after learning about the rock art. "Don't feel too sorry for her. I helped her set up camp and she brought enough stuff for a year."

Tom laughed. "All the same, it's a challenge for a city girl to transplant herself to the outback, out of contact with civilization for that length of time. Her idea of roughing it is probably turning off her side of the electric blanket."

"I don't know. Jo looks as if she can handle most things."

Tom traded looks with Shara. "Jo?" he asked.

"Don't start. All I did was walk her through a few survival skills."

"Like mouth-to-mouth resuscitation?"

"That does it." Blake moved Shara carefully aside and shaped up to his foster brother.

Not in the least alarmed, Shara felt a thrill of pleasure at being so accepted. She looked forward to meeting their foster brother, Cade, who was flying in from Perth for the engagement party later that day. Meeting the fourth brother, Ryan, would have to wait until he recovered from a heavy dose of flu. He couldn't risk infecting Des in his present state.

Judy slid between the men. "Could you two work off your surplus energy by setting up the barbecue?" She turned to Shara. "They'll probably still be carrying on like this when they're ninety."

Shara smiled. "I certainly hope so."

The cloth flew as Judy flicked it expertly across the table.

"I suppose it's better than turning out bitter and twisted like Max Horvath."

Hearing the name, Tom paused in the act of folding the ladder. "Is he hanging around again?"

Judy shook her head. "Not lately. After the threats he made at the cave, I was afraid he might try to sabotage the anthropologists' visit."

"Max may not have been around, but Andy's folks told him they saw Eddy Gilgai hanging around Dingo Creek," Tom said.

Blake's expression darkened. "What the blazes was he doing there?"

Tom propped the ladder against a wall. "Nothing good, you can bet."

He'd moved closer to Shara without realizing it, she noticed. "Isn't Dingo Creek where the journalist is camped?"

Blake swore. "I'd better get down there and make sure everything's all right."

"Any excuse to see Jo-o," Tom simpered, turning the one-syllable name into a singsong note.

"I think you should check on her, son," Des contributed seriously. "Max wasn't pleased when I paid the first installment off the loan. Jo's magazine made no secret that they're paying a hefty fee to use Diamond Downs for their story. Max might have hatched some scheme to make sure we don't collect."

Tom's arm tightened around Shara, thinking of the harm their neighbor had nearly done her by aiding Jamal. The latter was now in prison in Q'aresh, awaiting trial for treason, but Max was still free and more determined than ever to get his hands on the lost diamond mine said to exist on Logan land. He was quite capable of putting Eddy Gilgai up to sabotaging the journalist's visit if he thought it would achieve his aim.

He'd have to go through every member of the Logan family first. "Want me to come with you as backup?" Tom asked Blake.

"If I do, I'll call you. Look after your beautiful bride-to-be, and hold the fort till I get back," Blake said.

He had taken barely a dozen steps when Andy Wandarra

intercepted him, breathing heavily as if he'd been running. "You'd better come quick, Blake. A big crocodile is causing trouble at Dingo Creek. We think somebody's been provoking him."

"Somebody meaning Eddy?" When Andy nodded, Blake looked at Tom and Des. "Sounds as if you were right, Max hasn't given up yet. Handling the croc is my job. No need to let it spoil everybody's night."

Lines of concern bracketed Tom's mouth. "Just don't do anything foolish. I'm here if you need me."

"Can't do anything more foolish than get engaged." Blake's smile swung from Tom to Shara. "It'll be good to hand over Tom's leash to his wife. After taming him, a rogue crocodile will be a piece of cake."

Shara's radiant expression rejected Blake's claim. She didn't want Tom tamed. She loved him just as he was, as Tom McCullough and Barrak, the white dingo. They would deal with the crocodile problem the way Des Logan's family handled most challenges, head-on. If Max was behind the threat, they would deal with him too, and she'd do whatever she could to help.

Sliding her hand into Tom's, she squeezed it hard, sending a message of love and solidarity. "Do you think Horvath has any idea what he's taken on here?"

Tom shook his head. "No, but he's about to find out."

* * * * *

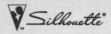

If you enjoyed what you just read,
then we've got an offer you can't resist!

Take 2 bestselling love stories FREE!

Plus get a FREE surprise gift!

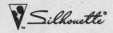

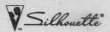

INTIMATE MOMENTS™

**Presenting the fourth book in
the thrilling continuity**

The Next Generation

No one is alone…

A Touch of the Beast

(Silhouette Intimate Moments #1317)

by award-winning author

Linda Winstead Jones

Rancher, loner—horse whisperer?
Hawk Donovan had always longed
to seek the source of his mysterious
power, and when a tip from a stranger
opens the door to his past, he takes a
leap of faith and begins to explore.
To investigate the old fertility clinic,
though, he'll first have to convince
Sheryl Eldanis, the beautiful vet who
has hidden the clinic's files in her attic,
that he can be trusted. But as their
search progresses, trust gives way to
passion—and when they uncover the
sinister information about Hawk's birth
mother, they unleash a deadly chain
of events that threatens Sheryl's
peaceful life. Can Hawk save his lover
from the danger he brought to her
door before it's too late?

*Available September 2004
at your favorite retail outlet.*